QUEST FOR THE WITCH'S CODE

SGT. HAWK BOOK EIGHT

PATRICK CLAY

ROUGH
EDGES
PRESS

Quest for the Witch's Code
Paperback Edition
Copyright © 2024 Patrick Clay

Rough Edges Press
An Imprint of Wolfpack Publishing
701 S. Howard Ave. 106-324 Tampa, FL 33609

roughedgespress.com

Paperback ISBN 978-1-68549-412-4
eBook ISBN 978-1-68549-411-7
LCCN 2024932002

To Kyle Clay, who was the only audience for my tales, every night of his childhood, until I was outgrown and put away, as we do with the once favorite things of our youth. Here's one more story for you.

QUEST FOR THE WITCH'S CODE

PROLOGUE

MANY YEARS AFTER THE WAR, MAXWELL HOECH DID AN
interview for a trade magazine, which has long since
gone out of print, and to date has been impossible to
locate. In the article, he discussed the origin of what
became known as the *Witch's Code* and stressed that it
had never been called by that name during the war. The
popular title attached itself to the encryption at a later
time, due to purely ancillary details, as you will eventually see. I gathered that he wanted to make it clear to the
world that there was no demonic influence in the
matter, as far as he was concerned. Nevertheless, Hoech
did allege an even more remarkable and supernatural
source for the strange method of communication. The
complete journal article containing his explanation is
lost, but the following paragraphs survived elsewhere,
in a more durable anthology. And so, in Hoech's few
remaining words:

"I lay on the floor of a horrid Japanese prison in the
dead of night, staring at a bloody, unseen ceiling, feeling
quite despondent, when I ran out of promises and

bargains to make with God to secure my release. We had become great friends, however, and I assured Him that I had no intention of going over to the devil in seeking the means for my survival. To pass the time, in the course of a prolonged conversation with my old Friend, I said aloud,

"Tell me something, God, something that no one else knows."

"I felt this a sort of consolation, you might say, for my remaining in my unenviable position, while still remaining loyal to my Creator. Since God knows everything, He has a lot of unused, but not always useless, bits of wisdom to share with the desperate.

"To my surprise, rather than speaking inside my head as was His custom, He sent one of his shining messengers in the early morning hours, who revealed to me something astounding and heretofore unknown to anyone. I was also informed that as unique as this fact was, it was now rendered unimportant, because I was the only person who would ever know it. The things that one person knows, it seems, are unverifiable and therefore of no use to mankind, and by definition, do not survive that person. Knowing my wonderful new revelation, and its prohibitive corollary, only left me more despondent. The messenger tried to explain to me that the most important things, important to God at least, are those that only *two* people know, because they are unique, yet they are also verifiable and able to survive. Beyond that, there is no great value in human experience to God, because of its commonality. The knowledge held by only two people holds the power of true wisdom within it, as well as the fabric of the spiritual universe.

"I suppose I should tell you, that right then and there, this other worldly conversation was the inception of the 'code' as a means of communication in my mind, and the means by which I was to ultimately *try* to secure my release. Other codes employed mathematical terms of precision, but I was to create one utilizing the imprecise elements of the human psyche to share a message. I felt I had to make every effort to put some of my divine interaction in this regard to a practical purpose. I admit to having no concept as to the amount of damage I would subsequently cause. We never fully understand the ramifications of what we do, or even care at the time. Now, of course, I've come to hope that I haven't angered God, or betrayed any confidences. Or made the world into a worse place in which to live."

1

IN THE BELLY OF THE BEAST

A PALM FROND BRUSHED LAZILY ACROSS THE CANVAS, camouflage-colored helmet cover of Sergeant Hawk. Mosquitoes floated without direction before his face and into his eyes. He surveyed the temporarily quiet and threatening scene spread before him. Beyond the apricot tinted sand lay the most recent problem sent his way, among an endless series of deadly problems. The campaign for the Helvedes Islands had progressed rapidly, with the successful landing on the largest island of the archipelago, Greater Helvedes. Moving inland on Greater Helvedes, however, proved to be a slower operation. The Japanese had learned a new strategy since the earlier campaigns of the war. Rather than meeting the Marines on the landing beach and trying to stop them there, the defenders now retreated inland, and forced the Americans to pry them out of the hinterlands. The superiority of the Americans in troops and materials had rendered the latest tactic a grim necessity. Fighting it out on the landing beaches had expended all of the Japanese strength far too early in the battles and had expedited the loss of most of their island empire. With their latest strategy, even if the Americans won the battle, they would pay a higher price for it, and have less manpower left to invade Japan itself.

The Marines encountered increasingly difficult lines of defenses as they moved inland. Trenches, pillboxes, caves, and tunnels all had to be conquered, along with their protective minefields, barbed wire, snipers, and machine gun nests in between.

Sergeant Hawk was not concerned with the grander strategy at the moment. His objective and his world, quite possibly his *final* objective and the *end* of his world, consisted of a fairly large enemy bunker planted in the middle of a sandy clearing in the tropical forest. The enemy had the advantage of a slight elevation, probably afforded to them by the builders when the fortification was constructed, in an effort to avoid flooding from the torrential rains. A dark viewport faced Hawk, and he could make out a concrete roof under the logs and vegetation piled on top of the bunker. Although he could not see it, he knew that there would be a machine gun in that dark recess, and that it was more than likely pointed at him right now.

Upon arriving here, and discovering the pillbox, First Platoon had initially settled upon attacking the rear of the formidable installation. They soon found, however, that the rear had a gunport of its own, and was quite capable of defending itself from that direction. No longer locked into the mindset of a frontal ocean assault, the enemy was ready for a protracted battle on two sides. For a predator, such as Sergeant Hawk, that still left a couple of other sides.

As First Platoon struggled with the forward, and

then the rear facing machine guns of the emplacement, they had the implicit control of the blind spots on either side of the pillbox. Unfortunately, their control of even these two sides did not last long. The Americans' free passage around the fortification was soon blocked by the arrival of a Type 95 Japanese tank. This effectively created two fortifications protecting the stubborn enemy, guns which were able to defend one another with interlocking and quickly adjustable fields of fire.

Hawk chewed placidly on a plug of tobacco as he studied the problem. His cold blue eyes shifted from the newly arrived tank to the pillbox as dozens of violent solutions flashed through his mind. This is what he existed for: to destroy these bastards. A learned critic of the battlefield, he admired the camouflage pattern painted on the tank, and its bright red, rising sun ensign. The enemy had a flair for such things, as opposed to the dull, amphibian-looking American tanks. Such things had a subtle way of putting the fear of God into you.

HAWK AWAITED the order to attack from Lieutenant Kirk and tried to settle on a reasonable plan. For the moment, both the tank and the bunker were pointing their weapons at his position in the front of the fort, as the enemy patiently waited for another assault. If necessary, the tank stood prepared to circle in front of the pillbox and face the rear, or it could also reverse itself into a position to do the same, like a boxer on his toes, ready to strike. The driver would have preferred the forward motion, due to visibility problems. The tank was mobile, but it was incapable of turning on a dime.

Reversing the engines caused a whole new set of problems for the men bottled up in the close interior.

The tank was the stronger defender of the two forces facing the Americans, with its 37-millimeter cannon, and two machine guns; all of which had a 360-degree mobility because of the rotating turret. As if to demonstrate this ability, the turret slowly adjusted itself, sighting in on a less well concealed Marine in the jungle, and letting loose with a thunderous blast into the undergrowth. The power of the cannon prevented the formation of stationary American positions and forced the attackers to drop back out of its range. Individuals could crawl through the forest for a look at their adversary, but as soon as any effective fire on the pillbox began, the tank swung into its jealously protective action, focusing on the center of the challenging Marine lines.

Either the tank or the pillbox, if standing alone, eventually could have been surrounded and overwhelmed by the Marines, due to the enemy's lack of maneuverability and clear visibility from their viewports. Together, however, the Japanese had created what, so far, had been an insurmountable problem. If the tank felt threatened, it could drive close to the pillbox, where the machine gunners ensconced there could defend the rear of the vehicle. This made trying to get a grenade into the hatch or the engine of the armored monster almost impossible, or very costly. The Marines could not train enough fire on the pillbox viewport, or on the tank view slits because the swiveling turret cannon always hunted them down when they crawled too close or raised too much of an alarm. The Americans had not been able to assemble in any sort of numbers for fear of attracting the cannon's fire.

Lieutenant Kirk told Corporal Joe Canlon to radio for satchel charges, a flamethrower and bazooka. That was the extent of the plan for now. Failing any success with that, the officer would ask for mortars busily engaged elsewhere to target the pillbox. His men lay scattered around the enemy position, and the lieutenant did not want to initiate a withdrawal if he could avoid it. The movement would only give the enemy more targets to shoot at or chase. The Marines would have to get back to a fairly safe distance if mortars or artillery were called upon, and the lieutenant was reluctant to concede even that. He wanted to deny the tank any sort of free rein to expand its area of control.

"What did they say?" Hawk asked Joe Canlon, who operated the radio, located in the pack on the back of the radioman, Blackwell. Joe had already delivered the answer to the lieutenant.

"They said they're trying. And asked if we wanted artillery? I told them not yet," said Joe.

"That don't sound good. We better do something before that tank gets a notion to come our way." Hawk rubbed his straight, narrow nose. "Or somebody takes a notion to drop artillery on *us*." Once entangled in the enemy lines, Sergeant Hawk no longer wanted to deal with artillery, specifically, the likelihood of it falling on him.

"Looks like you're about to get some answers. Here comes, Kirk," said Joe.

"They want us to wait here," Lieutenant Kirk informed Hawk. "Any ideas? I haven't run across tanks before. This is a new one for me."

"We could try the side of the tank, shoot up their windows," Hawk spat. "Or they used to tell us you could shoot them sprockets on the treads and bust 'em. I ain't never seen it done, for sure. But I know a grenade might blow the track loose. At least, if it did, the son of a bitch couldn't move."

"That's risky, getting close to that thing. The machine gunners in that bunker could see us trying to pull that off," said Kirk. "And the thing is still dangerous, whether it can move or not."

Hawk shrugged. "The armor ain't too thick on them bastards," said Hawk. As he finished speaking, the Type 95's cannon fired, the tank recoiled, and the blast ripped a black curtain shut, blocking out the jungle between them and the right flank. As the echo died away and the smoke swirled, they could hear men screaming. The tank had claimed several victims, without even advancing from the safety of its nearness to the pillbox. Smoke rose from the mouth of the tank's artillery piece. The cannon looked short and thin, like a cigarette dangling from the face of the fat, bullying tank.

"Okay," said Kirk, choked with emotion now. The cannon blast was decisively impressive. "Take six men over to the flank of that tin can and see what you can do. The tank and the pill box should be blind on that side."

Hawk nodded. "Yessir." Hawk raised his voice and waved at Joe Canlon. "Joe, get Baker, Osage, Turnage, and Murdoch. We're gonna try to slow up that thing."

"I got to do the radio," said Joe.

"Okay, *do* the goddam radio. Get me Gilmore, then. Shake a leg." The machine gun in the pillbox opened up on the place in the forest where the tank cannon's shell had landed, attempting to riddle any wounded, as well as attempting to kill any rescuers of the wounded. Hawk walked over to Canlon with a scowl. "Blackwell's the radio operator, what's with this radio shit?" he asked in a low voice.

"The lieutenant put me on the radio for now," Joe said with a bit of defiance in his tone. "I got a loud voice."

"Awright. Awright," Hawk said. "*Loud voice,*" he muttered with several obscenities. The five men had gathered around him. He turned his back to Joe. "We're gonna go off to that blind flank and put some rifle fire on their viewports. Might even be able to grenade one of their wheels if things turn out right. Somebody can get to the pillbox once that thing ain't guarding it."

Everyone bobbed their helmets, signaling that they understood, except Baker. He waved a hand.

"Did all that mean we're taking the pillbox, too? Or just the tank?" Baker asked for clarification.

"We're gonna see what happens," said Hawk. "The tank's the main thing for now. That's our job. They're supposed to be bringing up a flamethrower for the pillbox."

"Then why don't we wait for it?" Baker asked. He had been in many tight situations with Hawk. Like Joe Canlon, he was able to question the sergeant. Unlike Joe, he was *almost* always willing to take a chance, just for the hell of it. He had a slender and deranged looking face, with a permanent lopsided grin, and one eye sitting higher in his head than the other.

The tank cannon exploded again. A red and black fountain of flame lifted a clump of trees near where its first shot had landed and blew the uprooted timber back into the jungle. The tree trunks were launched like giant arrows deep into the forest, in what seemed like slow motion, and over the heads of the men immediately behind where the shell struck. The intermittent and horrifying displays of the machine's power had become commonplace.

"That's why. Let's go," Hawk answered.

The six of them disappeared deeper into the forest in order to make their way around to the right. They stopped to lie prone on the edge of the jungle, facing the two enemy juggernauts in relative safety, and within a much closer range than the men in the front and rear of the enemy.

Hawk opened up with his Thompson submachine gun, concentrating on the tank's side viewport. Murdoch threw the bipod of his BAR onto the ground and focused his fire on the sprockets and bogey wheels supporting the treads of the tank. Dozens of harmless sparks danced and whined in the mechanical recesses along the lower part of the vehicle. The remaining four men aimed their semiautomatic rifles at other targets of opportunity, including the engine cover, the machine gun barrels, and the top hatch. The hammering of all of the automatic weapons, resulting in a deafening roar of leaden rain inside the tank, startled the Japanese crew into immediate action. While a tank might resist high power ammunition to a considerable extent, this was not a large tank, and it was receiving an extremely heavy amount of close and well-aimed attention. The vehicle lurched forward a few feet, as if its driver intended to vacate the premises, in search of his attackers. The forward movement was only a lurch, however, and the next movement consisted of the slow rotation of the turret toward the side of the tank upon which Hawk's contingent lay. As the cannon brought its deadly open mouth in his direction, Hawk had to decide whether to keep up the effective barrage leveled at the enemy, charge the big steel turtle, or vacate the field. A charge did not look promising, as all of the hatches were tightly shut and there would therefore be no opportunity to get a grenade inside. Trying to insert a rifle barrel into the armored glass covered view slits did not seem possible. The hand operated turret slid around too quickly to allow for any prolonged thinking.

"Party's over!" Hawk shouted. "Withdraw!" The half dozen Marines jumped to their feet. They had yet to be fired upon, and would be able to make an unopposed retreat, if they moved swiftly enough. The pillbox could not fire in their direction due to the oblique angle, and it would take the tank another half a minute to point its cannon and 7.7 mm machine gun at them.

Realizing the danger of pulling directly back, once the mosquito thin nose of the tank cannon settled on their erstwhile position, Hawk led the men back along the same route, in the direction from which they had approached the enemy's flank, and back toward the front of the pillbox. By the time they had returned to the forest concealing Lieutenant Kirk and Joe Canlon, the Type 95 had unleashed another blast where they had been, leaving a smoking crater there.

"That didn't work," Hawk told Kirk, breathing heavily. "Maybe we should have run up and put a grenade in the tread first." He took out his canteen and opened it. "We could try it again, once they swing that turret back this way."

"That was close. I don't know if that's ever going to work. I want to knock it out, but I don't want to lose anybody, since we're supposed to have help on the way," said Kirk.

As they spoke, Hawk noticed the two green canisters hanging on the front of Kirk's utility jacket. Everyone had a grenade or two, but these two were a little out of the ordinary: they consisted of smoke bombs, rather than fragmentation grenades, used for marking locations for aerial observation, or at times, used to create a foggy screen.

"Smoke grenades might blind 'em enough to jump on that tank, or even the pillbox, sir," Hawk nodded at the canisters. "We could try both at the same time, blinding them and blowing off a track."

"Yeah..." the officer answered slowly. He was hesitant. "I don't know. Bullets go through smoke." Hawk raised his eyebrows and nodded in agreement. He couldn't argue with that one. It called for a drink.

"Ain't it past time for that flamethrower?" Hawk took another generous taste of the oily tasting liquid.

"Yes. It's getting that way. Do you want to try again?" the lieutenant asked.

"Well, sir, I wouldn't exactly call it *wanting* to. Let's just call it *willing* to. Before anybody else gets hurt."

"That tank needs to go," said Kirk. "The rest of the company is going to come stumbling into the damn thing any minute."

Hawk waved Blackwell and the radio over. He didn't see the temporary operator, the one with the loud voice, hanging around. He made the call himself. "Get somebody down the draw there, to warn anybody comin' up here that we got a tank aimed at us."

Lieutenant Kirk handed Hawk the two smoke

grenades. "See what you can do," he said in an unenthusiastic tone.

"Yessir." Hawk peered through the leaves at the pillbox. The tank had returned to its former position, beside the bunker and about half its own length in front of the fortress. The turret was facing forward again, in the same direction as the pillbox's machine gun. The machine guns on the tank, and in the bunker fired steadily into the forest, keeping the Americans pinned down. The open ground in front of the Japanese afforded them a clear field of fire, and domination of the battlefield, for the moment. History had shown, however, that an immobile emplacement of that nature could not hold forever. The confounding difference this time, was the mobile, hovering, and protective tank.

"If nothing else, lieutenant, they won't be able to see where to shoot for a while." Hawk held up the smoke canister. "Maybe y'all can get a bead on that pillbox gunport."

Hawk called his five men together again. "Let's give it another shot," he told them. "I got these things this time." He showed them the AN-M8 steel cylinders. Each could belch two minutes of hydrochloric fumes. The top of the cans had a mousetrap igniter, like a regular hand grenade, but with a shorter fuse. "Maybe we can smoke 'em out. These things can cause all kinds of shit."

As Hawk's party retraced the route through the jungle on the flank of the pillbox, Kirk ordered more pressure on the front of the bunker, in order to give them some degree of cover. The other Marines in the jungle crawled slowly forward, staying low and firing their Mis gamely at the enemy, hoping to get within grenade range. The machine gun in the pillbox managed to keep their advance at bay, occasionally hitting a target, and providing time for the tank cannon to pick out the best targets among the attackers. The Japanese machine gun set up a phalanx of exploding shots along the edge of the jungle, the pulsating blaze leaping to the height of a man, and effectively drawing a line which could not be crossed by the Marines. As the 7.7 mm's conical flash guard swung to the left of the arc of MI's facing it, a Marine on the right rushed out into the open and hurled a grenade. It exploded harmlessly between the tank and the bunker, and a line of slugs climbed up the American's back as he tried to retreat into the forest. His corpse shook violently as the gun sent another burst into him, to make sure that he was dead. The price of courage.

"Well, shit!" Hawk snapped upon seeing this. His five men had arrived at their position, and they were surprised to find Kirk trying to slowly advance on the enemy. Nothing productive could come of that. The Japanese machine gun played lines of fire triumphantly back and forth across the open ground in front of the bunker. Another grenade exploded harmlessly in front of the tank. The armored vehicle replied with the discharge of a blast from its turret into the concealing jungle. The gunner had learned to lower his elevation and had taken out a portion of the American lines. Still, Kirk refused to retreat, pressuring the already pressured defenders.

The enemy's latest success angered Hawk, the emergency making him temporarily forget his plan to use the smoke screen. Ordinarily a rather emotionless individual, anger was his weakness. The anger never lasted long, because it usually ignited into irrational rage. He dropped the two tightly clutched canisters at the edge of the jungle, as if having no intention of picking them up again.

"Pull back, like we did before, if that gun turns this way," he told Baker. "They ain't paying no attention to us. I'm gonna see what I can do."

"What?" Baker was incredulous. "What the hell are you doing?"

Hawk pulled a fragmentation grenade from his pocket and slipped the pin out. He held the safety lever down and ran out into the open space between the combatants, and toward the side of the tank. The Type 95 had a view slit on its side facing Hawk, though it was unlikely the crew was making any use of it, as all of their attention remained focused on the area facing the primary Marine force. The view slit was located in the center of a small, spring-loaded trapdoor that could be opened, but its small size only allowed for one of the tank crew to point a pistol out of it. Hawk had decided that he could deal with that eventuality.

He ran to the side of the tank, close enough to touch it. Bone chilling from a distance, the alien and familiar proximity of the angular pile of steel did not make the tank look any friendlier. Hawk had placed himself in one of those spots where human flesh did not belong. The cannon and one machine gun faced forward, and the other machine gun faced the rear. Other than the one little trapdoor viewport, Hawk was momentarily safe from view, in a hidden area on the side of the tank. He briefly inspected the idler, bogey wheels, and sprockets supporting the narrow tread, released the lever of the grenade, and laid it gently within the machinery, just under the mud-caked track. The

Japanese tracks were smaller than those of American tanks, and he fully expected the explosion from such a carefully placed grenade to result in causing immobilizing damage. He turned and ran back for the forest. While he had been attending to this, however, a crewman glanced out the little aperture on that side and spied Hawk's retreat. The trapdoor opened, and a hand clawing a Nambu pistol reached out, pointing at the fleeing sergeant. Baker and the others, observing from the concealment of the forest, aimed at the now wide-open view slit with their rifles, and opened fire. The pistol dropped from the disembodied hand, slid along the side of the tank, and clattered onto the ground. The bloody arm jerked back inside. Hawk's grenade detonated, obscuring the tank from view, as Hawk threw himself to the ground among the others. They all looked up anxiously, to see what fruit their labors had reaped.

Lieutenant Kirk, watching from the front of the pillbox, could see the action, and craning his neck said: "What the hell? He wasn't supposed to do that."

Corporal Joe Canlon, standing next to the officer, shook his head. "He's nuts."

The explosion caused a great deal of consternation within the tank. The ringing blast, the vibration, and the concussion within the thin-walled tank, rattled the thinking of the crew. Fearing correctly that the Americans had targeted their wheels, the driver threw the machine into gear and let out the clutch, to make sure that they could still move.

"Son of a bitch!" Hawk cursed as he saw the tank lurch forward as easily as it had before. He was amazed that the flimsy little sprockets had survived. "It didn't do a damn thing," he said.

"Oh, it did something," Baker corrected him. "They're coming this way." The tank spun the tread on the right side and held the tread on the left side stable, causing the vehicle to pivot in the direction of Hawk's party. The spinning tread threw angry clods of dirt in a whirling maelstrom.

"Uh oh," Hawk muttered. The crew was not going to turn the turret in the Americans' direction this time and allow them time to run away again. They were bringing the turret to their target. The machine gun already spat angrily at them as the tank wheeled around. This left Hawk with no time for planning, something he should have already done instead of risking the ill-advised maneuver with the hand grenade. He grabbed the smoke canisters. He pulled the pin on one, and the igniter spewed smoke.

Disregarding the machine gun fire, Hawk charged into the open space in what was now the front of the tank. The line of slugs streaming from the 7.7mm gun had not settled into a focused field of fire yet, instead, weaving wildly back and forth, jerking awkwardly at various heights. Hawk tossed the smoking canister about twenty feet in front of the tank, and in seconds the vehicle had disappeared in a white, boiling oblivion of fumes sprouting from several vent openings in the can. Hawk dove back under cover, as the machine gun finally managed to cross over the ground where he had been standing; although it was now firing blindly through the smoke. The tank paused in the cloud, as the driver tried to get his bearings. The five Marines poured fire into the oncoming armored vehicle, knowing that once it bulldozed its way through the smoke, it could pick its targets with deadly accuracy and firepower. Unfortunately, though they could see somewhat better than the Japanese crowded into the tank, the smoke obstructed the Americans' view to a fair degree as well.

As Hawk fired intensely at the front view port being used by the driver, whenever the smoke allowed him to aim at it, he understood that the tank was coming through the haze and after them, and more specifically after him. The driver did a strange thing at that point, however. Apparently, unable to see at all, he had lost his sense of direction in the cloudbank. His view port, like the one on the side of the tank, was centered in a trapdoor that could be raised for the driver to get a better view when not maneuvering in a combat situation. The opening was much larger than the spring-loaded gun port on the side of the tank, which only a pistol could fit through. A small man could climb through the driver's trapdoor. The driver flapped the door open and propped it ajar with a rod attached for the purpose. The zinc chloride in the grayish white fumes had stuck to his glass view slit and he was blinded, making it necessary to open the entire little portal to maneuver, if not just to breathe.

Above the clanking wheels and the blazing machine gun, Hawk's keen ears picked out the metallic slap of this port hole opening in front of the driver. He pulled the pin on the other smoke grenade, ran recklessly out into the open again, and with a powerful, pitcher's overhand throw this time, slammed it directly through the open driver's portal. In the instant that he threw it, with his fingers extended and pointing at the hatchway, he knew that the throw had been well aimed. The can clapped against something inside and rattled around on the floor. Within seconds smoke curled out of the driver's open window, and the top hatch in the turret flew open. A geyser of twisting smoke rose from the hatch, and smoke poured from around the view slits and from beneath the engine cover. The smoke engulfed the cramped interior and its occupants. A crewman climbed, choking and coughing out of the top hatch in the turret, and five gun muzzles directed a whirlwind of slicing lead into him. He tumbled down the side of the tank. The still moving tank swerved to the left and right, then stopped as the driver tried to climb out of his front window. He, too, met with a solid lead hurricane of fire, dropping him half inside, and half outside the tank. The third crewman had earlier been killed, when he tried to shoot Hawk with the pistol.

The Type 95 sat there like a furious factory chimney, spouting endless clouds of thick smoke, the engine still idling.

"Want me to drop a grenade in it?" Baker asked.

"No, wait a second," said Hawk. He had another idea. "I think they're all dead. Let the smoke burn itself out."

The men in the pillbox could not see what had happened to their big steel protector, off on their concealed side. They saw only occasional plumes of smoke blowing across their field of fire. Far from helpless, however, they continued to blaze away with their machine gun at the Marines firing at them.

Hawk crawled over toward Baker. "Hey, listen. Let's roll that tank in front of the pillbox and block their machine gun."

"Roll? Shit, that thing's on fire," said Baker.

"Nah, just smokin'. It's almost out."

"You can't *roll* that thing. You talking about getting in it and driving it?"

"Yeah."

"But that smoke is poison—all cooped up in that little bastard like that? Do you know how to drive that rig?" Baker asked.

"Shit, yeah. Don't you?"

"Hell, I don't know. Some crazy ass Jap shit like that? Probably not. The gears are different."

"We only need one speed. Listen at that old bastard, the motor's still runnin'. Just gotta throw it in gear, it's all ready to go. We pull that dead one out of the driver's hatch and go in that way," said Hawk. "We slam the top hatch shut and plow the shitass thing right into 'em. Jump out and run like hell. They can't do shit."

"I...guess...if you want to. Sounds like something that could really fall apart. Can you fit inside that thing?"

"Yeah. Might scrape off some of my hide."

"What am I supposed to do in all this?" Baker asked.

"For one thing, help me see. Always helps to have two. And help me get that dead one out of the way. I think there's another son of a bitch inside. He might not be real dead."

"Yeah. Okay. All right. I'm with you."

Hawk instructed the others to work their way a little farther to the left, but not directly in front of the pillbox. From there, they could indirectly fire at an angle into the bunker's view port, while not having as much of a risk from the machine gun swinging toward them. They no longer had to fear the tank. Hawk turned back to Baker.

"Let's go."

The two of them ran unopposed to the tank, its engine still idling. Only a thin, spinning, column of smoke continued to rise from the turret's hatch. Baker grabbed the jacket of the driver, who hung halfway out of his open escape hatch. The little doorway was small, and the body was jammed tightly into it. After tugging angrily, Baker finally flung the dead man to the ground. He hesitated to enter, however. Hawk, who had been watching the pillbox machine gun from its profile, did not hesitate. He raised a leg and bounded into the tight little steel container, tearing out large portions of his jacket. Baker followed, squirming through the dark opening more slowly.

The bitter smell of the burned zinc chloride threatened to become overwhelming. Both men coughed and squinted. They bumped against one another in the small space and stepped on the other Japanese crewman lying dead on the floor.

"Make sure he ain't playin' opossum," Hawk said.

"He's dead. Throw him out?" Baker choked.

"He's doin' awright," said Hawk, forcing himself into the driver's flimsy little metal seat. He disengaged one tread, pushed in the clutch and put the tank in what he assumed was low gear. When he let out the clutch, however, the transmission complained loudly, and the tank leaped forward with a giant lurch. Evidently, it was *not* in low gear. But the big beast was moving anyway and pivoting back toward the front of the enemy bunker.

"Damn! It worked!" Hawk shouted over the loud engine noise.

"You call this *working*?"

"Shit, yeah," Hawk answered, reaching out to grab the rod that held the trapdoor open in front of him. He let it fall shut.

"What about the top hatch?" Baker asked.

"Shut it. One of them bastards might try to jump in here," Hawk replied.

Baker slammed the hatch shut, and the darkness and stench increased in intensity.

"God, I can't breathe," said Baker. Residual smoke filled the small space of air between them. The smell changed from the predominating grenade bitterness to a deadly exhaust odor. They could barely see one another due to the smoke, metal dust, and darkness.

"Goddam son of a bitch. I can't see *nothing*," said Hawk. Smudge blocked out the glass on the view port.

Baker tried to look out the side view port. "I can't see anything, either." He rubbed at the thick glass with his sleeve, and it only smeared the smoke residue, making visibility worse. The thick armored glass did not afford the best of views under optimal circumstances. "I think we were headed toward the machine gun," said Baker.

"Yeah, but sideways. I wanted to go headfirst into it and try to push into the damned thing," said Hawk.

"I hear the bastard. They're gonna be blasting the side of us pretty soon."

"Yeah," Hawk answered. He had to be able to see. He couldn't drive the tank very well, even if he were able to see. It was lurching along in a higher gear than it should be for the speed he was giving it. The tank could very well stall after any one of the violent lurches. They bucked toward the front of the pillbox, almost in front of the machine gun. Hawk lifted the little trapdoor up about a quarter of the way open, in order to get some idea of where he was. This made driving more difficult, as a hand was required to keep the lid partially open. He managed to pull out a little farther in front of the bunker, turn, and face it directly.

"Okay, *now* I got it. Hang on. We're going in," said Hawk.

"Shit! Going in *what*?" Baker asked. He was standing and holding onto the side of the seat to steady himself. By then, however, the prow of the tank rammed the viewport of the pillbox, knocking the machine gun out of the opening and driving it violently back inside, in a mangled inoperable heap. The tank's cannon hit the concrete roof and broke into pieces, buckling the turret. Hawk accelerated as much as the pedal would allow, trying to knock down the front wall of the bunker. The tank's treads spun madly, but the reinforced concrete wall held against it.

"Where are we?" Baker shouted.

"Right in the opening. I think I bashed the gun out of it," Hawk answered. Baker was stunned. That meant the only thing between them, and the Japanese was the thin little driver's trapdoor in front of Hawk's face. Hawk pushed at the trapdoor and found that he could open it. It swung up and into the interior of the pillbox. He saw the men inside, scrambling around the remaining undamaged machine gun facing out of the rear of the bunker. The light from the rear viewport illuminated them enough to be able to tell what they were doing. Hawk quickly dropped the door shut.

"Goddam, we're damn near inside with them,"

Hawk informed Baker. He picked up Baker's rifle. "Quick, put a bayonet on it," he ordered.

"What the hell are you doing, going inside?" Baker snapped the bayonet hanging on his belt onto the M1.

"Nah, here you go," he handed Baker a grenade and gestured at some bailing wire that was coiled around an ammunition box on the floor, filled with the 37-millimeter rounds. "Wrap the grenade onto the rifle barrel with that wire. We'll give 'em a Bangalore torpedo."

Baker worked feverishly with the wire, the sharp blade of the bayonet, and the small, unsteady round body of the little bomb. The knobs on the fragmentation grenade made it easier to tighten the wire down on it. As he did this, Hawk continued grinding the tank against the front of the enemy fortress, in the hopes of pushing the front wall down. The motor sounded like it was about to explode, and the exhaust smell increased. The enemy within, still unsure of who was driving the tank, had removed the machine gun from the rear of the pillbox and began setting it up in the middle of the enclosure, facing the tank and the front wall, to be able to fire outside, should the wall fall inward.

Baker handed Hawk the rifle and grenade. "That ain't much of a Bangalore torpedo, we'll be about two feet away from the explosion," he advised.

"We'll give it a little help," Hawk muttered, and ripped the pin out of the grenade while holding down the spoon. "Hold up the stock. When I lift the door, shove it like a bastard as hard as you can into that son of a bitch!"

"*What?* What if it catches on something?" Baker shouted back.

"What do you think? *We're dead*," Hawk answered. "*Don't* catch it on nothing! Just shove that bastard hard. Use two hands."

Baker shook his head and grabbed the rifle stock. He put one hand on the butt and the other on the fore-stock. Hawk let go of the grenade's safety lever, and immediately lifted the driver's trapdoor upward, as far as it would go. Baker launched the rifle and attached the grenade forward with all of his strength. His brown forearm flashed forcefully, an inch in front of Hawk's eyes, covered with the red and black tattoo of a cowgirl, sitting on a corral fence. The elbow was moving with such force, it would have broken Hawk's nose if it had connected. For an instant he could smell Baker, more than the inside of the tank. Baker smelled like sweat and cigarettes. The rifle and grenade flew smoothly out of the tank's opening and crashed onto the deck of the dark pillbox, several feet away. Hawk dropped the trap-door shut. Almost immediately, a tremendous blast rocked the tank backward. Baker bounced against the sides of the tank and fell to the floor. Hawk's head drib-bled like a basketball against the front of the tank several times; the last time, without the protection of his helmet. The tank's body and the wall of the bunker protected the two Americans from the brunt of the explosion, in spite of being inches away from it. The Japanese inside the pillbox were shredded and tossed about as if by a steel tornado imprisoned in a concrete container.

Hawk and Baker sat in the captured tank, half suffo-cated and dazed. Fumes from the detonated grenade and ammunition inside the bunker drifted through the cracks around the view slits. It grew darker and smokier in their steel coffin. They heard Marines shouting outside and advancing on the pillbox, while firing into it. The tank no longer felt as if it were trying to move.

"Why the hell did you wire the grenade to the rifle?" Baker gasped. "You could have just thrown it in."

"I don't know," Hawk shook his bleeding head, semi-conscious. "Seemed like a good idea. I wanted to stick it up in there good, without them throwing it back out. It worked, didn't it?"

"Hell, yeah, it worked. They probably thought, 'what are those crazy Yankees throwing a rifle at us for?'" Baker wheezed. The hatch at the top of the turret opened, letting in light and fresh air. Joe Canlon looked down on them.

"Are you guys all right?" he called down.

"Yeah," Baker answered, still sprawled on the floor, and barely able to bend his wrist to wave at him. "Great. Great."

"Cut the engine, you might bust through the wall out here," Joe shouted.

Hawk shut down the motor. "That was the object," Hawk told him. Joe saw only blood where Hawk's eyes should be.

2

THE DEVIL OF A CODE

GENERAL DENNISON WELCOMED COLONEL CLARK INTO his office. The two shook hands and Dennison told Clark to have a seat. After only a minute or two of catching up on the well-being of their respective families, General Dennison went directly to the point.

"We have a situation here, Ben," said Dennison. "You have heard of the cryptologist, Maxwell Hoech? A bit of an eccentric, I'm afraid."

"Yes, I remember reading that he was kidnapped in Peru or somewhere, a few months ago. I never followed it very closely, or understood any of it. Or frankly, why anyone cared." The general smiled at the answer. "The newspapers seemed to think it worthy of note," continued the colonel. "If you or I were captured, would anyone care? I always thought the big to-do was because of his job, all of the mystery surrounding secret messages and the like. His lifestyle had a lot to do with it, I suppose. Personally, I don't know what good any of that business is. Was he killed or something?"

"I...don't know the answers to any of that at the

moment," the general answered. "Hoech was on a trip to Lima to meet with several South American intelligence agencies when the abduction happened. He was developing a code network and helping our allies there to expand their systems, presumably, interconnecting with ours. I'm sure it was all done to aid in our own war effort, basically, more than theirs. When the kidnapping incident occurred, no one knew who was responsible."

"They said it was the Germans in the beginning, I think," said Clark, "because of all the Nazi activity down there. And then when that didn't pan out, I believe they tried to blame the Italians, maybe," said Clark, waving his hand dismissively, as if it didn't matter to him who did it. "There's a lot of those in Argentina. But, you know who I would bet on? The Spaniards. They're Nazi toadies. Everybody gives them a pass because of that neutrality crap."

"There were many rumors," Dennison agreed. "We are past the rumors now. We know for certain that it was the Japanese. Hoech has surfaced. They smuggled him out of Peru and have taken him to Japan."

"The bastards!" Clark went from disinterest to outrage rather quickly, indicating that he could likely return to the same state of disinterest in short order.

"Yes. Indeed," said the general. "Here's the dilemma. Not long ago, we began receiving coded messages from Hoech; that's not exactly something you would expect from a Japanese prisoner. We weren't sure what to make of them. Was he sending them under duress, was he sending them secretly, or was it done voluntarily at the behest of the Japanese? Were the contents legitimate and true, or merely decoys? At length, we came to the conclusion that he had somehow found a way to send us clandestine, and legitimate intelligence information. We believe it is possible that he agreed to work with Japanese intelligence, on the surface, and has turned into a double agent. He may have been more acceptable to them because he was born in Germany, you may recall. He knew *a lot* of people in Germany, the right people. In any event, for the time being, the Japanese do not appear to be aware of his ability to independently communicate with us. Then again, maybe they are, and he doesn't know it, not to mention us."

"Fascinating," said Clark, his broad and unintelligent features tensed thickly in thought. "There's a lot of room for trickery there. That's why I never cared for all that."

"Yes, there is. Limitless room. The more you consider the possibilities, the farther you fall down the rabbit hole. Especially, as we puzzle through each message. You may or may not know that we broke the Japanese code before the war began. We were able to decode their messages from the beginning, with a few notable missteps, such as the attack on Pearl Harbor. We have inroads into the diplomatic messages, more so than those sent by the military. Hoech was instrumental in the early code breaking. He was an expert on Japanese code, dating back as far as the First World War. We suspect he has access to their coded intelligence, and they do not realize that he is able to decipher it.

"He is in a very unique position," the general continued. "We can read their code fairly reliably, but they have to send it out first, for us to intercept it. If it stays in house, going from one of their agencies in Japan to another, we cannot get it. And then, we have nothing to decode. Hoech obviously knows this and has been broadcasting their more sensitive messages for our benefit. He sends information to outlying Japanese bases who have no need for access to it, just so we can pick it up. At least, he sends some of the more important messages. In order to conceal what he is doing, he has devised yet another code of his own, so that they will not recognize his transmissions."

"Ingenious of him," said Clark. "If they planned to disrupt our communications by abducting Hoech, the plan seems to have backfired on them. He is doing them more harm than good."

"Yes. Almost. There is one...slight...problem with it all. His latest code is *too* good. Just like the Japanese, we can't figure out exactly *what* he is saying, much of the time. There were, and are, very few code breakers on his level."

"A shame," said Clark. "An artist without an audience."

"You could say that. Or an artist with a blind and deaf audience. We've had partial successes on some of his early efforts, such as plans for the development of a new and larger tank, and a grid layout of the mine defenses on one of our invasion beaches," said the general.

"Oh, good. All is not lost."

"Definitely not. But, just recently, we've had a devil of a time with one of his transmissions. He has classified it as *1Y-orange*. I don't know if you're familiar with that categorization, but it is a highly placed classification, based on several factors, and the implications of the information's weight on the war effort. Only two intelligence transmissions have ever met the criteria for such a high designation. Granted, this is Hoech's own personal grading of the message; his opinion, if you will. But he knows the significance of calling something *1Y-orange*. He has classified enough messages to know the criteria. It refers to something important enough to affect the outcome of the war itself, all by itself."

"My," said Colonel Clark. "I was thinking perhaps it had to do with his own rescue, or escape. But that would likely not rise to that high of a level of importance. Would it?"

"We considered that. No. It would not meet the objective criteria. But there is a caveat to even that. Because, the subject of the message *could* actually involve his rescue, even if the rescue itself was not the main thrust of the message. Perhaps Hoech believes that he must be rescued first, in order to deliver this *1Y-orange* message *in person*. So, a rescue could be interwoven in there. It's just a theory, we don't know. His recovery would be of significance to us, I don't want to minimize that. It's just that we have thirty people working on this, and that many more back in the States. Their consensus is that Hoech would not engineer his own rescue. Although, it my understanding it hasn't been ruled out."

"My word, this *is* complicated," said Colonel Clark. "I hope you have an adequate and qualified staff working on it. A most challenging problem."

"I am glad you think so. Because it seems that *you* are involved in this mysterious, all-important, last message from Hoech."

"Me? *What?*"

"Yes. It is a long series of words that seem to consist of nothing but gibberish, as most codes do. We have determined that we are being given a month to act before the information expires. We don't exactly know what that means. We have a month to do...what? Our cryptologists have a theory that the message is a series of names, mostly names of people, but perhaps not all of them. It seems that one name is able to identify the next name, following it in sequence. That is, the number one person is able to identify the number two person, the number two person can identify number three, and so forth. There are nearly a dozen. We are trying to merely skip to the last name and find the ultimate message, the mother lode, as it were, without following the sequence. But that's not working. It appears that it must be done in order. Hoech did this to confuse the Japanese, and I'm sure that it will, because it has confused us."

"Rather incredible. Hoech had to know more than the workings of a code to create such an intricate puzzle. He had to know these individual people, and something about them."

"Absolutely. Or he knew someone who knew them. He has to be quite a student of human nature, brilliant at recalling details and snatched bits of conversation about people. Well, more on that later. Nothing seems absolute in this matter. We considered that perhaps the names were in reverse order, that is, that the first name would be the solution, in order to cut down on the complications. Sometimes these codes work in that manner. It's one of the older variations in cryptology, no longer used much."

"I see," said the colonel. "I have heard a little about that very thing, in reading about Wake Island. I confess,

I never understood a lot about codes and code breaking."

"Nor do most of us. We have people that do, however. Here's the interesting part. We have determined that the first name in the *1Y-orange* message is actually—your name. In fact, that's how the Marine Corps ended up with this."

"Uh..."

"Yes." The general smiled at Clark's reaction. "So, I think we can rule out the number one name being our final solution. Unless *you* know something that you have been concealing from me in the last ten minutes? Do you know anything that could cost us the war? Something that Hoech told you, or you told Hoech? I take it by your expression, that you do not. No, we're fairly certain we're going to have to go through the entire list of names to decode the message, beginning with you. If this were not so, you would be able to tell us everything we need to know, right now."

"Strange. So strange. Why, and how, is my name on this list at all? As you say, I'm not the one with the ultimate solution. Or any solution. And mine is the *first* name? I never knew Hoech. Hell, like I told you, I've barely heard of him."

"That part, we don't know. And who really knows? You actually may be the one with the final solution, and not even know it yourself. We do have a built-in way of finding that out, however."

"Well. By all means, let's find out. How can we do *that*? I can't imagine knowing some top-secret information and not even being aware of it myself. Although, you have me wondering if anything isn't possible."

"If you know who the second name refers to, the

name that follows your name in the sequence, you are *not* the ultimate bearer of the solution. You are only a cog in the wheel, leading to the next cog. You are in fact, only the starting point in the sequence, and not the finish."

"Ah, yes. That makes sense. I wouldn't have thought of that. Clever. What is this name I am supposed to recognize? Or am I even allowed to know?"

"I might have simplified it too much. Hoech doesn't give us a name. If he did, we could simply contact the last person referenced. He gives us, instead, information that can only refer to one other person. It may be a word or phrase. It is, in effect, a clue toward the identification of a name. And logically, only *you* will readily recognize it. It does not mean that we could not have figured it out without you, given sufficient time. In other words, if there is a missing link in all of this, say if someone dies, we can hopefully go on, but it will take a good deal of time. We don't have a lot of time. We need answers right away. As I said, the whole puzzle collapses in a month."

"Why, certainly. I would like to aid in this effort any way I can, to the best of my limited ability. What is the identifying information I'm supposed to recognize?"

"The second entry in the code, after the information pertaining to you, is the entry: 'Delivalung recon non-com.' Does that mean anything to you?"

Clark looked down thoughtfully. "Why, yes, it does," the colonel answered without hesitation. "We had to do a series of classified reconnaissance patrols on the volcano itself, before the operation there at Delivalung. But actually, there were two sergeants leading those patrols, not one. Two particularly difficult areas had to be investigated simultaneously."

"Hmm," the general wrote something down. "Do you recall those two names?"

"Yes. One was Clifford Curry and the other, James Hawk."

"I see." The general wrote down the two names. "And are these two men still on active duty?"

"To the best of my knowledge."

"Hmm. As I say, we are still a little new at this. Perhaps there can be two names instead of one. Damn, this only gets worse. I wonder..." The general picked up his phone. "Corporal Jensen, please. Yes, Jensen, can you locate something for me? Yes. The report on the killed and wounded at Delivalung. Do we have that yet? Excellent. Can you bring that to me? Don't bother to knock."

The general looked at Clark. "I'm just curious. That engagement was fairly recent. If those two survived the campaign, they're probably around somewhere locally. In division, in the Helvedes." The general shook his head. "That brings up another unproven theory about this. The working theory is that all the names of these individuals are within the local theater of operations, perhaps very locally, as in the Helvedes Islands. The time limit would not permit us to search, say Omaha, or Persia, or French Equatorial Africa. We are hopeful that Hoech has limited the stage for us."

"Yes, quite likely those two are still around and involved here in the battle for the islands," said the colonel.

"*That* is encouraging on one level," said the general. "I can see how we might have figured that out without you. There must be some record of patrols leading up to the Delivalung assault. As I said, it would take a bit of time to find that out, and yet it did not take you any time at all to recall the names of the two gentlemen."

"Actually, it might not have been as easy as you think. The OSS was involved in that operation. The whole thing was hush hush. The records of those patrols are long gone, if they existed."

Corporal Jensen walked in unannounced and handed three sheets of paper to the general, saluted, and left. The general picked up the top leaf and began reading.

"392 killed. Those were heavy losses for an operation of that size. I see here, right off, Clifford Curry, killed in action," read the general.

"Oh, no," said the colonel. His disappointment had more to do with solving the coded message, rather than the misfortune befalling Curry, as demonstrated by his next, quickly asked question. "How about...Hawk?"

"Let's see. It's alphabetical. No, I don't see him. Oh, yes, here he is, on the wounded list. A minor wound evidently treated and released. So, this fellow is around, alive and well."

"And he will be able to identify your third name?"

"Hopefully. That's the theory. I wonder if Hoech knew that Curry was dead." The general frowned. "Or, if he knew these two at all. You say that he didn't know you. But it is a coincidence, I suppose, that there is only one living name, when it could have been two. And yet, I somehow doubt Hoech was only coincidentally right."

"This may not be too bad, after all. I mean, in a month it could be done easily. We have already found two names."

"Yes. Only one, for certain, I'm afraid. We'll have to

confirm this Hawk fellow. Do you know him, or anything about him?"

"Some. He's been in on a lot of dirty details, and they didn't get any cleaner because of his involvement. He's a character you meet in the shadows. He gets the bad assignments because he is expendable. The 'bad' tends to stick to him. Better to deal with him quickly and move along to someone else."

"Oh. Sorry to hear that," said Dennison.

"Why, sir?"

"I mean, it appears you relied upon him at Delivalung. I was trying to think of someone to run with this thing, to connect the dots. If these names, these people, are all involved in the local campaign, it might take a combat experienced individual to help locate all of them."

"Well." Clark laughed abruptly. "No argument there. He *is* that. If *that's* all you want." Clark shook his head. "But we're not talking about a genius here," said the colonel. "This is a pretty sophisticated undertaking. He's more of a...one time, shoot to kill, suicide mission type of operative. He's just as reckless with his own life as he is with others."

"And yet, he keeps getting new missions?"

"Well, yes. But, like I said: they are not code breaking, sophisticated missions. They are more of the blood and guts, desperate type of operations. Always plenty of those."

"I'm afraid," said the general, "that may be what we need as this progresses. It could turn into that. We may become desperate. And maybe, for someone to consistently survive the missions you describe, this man may be a little more sophisticated than you give him credit for."

Clark shook his head. He figured he knew James Hawk well enough. "I doubt that."

* * *

FIRST PLATOON HAD BEEN GIVEN a rest after their triumph over the pillbox and the tank. Company headquarters was relocated nearby, and the rest of the company continued in the push forward. The men in Hawk's squad were relieved that no one had been severely injured within their small unit during the operation, as the rest of the platoon had not been so fortunate. The Japanese tank had served the enemy well, before its encounter with First Platoon. As they sat in a loosely defined circle before the pillbox, normal life resumed, or at least, what had become a normal life for them.

Marchand, a large, foul tempered man, had for some reason taken a dislike to young Osage. The teenaged Marine was quietly cleaning his rifle in the lull following the action. Osage, like many, if not most Marines, had been in high school less than a year before. His life had been turned upside down by the war in the Pacific. Unlike many others, however, he had adapted well to his new world, due to an innate inner toughness that had sustained him.

Marchand, somewhat older, had not adapted as well. He had been horrified by the life and death struggle for the pillbox that the other men had taken in stride. He was used to receiving deference from others because of his great size and found himself lower in the tier of respect here than he liked. He was especially irritated by the smaller, wiry, young Osage, who all of the others liked and appreciated for his courage. Marchand suddenly decided, for better or worse, that this would be a good opportunity to raise his own stature within the group by lowering that of Osage. This had been a tactic of his since boot camp, and he felt that it had worked so far. He needed to fit into his new squad, and he needed respect. Unfortunately, the tank and pillbox incident did not afford him any, and he hoped that perhaps he could steal some of the luster from Osage.

"I didn't see you do much out there, Osage," said Marchand.

"Probably not," Osage answered, disinterestedly. He had the trapdoor on the buttplate of his MI open, with the little cleaning tools all taken out of the kit and lying about on a log next to him. The task did not require a great deal of attention, but it required some, to be done right, and he was doing it right. "I was on the other side, with Baker and them. We were out of sight," Osage informed the big man quietly. Joe Canlon looked up as the two men spoke to one another. He could tell by Marchand's tone that this might not end well. He knew Osage a lot better than did Marchand and knew that whatever the big man had planned might not work out as well as he thought.

"That's right. I was in the front getting shot at," said Marchand. "You were laying over there on the dead side of everything. No wonder I didn't see you. What kind of pull does it take to get that kind of assignment?"

Joe cleared his throat anxiously. He did not feel Marchand was properly addressing someone who had just participated in destroying a tank; an incident in which several men had died. Joe still felt a little guilty about his own claiming of special status as a radio operator, with a loud voice. Joe sensed it was too soon for any joking, much less childish bullying.

* * *

OSAGE, failing to pick up on the significance to any of this, including Marchand's tone of voice, ignored the whole thing and continued cleaning his rifle. He was a little numbed from the combat experience, having had a ring-side seat for all of it. It was easier to adhere to combat etiquette when one was a participant.

"Next time, you better pull your weight," said Marchand. Several of the men looked up in surprise at the sharp rebuke. There had never been any question of Osage pulling his weight, in any circumstance. Marchand's tone was less ambiguous with the last barb. Osage was a little surprised himself now, picking up on the gist of this.

All he could think of to say to the unexpected and unwarranted attack was: "Is that right?"

"Damn right, it's right," said Marchand.

"What are you gonna do? Court martial me?" Osage asked.

"I'm the one that's gonna break your goddam little skinny arm," said Marchand.

"You're the one they're gonna be callin' old one eye, too," said Osage, without a smile. Joe Canlon decided this might be a good time to intervene. Marchand was full of shit, but Osage was not.

"Hey, Marchand," Joe said, "here comes Hawk. Why don't you break *his* arm?" Everyone grew silent and looked at the ground as the sergeant approached them, including Marchand.

Hawk walked up to the group, adjusting the Thompson hanging on his shoulder.

"Hawk," said Joe. "How's your arm?"

"My arm? It's okay. I busted my head a little." He took off his helmet to show a deep gash in his forehead. Actually, it looked like something that should have killed him.

"Oh, yeah," said Joe, "quite a shot there. Somebody was worried about your arm," he added. "Kept talking about your arm."

"Nah. My arm? Shit. It's awright. Look, y'all, I gotta go see the captain. Take care of things here for me," said the sergeant. "He's probably got something else lined up for us, so look sharp." He replaced his helmet, winced, and walked away.

"That was your chance," Joe told Marchand. "Had his arm all ready for you."

"You're a real wise guy, ain't you, Canlon?"

"What's the matter? Want me to catch him for you? I can get him back. We're old buddies." Joe smiled.

Marchand tightened his lips and looked down. In addition to the spoken taunt, it so happened that Joe Canlon was a corporal, as well. Marchand was placing himself in disfavor with those in the most immediate positions of authority over him, for no particular reason. He did not like the outcome of the episode and continued to simmer. Osage, still largely indifferent to it all, continued cleaning the rifle. If he had to deal with Marchand, he would. If not, he might end up saving the bastard's life someday. Who knew what would happen in this crazy place?

Hawk entered the tent of the company commander, Captain Macintosh. Even with the front and back flaps clipped open, it was blazing hot inside. The sergeant took off his helmet.

"At ease, Sergeant," said the captain. "I have an unusual little request of you. Nothing serious. Have a seat there. It'll take a minute."

Hawk sat in the wobbly wooden folding chair. One leg of it sank into the ground. He stood quickly, pulled it out, and moved it a little before sitting down again. He maintained his dignity and military courtesy throughout the incident.

"I'm a little hard of hearing this morning, Captain. Stuck my head in a Jap tank," said Hawk. "I heard about that. Got a nasty abrasion there. You didn't want to get that treated?"

Hawk touched his forehead. "Oh. No, sir. It's awright. Some fella did something to it. My arm is okay, too." He touched his forehead again. The damn thing did sting.

"Oh. That's good." The captain glanced at the sergeant's arm. "I called you here because the general wanted me to ask you a few questions. It won't take long. The question won't take as long as the explanation, I'm afraid."

"The *general*? Probably wants to know when I'm gonna move in on Japan, sir." Hawk smiled.

"Yes. When are you?" The captain laughed. "We've all been waiting. No, it's this odd thing about a...code. I don't suppose you've heard of Maxwell Hoech?"

"Not that I recall, no sir. What outfit is he with?"

"He's not a part of the military, to my knowledge. He's a government employee, a cryptologist and sort of a celebrity, and most recently—a Japanese prisoner. He has sent us a message, that it seems, only you can decipher."

"Only *me*? I don't know what that would be, sir. Unless it's something out of the funny pages."

"The code is a series of messages that have some sort of personal reference to the recipient. We need your input before moving on to the next recipient. In fact, you should be able to tell us who the next person is. Am I making myself clear?"

Hawk stared blankly at him. He had no idea what the officer was talking about. He suspected that parts of the story were being deliberately left out, to make certain that he would never understand what was going on. That was the way military higher ups handled problems that they didn't understand themselves. He could not even guess or make a joke about this one. He knew that he was supposed to say "yes." You didn't tell officers that they weren't making themselves clear. But he wrestled with it for a moment.

"Yessir."

"Good. Here is the phrase that you are to identify. The phrase is associated with a person you should recognize." The captain frowned as he read the page in front of him. "I'll tell you what. Why don't you just read it?" He slid the paper across the surface of the little camp desk. Hawk spun it around with his smoky hand and grime covered fingertips, and leaned forward to read it. "Aloud. Please," said the captain. "We don't want any misunderstandings." The message was in capital letters, and other than Hawk's name, nothing else was printed on the page.

"Do you love me now?" Hawk read the five words

slowly. He frowned and shifted in his shaky little chair. It felt like a different leg of it might be sinking into the soft earth again. His mouth was slightly opened as he stared at the page. His lips moved as he read it to himself again.

The captain smiled. "Does that mean anything to you? Does that bring anyone to mind? A person?"

Hawk hesitated. He could not imagine what this was all about. But he also knew that the message meant something to him.

"Yessir. It does. It's a...thing...something this woman that I knew used to say to me, sometimes."

"Really? A civilian woman? An American woman? Where is this woman?"

"Well, she was...a civilian, I think. American. She was married to Captain E. W. Orr, out of Able Company. I don't know where she is. Maybe in Los Angeles, or something. That's where they were from. I ran into her on Ayermo. And that's the last I saw of her."

The captain began writing things down. "E. W. Orr? Marine Corps? Where is he now?"

"I reckon he's dead, sir. He was missing in action, but somebody reported seeing him dead. Somewhere on the island. That was kind of a mess. A lot of things got skipped over out there, when it came to the clearing all that up. We barely got off Ayermo."

"And she said these words to you after Orr died?"

"Oh...yessir. But...I mean, if it's important...I don't imagine that mattered much to her. I don't think she knew he was dead."

"So, you're saying, a captain's wife told you this?"

"Yessir. It was just some crazy thing she was always

saying. Kind of a running joke. It didn't mean much, I guess. If that's what you're thinking."

"In other words, in your mind, she is the *only* person —you know--- that this line could be referring to?"

"Yessir. Nobody else ever said anything like that to me. I mean, you know, maybe once, somewhere. But not over and over like that, like a joke. Like she did. She was always joking. She thought she was funny. But she wasn't."

"Interesting. Interesting woman. What is her name?"

"Vera Orr. That was her name, then. I guess it still is. You know women."

The captain wrote it down. "V-e-r-a?"

"Yessir. And...she's...a little different. She's not just some woman."

"How do you mean?"

"She knows a lot of people. She's got a lot of money. She does a lot of...things. I guess you'd say, she's connected. She could turn up anywhere, and I mean anywhere. She popped up on Ayermo in a submarine. She knew Colonel Clark. I think she knows people in Washington. All over the East Coast, mainly. But California, too, I imagine. They lived out there for a while. She does whatever she wants to do."

"That is so interesting. Maybe she knew Hoech personally. She must have. I am guessing all of these people in this code are unique like that. Except for yourself, of course," said the captain.

"Yessir. Nothing unique about me. I ain't got nothing, and I don't know nobody," Hawk laughed. "I got in the line to meet Veronica Lake one time, but ended up with Loretta Young——at the Hollywood Canteen. That's about it for me."

"Is that right? Veronica Lake?"

"Yessir. She was in this picture where she blows herself up at the end with a grenade and kills all the Japs. I kind of wanted to meet her. They'd move you around, if the line got too long, so I got shifted to Loretta Young. But I got nothing against Loretta Young. She was real nice."

"Yes! I remember that movie with Veronica Lake. Can't remember the name of it."

"Me, neither. It was something about the flag."

"Well, the way this code thing is going, we may meet her, after all," said the captain. "No telling how many people are involved in this business. She may have known Hoech."

"Yessir. This Vera Orr ain't too shabby, herself. Captain Orr said they wanted to put her in the movies," Hawk informed him.

"You haven't seen her since Ayermo?"

"That was it. We didn't part too friendly. It was a real tangled up situation. Me and her. She's...hard to figure. I didn't try."

"I suppose they will be able to find her easily enough, if her husband was in the Corps. I hope they are finished with us on the whole detail, after we close this out. I don't know what it all means. It's supposed to be some important message that can win the war, or lose the war, when you put it all together."

Hawk shook his head. "Yessir. That all sounds a lot like Vera Orr. That's the kind of thing she would be mixed up with. She'd be a good one to stay away from, if you have a choice. I bet the colonel could probably find her."

"I'm curious as to how all of this works, Sergeant, as

I am sure you are," said the captain. "I wonder if she *knew* Hoech." Hawk sat stoically with his fierce, expressionless face, and without having the slightest curiosity about anything. "When you read that message, you *knew* immediately who it referred to?"

"Yessir." Hawk readily admitted it.

"And yet, it's only five common words. Don't you think this woman could have said them to anyone else?"

"That wouldn't surprise me none. Yessir."

3

CLIFF AT THE END OF TOMORROW

SEVERAL DAYS LATER, TO HIS SURPRISE, SERGEANT HAWK was again summoned to the headquarters of Captain Macintosh. An even greater surprise awaited him there. After he had entered the tent and saluted, another officer stepped out of the shadows behind him. Although his combat saturated instinct urged him to turn and strike the unidentified stranger, he had just enough military bearing to control himself, and remain at attention. Colonel Clark walked around to face him. Hawk saluted again. Macintosh arranged the chairs in front of his desk. This time, the chairs were set on a sheet of plywood, and did not sink into the ground. The two officers sat down and Hawk remained at ease.

"It looks like we are revisiting the subject of the Maxwell Hoech code, Sergeant Hawk," Captain Macintosh informed him. "I believe you know Colonel Clark, from regiment."

"Yes, sir. How are you, sir? How is Major Bearn?"

"I'm doing well. He's mean as ever. Working on that lieutenant colonel thing. And how are you? You look fit as a fiddle. I could strike a match on you," said the colonel.

"Yes, sir. Still around. Somehow," Hawk said. "Got this dent in my head, but my arm is okay."

"I'm told Captain Macintosh filled you in on this... code affair?"

"A little, yessir. I was a part of it somehow," said the sergeant.

"Yes, you were. You and I have something in common there. I was the first name on the list, and you were the second. We have mutual acquaintances," said the colonel. "One in particular, I believe: that would be the third name, whom you identified."

"Mrs. Orr? Yes, sir," said Hawk. "I was surprised to hear her name come up."

"Not too surprised, I hope, since you were the one that brought it up," said Clark.

Hawk thought about that. Was he being castigated over this stupid code business? Was he supposed to leave Vera Orr out of it? Did they want to know the truth, or not? He was enough of a student of human nature to know that the last thing some people want to hear is the truth.

"I was surprised, sir."

"I'm an old friend of Mrs. Orr. She probably told you that?"

"Yes, sir. She mentioned that."

"She had a lot of pluck, to go on that mission with you into Ayermo. That was not a walk in the park," said the colonel.

"Yes, sir. But everybody knew that, going in. We don't do walks in the park."

"No, indeed. That, you don't. She told me a few of

the details of that adventure. It's nothing short of a miracle that any of you are alive." The colonel looked at Macintosh. "Maybe we could get another chair in here. This feels like a cross examination. I think the sergeant would be more comfortable sitting down. We are going to have a little discussion here, and I don't want to get a crick in my neck from looking up." Another chair was brought in shortly. Appropriately, it was a shorter and older chair, so that the other two leaned over Hawk slightly, in order to make him feel small. Of course, he didn't. A lot of arrogant nuance was often wasted on him.

"Based on your testimony, Sergeant, I was required to pay a visit to Mrs. Orr, and renew old acquaintances." The colonel's face was much closer to Hawk's now.

"Sorry, sir. I didn't know that I was giving testimony."

"Oh, nothing to be sorry about. You filled in a part of the puzzle. And quite well, as it turns out. I should start at the beginning. I was first on the list, and I identified you. Then you identified her. I had her tracked down. She is staying in Hawaii. Were you aware of that?"

"No, sir. I ain't had nothing to do with her."

"Well, I suppose I should thank you for getting me an all-expenses paid trip to Honolulu. I had quite a chat with her. She recalled you very well." The colonel laughed.

"Yes, sir. The feeling is mutual," said Hawk.

"Yes. She spoke highly of you." This surprised Hawk, but he was glad his comment had been vague enough to not have been taken as a disparagement. "And she has identified the fourth name. It is an individual with whom we are somewhat familiar in the

Corps. Command, that is. No one that you would know, I'm sure." The colonel waved his hand impatiently.

"That's good," said Hawk, having no interest whatsoever in anything related to secret codes, Vera Orr, or Colonel Clark.

"You're probably wondering why I made a special trip to see you here," said the colonel. Hawk had not been wondering. He had not known the colonel made a special trip to see him, and therefore had nothing to wonder about. "Well, I'll tell you." Colonel Clark took a drink of water from the desk of Macintosh. The officers' water did not taste like oil.

"After speaking with Mrs. Orr, I went back and spoke with General Dennison. He's the Marine Corps liaison in charge of this Hoech mission. We kicked it around, and we realized that we need a man on the ground with this operation. We can't just have different hit or miss messengers all trying to put this giant thing together. By that, I mean, it's all over the map. Mrs. Orr suggested that you were excellent at organizing and running small operations. And you have an unusually good rapport with your men."

Hawk could not help himself, even though he was conversing with a colonel. "You said you were kicking it around, sir? And Mrs. Orr was in on the talk?" He knew it sounded impertinent. But he knew Vera Orr. What was Vera Orr doing "kicking around" a top-secret classified military mission? And the name of James Hawk?

"Well, to a limited extent, of course. She had to be told certain aspects of the matter, in order to tell us the fourth name in the code. Nothing was compromised. When I told her that I felt like a mere errand boy, she suggested your name to get me off the hook in the matter of making these contacts. And when I got back to the general, we discussed the situation more fully." Clark seemed a little nervous to Macintosh, as if Hawk had caught him in something. Hawk suspected that he likely had. The subject of Vera Orr could make you nervous.

Hawk sat sullenly, not looking pleased with the answer or the situation. The implication, so far, was that the three of them had decided that Hawk would make a dandy errand boy.

"When we got to this fourth name, it became clear that the decoding was turning into something a little more sensitive. It was no longer a matter of pulling out the phone book and making a few calls. The next man, for example, is a coast watcher, in a potentially dangerous location. Contacting him will involve a totally different set of circumstances than the first three names. We were hoping to make use of your expertise in long range reconnaissance patrols."

"Them fellas got radios, sir," said Hawk. "Is he an American?"

"He is not an American. He is a civilian of German birth. Now, it has been arranged to enroll all of the coast watchers in the Royal Australian Navy Volunteer Reserve, or RANVR. That gives them military status, to prevent the Japanese from executing them as spies."

"I wouldn't count much on that, sir," said Hawk.

"No. I know. But it made someone feel better to do it. And we cannot radio the man because this code is too sensitive to have any portion of it exposed to the open airwaves."

Hawk nodded. He had heard that one before. Things were usually too sensitive to use a radio for as long as he was involved. At the point when anyone else got into a bind, however, a banned SCR-300 magically appeared—along with a guy with a loud voice.

"The three of us were of the opinion that this coast watcher may just be the beginning of a much more difficult to reach series of connections. Combat may even be necessary. Maybe not at every contact, but at least some of the time. Hoech obviously did not plan on having a regimental level detective, such as myself, solve this mystery." Clark laughed, quite impressed with his own newly promoted importance. "Not that I haven't seen a little action in my day, I can tell you."

Hawk noticed that the "three of us" were back in the decision making. Vera Orr was up to her...neck...in this; with generals, and God knew who else. Hawk knew that she had something on Clark. But did she have something on *everybody? Son of a bitch!* He sighed. *She ain't got nothing on me.*

"I was reluctant to drag you back into this. I know you thought your part was over. But then, fighting through the Helvedes is no picnic, either, is it? I'd like to have you on board. I'd like for it to be voluntary, and for you to have about a squad of handpicked volunteers to travel with you. I would need an answer fairly soon. We have a time limit, of course."

Of course, thought Hawk. A time limit for me. I need to get busy, because everybody else had been "kicking it around" for a while. Vera Orr had made a practice of insulting his intelligence the entire time he was with her. He was sure the "three" of them had "kicked" him around pretty good. But when they needed somebody to decipher their super-duper indecipherable code, whose door did they come knocking on? Sherlock

Holmes? Charlie Chan? No, they stopped off a little closer to home. Because somebody could get *killed*. Better to delegate this baby to someone less...intelligent.

"I don't mind helping out, sir," Hawk said, at last. What difference did it make? He could say no, and Kirk would have him charging another tank before dark. As long as there was a Japan, this was his life. And that was fine.

"Excellent. Mrs. Orr identified the fourth name as that of Otto Ranke, who is a recent transplant from New Guinea. He had a plantation there, and we moved him over to Caratu for the purpose of observing the strait there for us. He has a coconut and rubber plantation, but it's more or less a cover, not very profitable. You will have to question him as to his knowledge of the fifth name. That means you will have to be given the code itself, which I don't need to tell you, is very sensitive. No one is to have access to this code but you. It may be virtually impossible to figure out, but we don't want to count on that."

Hawk listened silently. He instantly recognized the name that he was not supposed to recognize. He had dealings with Otto Ranke when the German was in New Guinea. While that was intriguing enough, it also occurred to him, that he knew all four of these people listed in the code: Clark, himself, Vera, and now Ranke. Coincidence? Should he mention it? Hawk suspected Clark already knew the sergeant was no stranger to Ranke. If the colonel wasn't laying all his cards on the table, neither would Hawk. There was already one other matter, obvious to both Clark and Hawk, that they were not being candid with one another about: their respective relationships with Vera Orr.

"There will be a little more briefing, and then you'll have to brief your men, and get fitted out. We should be able to shove off before the end of tomorrow." The "we" part appealed to Hawk's cynical sense of humor.

"Yessir. The end of tomorrow."

* * *

CARATU WAS a desolate island on the edge of the Helvedes. Its rocky coast and barren interior made it of little worth to the combatants in the Pacific Theater. Even the location had little to offer. Clark assured Sergeant Hawk that the Japanese were unaware of both the Hoech communique, and of Hawk's mission to Ranke, and that as long as everyone kept a low profile, there was no reason to expect any *major* enemy contact. Hawk's patrol would simply get in, get the information from Ranke, and get off Caratu. The enemy was fully engaged on several other islands in the Helvedes, however, and it would not take a great deal to draw them into a conflict, if the Americans were indiscreet. Clark was a little vague as to whether the Japanese knew of Ranke's presence on the deserted coast, but the implication was that they were not, or at least, were not very interested in him. Hawk had his own ideas about that, since the German must have been sending radio signals to someone in his role as a coast watcher, and that *someone* could always be Japanese, whether intentionally or unintentionally.

Hawk had never doubted Ranke's loyalty to the Allied cause, in spite of his German ancestry. He had known the rugged farmer to engage in open hostilities with the Japanese on occasion. Perhaps his alignment would be different if they were in Germany, but Germany was a long way off.

Ranke had been set up by the allies on the northern shore of Caratu, in a quickly assembled rubber and coconut plantation front. A Higgins boat landed Hawk's patrol of twenty men on the western shore in order to draw as little attention as possible to the mission. If a casual observer became aware of both the location of Ranke and that of the Americans' landing, perhaps they would not associate a connection between the two. The western shore allowed the fastest access to Ranke's plantation, other than the northern shore itself, with the visitors having only to round a rather high cliff face along that coast before presenting themselves.

From the narrow western beach, Hawk's patrol would climb the wall of the cliff along a northward leading trail, zigzagging through the middle of the solid rock on a ledge, at a slightly upward leading angle, until it reached the top on the northern side of the island. The daunting, flat cliff faced the ocean and blended from a white to a cream-colored limestone several hundred feet tall. Upon being set at the bottom of it, Hawk immediately didn't like the setup. From a distance, his men would look like insects crawling on a white wall, well defined, and vulnerable.

As the others disembarked, Hawk lit a cigar and stared up at the cliff, his head tilted far back.

"That don't look like no concealed approach," said Canlon.

"No. Nobody knows we're coming, though. It should be okay," Hawk answered, hiding his own misgivings.

"And the Japs don't know *nothing* about this code, or

us?" Joe asked. He had been given an outline of the operation.

"Yeah. It's supposed to be the most secret classification they got," said Hawk. "Safe as it gets."

"I don't know," said Joe, looking up. "If it was so secret, and so safe, I got a feeling that we wouldn't be the ones here."

Hawk blew smoke into the high wind. "Yeah, that thought crossed my mind." When the men and equipment had been quickly unloaded on the beach, the boat backed noisily away and pulled off. The lonely sound of the waves crashing on the rocks sounded less friendly. "Well, you cain't complain about the landing, anyway," said Hawk, ignoring the spooky atmosphere. Spooky was better than getting shot at.

Joe wasn't as sure: "That guy sure took off in a goddam hurry."

"I guess he's got shit to do. Let's get on up this bastard and get this over with."

"What exactly the hell are we doing? I didn't quite catch all that at your two second briefing, where you volunteered me for this," Joe asked as he picked up his pack and weapons.

"Just gonna ask the fella a question and come on back down here and go home. Easier than fallin' off a log." Hawk drew on the cigar. "I know the man. You've met him. He's reasonable, sort of. For an old bastard."

Joe shook his unstrapped helmet. "I think I'm missing something. This top-secret stuff must be over my head. Seems like a lot of extra trouble for nothing."

"Well, shit. Everything's over your head, except a frog's ass. Get 'em in a line. Looks like that ledge will only take one man at a time. We're gonna be strung out all over hell and half of Georgia."

They began the laborious climb upward. Their equipment, already heavy on the flat earth, grew heavier during the trek up the ascending angle. The ledge jutted a fairly uniform five feet or so from the side of the cliff, evidently having been carved out of the rock at some point by human hands. The narrow avenue had no appeal to those who were sensitive to heights, as there was no handrail. The only concession to safety, designed into the construction of the path, consisted of the slanting of the walkway inward, so that it formed a somewhat triangular ditch. The higher, outer edge of the gradient therefore kept an errant foot from pulling a traveler off into oblivion. The few inches of slanting, however, also made the walking more difficult, as one's foot remained in an uncomfortable contortion. To the left of the climbers fell the open and massive drop to the rocky beach below, and to the right soared the solid, uncompromising wall of the cliff, leaning toward them, almost pushing them away from it.

Joe Canlon climbed behind Hawk. Since it would be difficult to change a position in the single file of men, once they reached the greater heights, Hawk chose his place carefully. It would be difficult to bypass anyone on the narrow ledge. Ordinarily, on mother earth, he would have taken the lead, and periodically made his way back to the rear, checking things as he went, while the hike progressed. He now had to pick a place and stick with it, on the unfriendly cliff face. He chose the middle as a compromise between the front and rear spots.

"This is dangerous," said Joe. "There ain't no better

way to get to this guy than this?" He tried not to look over the edge, but the endlessly swirling ocean drew his eyes to it.

"Yeah, I *told* you. We could have landed right on his coastline. They were afraid the Japs might be watching that," said Hawk. "It ain't my idea. All I saw was a map, and this looked flat on that stupid son of a bitch."

"You need to check the elevation key next time," said Joe. "A lot of times, they'll put a guy that can read and write over a patrol like this. It pays off, too. I think I'd rather have the Japs watching me on that other coast than climbing this bastard. This is dangerous."

"We gotta come back this way, too," Hawk warned. "There ain't no boat wants to go along that northern coast. That's probably the real reason why we're here on this thing."

"That really pisses me off. The Navy and the Air Corps, and everybody else, gets to say, 'that's just *too* damn dangerous.' The Marine Corps says, 'climb that crazy son of a bitch, you dumb ass.'" Joe looked up. "What if I get way up there and get too scared to go any higher? Sometimes your legs just won't go, you know?"

Hawk ignored that possibility. "At least nobody knows we're here. I wouldn't want to run into something on this rock. There is a good side to being top-secret."

"Yeah. Just like they don't tell your family you're dead on these top-secret deals. Old Joe? No, we don't know nothin' about him. Did you check over in Newark?"

Hawk felt his leg muscles pulling as he climbed. The narrow ledge, and the slant of the surface of the pathway seemed to push him more and more toward the ocean, affecting his balance. He could see down quite well, where sharp, murderous rocks beckoned to him. Above him, however, stretched only an endless, straight wall, and about half of the sky. Near the top, looking very tiny, shore birds circled and screamed.

"I think you're right. This *is* dangerous. I wonder how many customers the Caratu tourist bureau loses every year," said Hawk. He had the urge to hold on to the cliff wall, but once he put a hand on the smooth surface, his hand seemed to push him toward the other side, and then drop into the ocean.

"You're sure nobody knows we're here?" Joe asked, growing breathless.

"Nobody. They didn't even tell Santy Claus."

"Well, the secret's out. I see a damn airplane way out over the ocean. He acts like *he* sees us. He's just kinda floatin' around out there."

Hawk paused and shaded his eyes with his hand. "Oh, yeah. I see him. He's probably wondering what those crazy bastards are doing."

"Maybe they sent us a guardian angel," said Joe. "They might visit that coast watcher guy every once in a while, to bring him supplies and shit."

"Yeah." Hawk returned to climbing. "That's probably what that is."

Behind Joe, Blackwell called out. "Man, I want off this thing."

"Only two ways off," Joe called back, "the fast way and the slow way."

"I think you're supposed to crawl up this thing," shouted Turnage, the man in front of Hawk. He was half bent over, resting his hand on the rise of the outer ledge, enabling him to push himself back toward the cliff and away from the drop as he walked. He was covered with the whitish, salty dust of the cliff. The wall had not been dusted in several million years.

Joe reached out and pressed his hand against the outer ledge, using Turnage's method of climbing. "Hey that's a good idea." His pace slowed. "Kind of gets to your back, though. But you don't feel like it's pushing you over the edge as much."

"It ain't much farther," said Hawk. "We're halfway up the...thing."

The tiny plane in the distance loomed larger. The faint sound of its engine grew audible. Hawk stopped and shaded his eyes again. Something about the sound of the motor drew his attention. He had heard that smooth, predatory hum before.

"You know what?" he asked Joe. "That might not be *our* plane." Joe stopped, stood up straight and shaded his eyes.

"It sure better be," Joe said. The plane advanced rapidly, head on, making identification difficult, and then banked a couple of miles or so away from the cliff. Finally, the rising sun emblems stood out bright and clear on the wings of the Zero.

"*Shit!*" Hawk faced Turnage. "Tell Baker to stop! Pass it up! Get everybody to lie down in the trail!" He gave Joe the same message, to be passed down to the men in the rear of the file. The Zero lazily turned back and forth, enjoying the open ocean air, studying the strange sight on the cliff face, and making a few calculations of his own. His motor warbled louder now, growling interestedly, and echoing off the flat stone of the mountainside. The mechanical vibration settled into the nerves of the trapped American climbers. They were nailed to the dart board of a target with nowhere to run.

"What's he doing?" Joe asked.

"I don't know. Maybe he can't figure out whose side we're on," said Hawk.

"I think maybe somebody besides us knows about your top-secret mission," Joe said, watching the Zero glide calmly back and forth in front of them. The pilot had lots of time to figure this out. Turnage squinted fearfully, but his only thought was how much fun it must be to cruise in the pure air above the ocean like that.

"Yeah. And they might want to put a stop to it," Hawk admitted. "Maybe they read a leaked transmission about us. It couldn't have been from too long ago, because they just decided to send us here."

"The Japs sent an airplane after us. They gave us the express service," said Joe. "Our guys give us a boat and hiking boots."

"Maybe if I wave at him, he'll go away. Maybe he thinks we're Japs," said Hawk.

"Yeah, right. We're just laying down here with a tight pucker because we're bashful," said Joe.

The plane banked and came straight toward the cliff. Any doubts about its intentions were soon dispelled. It opened up with its 20-millimeter machine cannon on the side of the mountain. A line of lightning bolts with jackhammers on the end of them stitched into the stone just above the heads of the men lying inside the shallow ledge. Deafening metal pounded the rock, and dust choked the narrow depression concealing the Americans. Smoke floated above the trough. After half a minute of the drilling of metal on stone, the plane soared over the top of the cliff and out of sight.

"So much for making friends," Joe shouted. "We ain't got no cover here, those rounds can go right through this little piece of rock."

"Just keep low. He can't hit what he can't see. He has to keep coming straight at us." Hawk answered. Joe had no reply for that. It was the only advice he was getting, and he was stuck with it. The men tried desperately to disappear behind their few inches of stone on the side of the upward tilting trail.

The plane swung far out over the ocean in order to position itself for another run straight toward the cliff side. Less than a mile away, its machine guns opened up, brightly streaking from the wings on either side of the fuselage and colliding with the stone outcropping down on the beach. The double outpouring of flaming lead climbed the wall of the cliff, ripped through the ledge in two corresponding places, and rose higher up on the mountain, before the plane pulled up to pass over the Americans again.

"Anybody hit?" Hawk shouted.

"No. It went off to the left of here!" Murdoch screamed back at him. The plane prepared for another run. This time it looped closer to the cliff, to attempt to skate along the side of it, parallel to the men concealed by the ledge. The massive, plowing steel shells scraped just above the entire file of men, digging out a trench in the side of the cliff, before banking out over the ocean again.

"He can't get a good shot at us from that direction," Hawk shouted.

"Good enough for me!" Joe shouted back. "Did you see that bastard turn on his side and slide along that rock? Should we climb? We can't just sit here. That Jap knows what he's doing!" Before Hawk could answer, the plane was flying directly toward them again, firing from a mile away and rapidly closing the distance.

Hawk slung his Thompson machine pistol over the ledge and fired back at the invincible hurtling monster. With the limited range of his submachine gun, and the incredible speed of the Zero, Hawk's fire had only a few fleeting yards within which he could possibly connect with the plane. Factoring in the rate of fire of the machine pistol, only one or two rounds would mathematically be able to strike his adversary. Though lightly armored, the Zero had little to fear from one or two forty-five slugs accidentally striking it.

Resistance, however, is self-perpetuating. The other men opened up as well, after hearing the report of their leader's automatic weapon. Baker aimed a BAR toward the plane, and several other men had been issued .45 caliber burp guns for the special mission. The others pointed long rifle barrels over the ledge and aimed their M1s at the cockpit of their tormentor. It was not promising, but it was all they could do. The rifles had good range, and they could fire at the plane both going and coming. But again, the aircraft's speed thrust it so rapidly through their field of fire that the Japanese fighter was only exposed to perhaps twenty wildly thrown, and relatively small, rounds during each pass.

The plane swooped low over them, once again passing parallel to the cliff. The line of machine gun bullets issued from one wing struck harmlessly, high up on the side of the cliff, but the fire from the other wing danced along the top of the ledge, exploding portions of it to smithereens, and eliminating the meager cover it afforded. At the end of the pass, a one-hundred-thirty-pound bomb cartwheeled from beneath the Zero, and exploded halfway down the cliff, between the cringing Americans and the ocean. The plane rose into the sky again.

"He's got us pinned here!" Joe shouted. "We can't do shit!"

Hawk changed magazines as the plane started firing from far away, coming straight at them again. He feared that Joe was right. The only hope was that the plane would run out of ammunition, and that could take a long time. The Japanese fighters were generally conservative with their bullets, because they never knew when they might encounter the superior numbers of the Americans in the airways. The fellow attacking them today seemed to have a different mindset. He evidently had been ordered to go all out in his efforts to destroy the patrol. And the Japanese pilot could not have found a better place to do it.

Although it was not at all logical to believe that Maxwell Hoech would have gone to all the trouble of devising his elaborate code to eliminate one small patrol, Hawk was not thinking logically at the moment. He did not harbor friendly thoughts about the code breaker or his loyalties. A hailstorm of 7.7 mm machine gun rounds fell all about the sergeant, making it impossible for him to fire back at the attacker. He could see nothing in the cloud of smoke, fire, and dust, and heard only explosions and the roar of the engine passing just overhead. Most of the explosive sounds came from the gunfire of his own men, rolling powerfully up and off the wall of rock. While the American automatic fire had no effect on the flier, the longer ranged and more precise M1s might have been able to strike a blow in their own defense. Osage claimed that he saw the glass in the cockpit shatter. Perhaps a .30 caliber round had by sheer chance hit the reckless mark.

The next burst from the plane fell around Joe Canlon, just as the last one had sliced along the area close to Hawk. Joe shrieked in terror as the rounds endlessly struck at his position. The front of his ledge was vaporized, turned into dust by the flashing leaden storm. Several rounds chewed even closer, almost striking him, and melting away part of the ledge trail itself. In horror, Joe saw only thin air beneath his knees, and he slid down the wall of the cliff.

Hawk dropped his weapon onto the trail and latched on to Joe's flailing arm as the plane passed over them. Joe's weight pulled him down the sharply angled ledge and toward where Joe was hanging out into the open air, kicking his legs. Hawk could not stop their fall. Joe's weight, equipment, and the steep angle overcame Hawk's ability to stop them from both sliding. Not only was he going to lose Joe, he could not prevent himself from plummeting downward now, even if he let go of him. He felt the hands of Turnage sink into his jacket from behind. He stopped sliding. Sensing the new stability coming from above him, Joe began climbing frantically up Hawk's legs, and finally over him. He discovered Turnage and two other men were grappling to hold Hawk, and he joined in. The plane passed over them, firing wildly in the general direction of the struggling pile of humanity, and missing everyone. They slithered to the higher side of the trail, which was still in the process of slowly collapsing, and tried to get back under the cover of the still existing ledge before the plane returned.

The plane soared parallel to the cliff again and the machine cannon fired its last few rounds, directly striking the ledge at the end of the column, blowing it completely free from the side of the mountain, and killing the last three men, who rolled with the pulverized stone all the way to the rocks in the ocean below. As the plane pulled up, it dropped its second and last one-hundred-thirty pounder, which exploded on the beach beneath the patrol. The pilot had been unable to aim either bomb with any precision. He was likely preoccupied with avoiding a deadly scrape along the wall of the cliff with his wingtip. As Joe had observed, much of the time the pilot had to fly turned completely on his side, wings parallel to the horizontal cliff. When the flier pulled up, Hawk saw his white scarf blowing in the hundred mile per hour wind through the broken glass of the cockpit. Osage had been right. At least one bullet had gotten the attention of the flier, if little else had.

The plane soared out over the ocean, but this time, appeared to keep going, until it was just a droning speck in the distance. Hawk sat up. His helmet had been knocked off, and streaks of blood ran down the side of his head where rock dust had been blown into him at high velocity.

"Tell Baker, double time, get to the top of this son of a bitch," Hawk ordered Turnage. Double time, however, degenerated into merely crawling, this time. The protective side of the ledge had been blown off in many places. The dangerous path had turned into an almost impossible one. The climbers had to help one another across the newly opened spaces along the route.

"It's a damn good thing this is all top-secret," Joe gasped.

The confrontation with the airplane slowed the trip considerably. By the time they reached the highest point of the cliff, it did not appear that they would reach the Ranke plantation by dark. Having lost some enthusiasm for his unusual mission, and not wanting to push his luck, Hawk decided to camp some distance from the western shore. They came to a lower elevation in a sparsely wooded area dotted with palms and ferns. Hawk set up a perimeter and a guard. He believed the mission had been compromised. He did not think that the airplane had randomly happened upon them. He discussed this with Canlon as dark approached.

"You're the second in charge here," said Hawk. "I gotta make a command decision."

"That's just what I want to hear right now," said Joe.

"Yeah. That plane made me think. I could get bumped off pretty easy on this detail. I wasn't planning on all that. They made this sound pretty simple. Looks like it ain't going to be. We may be in for a little opposition."

"I would call that opposition. Yeah. That guy we're after may be dead, if we ever get to his place. If they'd try to kill an armed patrol, they'll try to kill some crazy old guy on the beach," Joe said.

"Right. It's a horse of a different color, now. I gotta tell you more about what I know. I wasn't supposed to tell anybody what this code thing says. But I think it's time to write our will and testament."

"Aw, shit. Can't we wait on that? If you get killed, they'll just bring us in and get somebody else. Or, more likely, forget the whole thing."

Hawk took a piece of heavy paper out of his shirt pocket.

"No. You'll have to keep going. Look at this thing. This is what this is all about. This guy Hoech is a prisoner and he sent this message, and we have to figure out what it means. And 'we' may end up being 'you.' They've kind of dumped it on us."

"You know what that means?" Joe interrupted. Hawk frowned. "What?" Joe took the page. "It means they don't care what happens anymore. It was too much trouble for them to deal with. If we can figure it out for them, good. If we can't, they go back to the officer's club for a snort."

"I don't know about all that. Since it's Clark, no telling. He's kind of a bastard."

"I wish they would put Bearn in charge. If it's anything important, they put Bearn in charge, and send Clark out somewhere to count tent pegs," said Joe, opening the page and reading a couple of the lines out loud.

"What the hell is this: 'Kill Saipan ridge commander Delivalung recon non-com do you love me now Berlin philharmonic bracelet soul green bottle'..." Joe stopped and shook his head. He read the rest of it to himself. *Better that a millstone be hung only one could be students president saved by the enemy with syringe robber messenger of the sea me like a bird summer lake apple pie.* "What the hell is all of this? This don't make any sense. It ain't no code. I've seen code, and it don't look like this. This is just words."

"See, that's because you're ignorant. When you get to the end of it all, it's supposed to tell you some big project the Japs are pulling off."

"I got to the damned end fine. It's just words, unconnected words."

"No, it's a list of people, stupid. The 'Saipan commander' thing is talking about Clark. So, they ask Clark who the next guy is. 'Recon non-com', is me, get it? They had to go to Clark and Clark knew that the next name was me."

"Everybody knew that. They didn't have to go to Clark to get that."

"Not everybody. Two seconds ago, you said it was unconnected words, you *didn't* say it was me," said Hawk. "You didn't know shit till I told you. It's like the horse races on Tuesday. You're a goddam genius on Wednesday, because you already know who won."

Joe stared at him. "All right. Do the next one," he finally said. "Who is that?"

"'Do you love me, now'? That's mine. They asked me that, see? And I said, that's from Vera Orr."

"Hmm. Vera Orr. You knew that?"

"Yeah, she used to say that all the time. So, then Clark goes to her. He flies to Hawaii, instead of just getting her on the radio, so he can see her, I guess."

"No, he goes because it's top-secret," said Joe. "It's done personally. Like us gettin' our ass shot off on the side of a mountain. You gotta do that shit in person. I would have rather had the Hawaii part, too."

"Right." Hawk decided not to think too much about Joe's logic. "And when he gets there, he reads Vera the next line. That's another thing: you don't let *anybody* read the whole thing because they might figure it out. You only let them see their part of it."

"I thought you wanted to figure it out," said Joe.

"Yeah, you do. But you don't want anybody else figuring it out. Like say, Vera Orr. Or the Japs."

"Shit. I bet that bitch already knows the whole thing.

And so do the Japs. Isn't it something about *them*? Why would they *not* know? That means Clark told her this..." Joe looked down and read quickly. "...'philharmonic bracelet' thing, and she knew that had something to do with Ranke?"

"That's right. I kinda knew the others, but I never would have known that," said Hawk. "She must know the German and got a bracelet from him or something."

"How do you know she knew? She could be wrong," Joe asked. "*You* could have been wrong. Why would she say something like that to you? The 'love' thing?"

"She was always joking. Everything was funny with her. A big joke. I don't like that kind of shit. But, the people will know if you're right. Each person knows. I knew I was right. This Hoech guy knew, somehow, that I would know what it meant. And if I get killed tomorrow, this next one is what you ask Ranke: 'soul green bottle.' And he'll know what that means. You can bet on it."

"Okay. Those words make no sense at all, but they will make sense to him?" Joe asked.

"Right. See, you ain't so stupid."

"Maybe I'm not. Gettin' smarter all the time. Tell me this. What's this thing at the beginning mean: 'Helvedes coordinates'?"

"I asked about that. The colonel said it doesn't mean anything. They sometimes put stuff like that in there to mess you up. Like if you mix numbers in with some words, the code people know right off to skip the numbers."

"If we go back with this new name we get from Ranke, are we out of this chase, then? Or, are we gonna be running all over the islands, getting shot at for this crap? These words go on forever. You know the Japs already know the answer, don't you? They're gonna be right there waitin' on us every step of the way. That's the message I'm getting from them today."

"I ain't sure about that, yet. I hope not, I hope this is it. But Clark did make it sound like I was gonna be the one running around figuring all this out."

"Why would they do that? If this is so important, why turn this whole complicated puzzle over to some dumb ass like you?"

"I think you just found that out today. We're gonna be running into a few roadblocks. You don't want geniuses wrassling with roadblocks, do you? And, I guess, this part ain't that complicated anyway. If you just get the right answers for them. I mean, the middle of it ain't complicated, you go out there and get a name. Maybe getting to the end of the riddle is a little different. That's where the experts come in. Because Clark seemed to think that all you have to do is find the last person at the end of the code, and you have the message." Hawk looked at Joe's face for some affirmation that he was following the line of reasoning. He saw nothing of the kind. He decided to confuse him a little further. "If the last person already knows the message, why do they need Hoech to tell anybody anything?"

"I guess, because the last person doesn't know that he knows," Joe answered. "But Hoech knew that the last one knows, and he wants us to find him. Or maybe Hoech is going to tell the last person the message when we get to him." Now it was Hawk's turn to look puzzled. Sometimes, Joe wasn't as stupid as he seemed. "I don't know," Joe continued. "This is the kind of thing that gets deeper the more you think about it. I can tell you, getting blasted by that plane today was deep enough for me."

Hawk shrugged and took the paper back. He folded it and put it in his pocket. "Anyway, now you know what we're doing. I think. Who knows? You're so goddam ignorant."

"Yeah. Thanks. A guy likes being appreciated."

"Ain't that the truth."

4

AMONG THE TREE SNIPERS

NINE THOUSAND MILES AWAY, IN WASHINGTON, D. C., Wilhelm Volmer stepped briskly off the streetcar near the Lincoln Memorial. With a newspaper under his arm, he left the side of the street and entered the trees along the reflection pool. Finding a grassy spot, he sat on the Mall and waited for his companions. He opened the paper and shook his head as he glanced through the headlines. Within a few minutes, Setsuko Takemitsu joined him, tossing down several books and lying down next to him. Small talk followed, until almost half an hour later, when the last member of the trio finally arrived. Stefano Calvino stood over them for a moment before sitting down.

"How goes the war?" he asked. "Is there any good news?"

"None," said Wilhelm. "If they are telling the truth. You can't trust American reports."

"None," Setsuko agreed. "But Japan is doing the best," she added. The three, by all appearances, conventional graduate students, sat in a circle and opened the books in front of them. "You can't tell a book by its cover," said Setsuko, holding up the cover of her book. It read, 'American History: Colonization through Reconstruction'. "I heard someone use that expression today. I had read it before." She lay open what was actually a medical treatise.

"Yes. Amusing Americanisms," said Wilhelm. He closed his newspaper and waved it meaningfully at them. "By all indications, our time is running out much more quickly than expected."

Calvino made no reply, only turning the girl's book around that he might read it. He looked up at her with his charming smile.

* * *

THE PATROL RESUMED AT DAYLIGHT. The open and airy palm forest soon evolved into a thicker tropical blend of flora as the elevation descended toward the northern coast. Hawk took the lead now, expecting indications of the outskirts of a plantation, such as clear-cut ground. He had seen enough rubber and coconut plantations to know better than this, but being from Mississippi, his default expectations were of manicured farmland, and expectations are hard to change. According to his map, they were nearing the coast and had to be approaching their destination, unless someone had made some grave errors.

His patrol moved with relative silence for a party of its size. They were skilled jungle fighters and travelers. The noises that Hawk heard ahead of him revealed the presence of something, or someone, who was not as careful. Because animals were few and far between in the islands, and Japanese were *not* few and far between, he assumed that human beings were approaching. It was not a large group, perhaps only one or two men. The unidentified sounds would have caused apprehension in anyone else in the secluded wood, but James Hawk, with a submachine gun in hand and seventeen men behind him, was of a different temperament. He stood unbowed and waiting, his fierce and cruel features immobile, another feature of a predatory jungle. The face was not accustomed to tolerance of apprehension.

Two figures burst through the foliage upon him, but he made no move to raise the muzzle of the Thompson. They were obviously startled and appeared terrified. Hawk immediately recognized Otto Ranke. He was a large, well-built man, heavily darkened by the sun, with light blue eyes shining out of his weather-beaten face. Ranke was accompanied by a Melanesian islander.

"How you doin' there, Mr. Ranke? James Hawk. I came to see you for the government, again. Remember me?"

Ranke, having gasped in horror until his breath was gone, shuddered and recovered himself after a moment. His companion remained fearful.

"Mr. Hawk! *You!* Yes. Of all things. Thank God," said Ranke, with a German accent. "We thought you were the Japanese. They took over the plantation house, and we barely escaped. We could not even pick up a rifle."

"I'll be damn," Hawk replied, trying to sound as if he found this upsetting, instead of part of his average day. "They ain't supposed to be here. We've already run into them once. I'm sorry about all that. Somebody got their wires crossed when they said this was supposed to be a secret meeting."

"Secret? Here? There haven't been any Japanese here in the entire five months I've been here. They came out of nowhere, and there are a lot of them."

Hawk, being of a military mind, seized upon the "lot" referenced in the report. "About how many would you say that was, sir? Say—in numbers?"

"I saw at least a dozen, maybe two dozen, before we ran. I don't know how many more followed. There could be *any* number."

"That's gonna make it tougher for us to get outta here," said Hawk. "We came up the cliff and a plane started drilling on us. I don't think we can go back that way. Somebody done ratted us out."

"Good god! That must have been horrible!" Ranke exclaimed.

"Yeah. Damn sure was. Any other ways out of here?"

"We always used the dock on the coast. But the Japanese are there now. They knew I was here on Caratu, but had never attacked me before. I have a radio that I have been using to inform Australia about ship movements through the strait. I always suspected the Japanese knew of it, and they permitted me to transmit, just so they could eavesdrop."

"I wonder if that's how they knew about us," said Hawk.

"No, because I didn't know about you," said Ranke.

"You didn't?" Hawk pulled out a block of tobacco and looked back toward the jungle that had produced the two fugitives. "Was anybody chasing y'all?"

"I hope not. We left as fast as we could."

Hawk nodded. "Well, we got us a couple of problems

here. Maybe we should go back the way we came, in case somebody is behind you. I have this—message— for you. We might have to do some fast talking, and settle our business, before we get our ass shot off." He bit off the tobacco. "That would leave some highly placed people real disappointed."

"Excellent. We are subject to your wishes. Lead the way. I confess that I have never been more delighted to see anyone in my life," said Ranke, still visibly shaken. Being taken prisoner by the Japanese was not a pleasant prospect. And being taken prisoner was only a short-term prospect.

Hawk gave an abrupt laugh. "Better be careful. Nobody ever says that about me for long. I got kind of a cloud that follows me around." They turned, and the patrol reversed its course, returning generally in the direction of the cliff on the western coast. Due to the confusion after the unplanned meeting, no specific destination had been settled upon. They halted in a rock-strewn, sandy floored haven, with few trees, about a half mile from the cliff. The ring of large stones impressed Hawk as being defensible, if they had been followed. He had an eye for such matters, based on considerable experience, rather than mere theory. It made a good spot to bring up his men and wait.

"Have a seat," Hawk told the German, as the others formed a rough camp. "We gotta get a few things out of the way, you and me." Ranke sat on a rock, a little unsure of Hawk's tone. The American could be frightening, even when he had no ill intent. "Here's the thing." Hawk remained standing. "They sent me here to get some information from you."

"Why didn't they radio?" Ranke asked. "I am in regular contact."

"Looks like we're finding out why right now," Hawk answered. "Somebody, somewhere, did some unauthorized radioing. I'm here because of a coded message from out of Japan. Big doings, see? There's a little part of it that only you can understand or interpret," Hawk added.

"I'm afraid you've received some bad information. My Japanese is very poor. I could not interpret anything," said Ranke.

"No, it ain't in no Japanese. You speak good English, and that's all you need, because what I got is in English." Hawk took the paper out of his pocket. "In fact, I need an answer right now on this, and not afterwhile, in case one of us catches a bullet in the head." The sergeant roughly flapped the recalcitrant page open a few times. "Just so you understand, this is some kind of information that only you would know...about somebody else...another person," Hawk explained, before resorting to spouting off the nonsensical words. He felt embarrassed at the absurdity of it all. He decided to give Ranke some background. Perhaps that would be more conducive to clear thinking and avoid confusion. "Well, I'll tell you how we found you. Do you know this lady, Vera Orr?"

"Vera Orr?" Ranke registered surprise upon hearing the name. He smiled; something that Hawk did *not* do when he had heard the name. "Oh, yes. The wife of Wendell Orr. I met her in Prenzlauer Berg. A very beautiful young woman. A delightful woman. So vivacious."

"Yeah. Maybe so," Hawk replied, somewhat less enthusiastically than Ranke. "She's vicious, awright.

Anyway, they asked...this woman...who the words 'Berlin philharmonic bracelet' reminded her of, and she gave us *your* name."

"Ach!" Ranke rocked back and laughed. "What a sweet young woman! I wish that I could see her!" Hawk spat. *Quite a reaction*, he thought. Vera Orr had worked her magic on this fool. She was irritating Hawk without even being here. "You see, she lost a very old, unique and expensive bracelet at the symphony and I was fortunate enough to find it for her. I tracked her down through the box office and returned it, in a small town near Berlin. She was ever so grateful. That husband of hers must be fabulously wealthy. The stories that bracelet could tell! It carried the history of Europe behind it. This Orr was a very nice man, but sort of a... nebbish. I can't think of the right English word. Something like that."

"Yeah. He ain't so wealthy no more. He's dead."

"No! How did Mrs. Orr's husband die? Was he killed in the war?"

"Yeah. Well, no. You might say that. He kind of fell and bumped his head. Unexpected like."

"She must be devastated. Unbelievable. So unfortunate, so much to live for."

"That's what they said, awright. A Rhode Island fella. Lot of connections. So, the thing is...where we're at now...it's your turn to tell us who this next person is, so we can get on with figuring out the code. This here code...it tells a story when you put it all together...of something big the Japs are up to. See?" Hawk doubted his powers of explanation, but Ranke did not seem puzzled.

"Very well. Who is this person? This is very strange."

"Right. Here you go. Your words are: 'soul green bottle.' That's s-o-u-l." Hawk folded the paper up. It occurred to him in the moment, as the paper returned to his shirt, that this was all going to be a major disaster if Ranke had no response. "You can think about it. It's kind of...wild."

"Soul green bottle? Yes, I know who that refers to," said the German. The expressionless Hawk gave a mental sigh of relief. "It pertains to a witch doctor or shaman, a medicine woman of sorts, here in the islands. She casts spells, and cures the natives, and curses their enemies. Things like that. One of her more spectacular tricks is capturing your soul and putting it in a bottle. She only puts souls in the *green* bottles. I suppose she gets these bottles when they wash up on the shore. Or she may have stolen a supply of them off a ship. She has her minions. In any event, souls only go in green bottles, and she will sell them to you. Even *your own*. She has other colored bottles, for other things. Ghosts, or, I don't know." Hawk stared blankly at the explanation. "You think it incredible, no?"

"Uh...yeah. That *is* incredible. Did you say a name? I heard she was a 'witch doctor,' but I didn't get no particular name."

"They just call her *Vuniwai*. It's the only name I know."

"Oh, yeah?" Hawk took the paper out again. "Catchy name. Ain't run across that one. I was hoping for Sue Ann. And where is she? Or where did you last see her?"

"On Papanuca. That's the only place she's ever been, or will ever be, I'm sure."

"Could you write that down for me? I might get some of the letters out of place, on account of the way I write so fast. Hey, anybody got a goddam pencil?" he shouted.

Joe Canlon handed him a dull pencil. Ranke scratched, more than wrote, the names of the person and the island onto the paper. Hawk studied the deep carvings in the surface.

"Yeah, okay. I got it. I can make that out. She must be Irish."

Ranke didn't get the joke.

"I can do it better if you sharpen the pencil," said the German.

"No, shit, no. That's fine. It's better this way. It's like that disappearing ink stuff, you know," said Hawk. "Real top secret. Like me." Again, Ranke missed the humor. "This is good," Hawk sighed. "This is what we came for. It sounds to me like that line out of the code could only mean this witch doctor, right? Nobody else?"

"Absolutely," said Ranke. "I would wager you could travel the world over and find no one else that phrase might refer to. Who puts souls in green bottles?"

Hawk frowned and shook his head. "Now what would some son of a bitch like that know about *anything*?"

Ranke tried to be helpful. "I suppose...she, or anyone, only has to know another name in the sequence. Am I correct? Until, I am assuming, the last name is reached. She need not know anything else."

"Yeah," Hawk agreed, somewhat relieved. "Any crazy old bastard can know that much."

* * *

HAWK SENT OUT SCOUTS, back toward the cliff, and north toward Ranke's house. He had accomplished his mission, but still had the problem of escaping Caratu, and relaying the knowledge he had gathered. A radio could have provided a simple solution. Since awareness of the mission had already been compromised, the absence of a radio did not give the patrol any kind of protection. It only left them trapped here. While it was perfectly logical for command to abandon Hawk to his fate, as it often had, it was not logical for them to make it impossible to receive the message that they so much wanted, concerning the next stage of the code. Military purpose was so ingrained in Hawk that he essentially adopted his superior's lack of interest in his own personal safety and welfare. As the day wore on, and they waited for the scouts to return, Hawk and Ranke discussed their options.

"I must return to my home. I left with nothing. All of my belongings are there," said Ranke. "Your force, armed as they are, could help me to recover it. Only I and Charlie Vutu are left," he said, referring to his traveling companion.

Hawk nodded. "That might be a big job. We don't know how many Japs are there. I don't mind a little scrape, if it ain't something somebody gets killed doing. But I *got* to get this message back. We'll see what the scouts say. You say you got a radio there, and it's working?"

"Yes. If the Japanese haven't destroyed it. I suppose they may have done just that, if they are leaving. If they are going to stay there, they may have wanted to keep it."

"I'd like to get ahold of that son of a bitch. We could

ask the colonel if he wanted this name, over the air, and ask 'em how we're gettin' off this shitpile. If we don't make it, he's gonna want this name."

"You could always follow through with your original plan and go down the cliff to the beach. I'm sure they will have a patrol boat waiting for you there," said Ranke. "When in doubt, do as you're told."

"Yeah, but things have kind of changed since we landed. It looks like the Japs know all about us, and I don't want to get stuck out on that damn cliff again. I at least want to be able to fight back." At about that time, Baker returned from reconnoitering Ranke's property. "How does it look, podnuh?" Hawk asked.

"There's over a dozen of them there. I think they have a machine gun in the farmhouse. It's not small potatoes. We might be able to surprise them, but there's a lot of cleared ground around the house, so we'd be in for a fight. It won't be easy to sneak up on. I saw a landing barge down by the shore. The way it looked to me, they might be waiting for somebody. Like us."

"A landing barge? Maybe we could steal that," said Hawk.

"That would be a stretch," said Baker. "I hope you can drive Jap boats better than you drive Jap tanks. I don't know if I would try to do any wandering around between that house and the beach. It's a tight fit. They would see you."

Ranke agreed and shook his head. "They would see you for certain if you tried to get to the beach. The house is too close to it. Do not try that."

Canlon had been standing nearby, near enough to hear the report. He watched Hawk's face as the sergeant listened to Ranke and Baker advising him not to try to commandeer the boat. Hawk was not one to take sound advice. About that time, the other scout, Osage, returned from the cliff. He had found no indications of the enemy's presence in that direction.

"Maybe we could send one guy down the cliff to see if the boat showed up for us," Joe suggested. Hawk looked up solemnly.

"Yeah. Could do that. I'd like to get that damn radio, though," said Hawk thoughtfully.

"Get in a big fight over a radio?" Joe asked. "It's not worth it. They probably busted it to pieces. If we stay here long enough, they'll come looking for us, anyway. We just need to hide out or get out."

"Maybe," Hawk answered, "but Mr. Ranke, here, wants his place back. He's left all his stuff there. He buried his sock full of nickels in the yard, and all. We kind of owe him a little help, on account of how we brought all this down on him. And that radio..."

"And get everybody killed? And nobody gets the code message?" Joe countered.

"The thing is," Hawk answered testily, "these Japs are probably here after us on account of that damn message. They aren't gonna wait till somebody at head-quarters decides the weather is nice enough to come get us. If we don't go to the Japs, they'll be coming after us. We *need* that radio. And they need us dead."

Joe decided to shut up. He was obviously driving Hawk into a defensive reasoning process that made a lot of sense to himself, and no one else.

With plenty of daylight left, his mind made up, Hawk set out for the Ranke plantation. He wanted to attack it well before dark, and have the issue of its control settled, before the concealment of nightfall made the fighting much more deadly. Baker led the way, showing the others the route that he had taken to the northern coast. Unfortunately, they did not reach the farmhouse before the Japanese learned of their presence. Unknown to Baker, he had been observed and allowed to pass by in order for the enemy to await the return of the larger force.

Before they could enter the open grounds of the plantation, and while still in the congested terrain of the palm forest, sniper fire opened up on the Americans, wounding a man, and killing another. The Marines flattened on the ground, unsure of where the fire came from. The Japanese were ruthless at this game, using rifles that were virtually smokeless and without a flash. The light 6.5 mm ammunition gave off a sharp crack that tricked the ear, and might have issued from anywhere. Additionally, the enemy snipers usually had telescopic sights, and judging by their accuracy today, this was the case. The Imperial soldiers were not interested in marksmanship for the most part, preferring to get close to their adversaries with a bayonet when possible. Snipers, however, were the exception.

"Did you see where that came from?" Joe asked Hawk. They lay in a clump of spreading ferns, more useful for concealment than any bullet stopping power.

"No. They must be in the trees. We didn't run into them head on, so they can't be on the ground. They saw us first. They like that tree shit." An enemy rifle fired again. The bullet slashed through intervening leaves. "Yeah, I think that's comin' from above us."

"It must be more than one," said Joe.

"Yeah. We gotta flush 'em out."

"What do you have in mind?"

"Try to find 'em. Circle around behind 'em. Listen for 'em." Hawk gestured to Baker, who ran to him. "See if you can swing wide and get around these assholes. Come up behind 'em and try to spot them when they shoot at us."

The sniper fired again, the bullet striking the earth near Joe, and blowing a handful of dirt into his face.

"Shit!" Joe shouted and rolled to the left to find a better source of cover.

"That Jap ain't no slouch," said Baker. "That was close."

"No, he ain't. Go back and swing wide around him. I might draw his fire once you get behind him. We gotta see the bastard before we can do anything," said Hawk.

"I bet there's more than one. They usually get set up in a way to cover each other," said Baker. "Better watch that drawing fire stuff."

"Don't worry about that. I'll be looking for him. He'll probably try to pick you off. With two of us running around, and them stuck up in a tree, they probably outsmarted themselves. We gotta see them eventually."

"Right." Baker signaled Joe to hand him the M1 Joe carried. Baker did not want run into the forest under sniper fire carrying his heavy BAR. Joe pushed the rifle into the air with both hands, and Baker caught it. The flash of activity drew another shot, and this time it was more obvious that the enemy fire came from somewhere above them. Baker twisted around, stood, and ran into the jungle behind them. The sniper fired again.

"Did you see that?" Hawk asked Joe. Joe had his head down.

"Shit, no. But it hit right behind me," Joe answered.

"Nah, it hit by Baker. You gotta pull your head up if you're gonna see the son of a bitch."

"Pull my head up? Shit on that shit."

Hawk muttered a few obscenities as he waited for Baker to get into position. He heard two or three Marine rifles fire.

"Who fired? Do you see him?" Hawk shouted.

"No!" Osage answered. The others who had fired remained silent. "But I think he's in that tree in front of me. I hear him screwin' around," said Osage.

"Okay," Hawk breathed quietly to himself, and then shouted again. "Watch that tree, I'm gonna draw his fire. See if you can hit the top of it with a rifle grenade."

"Wait a second," Joe cautioned. "Give Baker more time. You can't just run out there like a dumb ass."

Hawk rolled on his back and looked up through the palm fronds. "I used to know an old guy at the dump. He spent all day shootin' rats. He would get 'em when they stuck their head out of a hole, or when they ran in a straight line, like on a wire or something, where you can get a lead on them. But he never could hit one that went zigzagging around."

Joe looked up and shook his head. "Great story. I'll write it on your tombstone. The jackass that thought he was a rat."

Hawk leaped to his feet and ran directly toward the tree indicated by Osage. After a few feet, however, he swerved suddenly to the right and dove behind a large, forked tree. First one and then another shot struck the earth in the pathway in front of the tree, where the sergeant should have been, if he had continued on a straight path. As Hawk reached cover, Osage opened fire on the top of the suspected tree. Hawk peered from around the fork of his covering tree. To his surprise, Baker was standing right under the sniper's tree, behind the enemy's line of sight, and firing upward.

The sniper shrieked in pain. A rifle with a large attached telescope cartwheeled from above and clattered on the ground. A human body plummeted from the upper trunk, but stopped, as if it were a yo-yo on a string, and bounced up and down. The sniper had been tied around the waist by a rope to the tree. A helmet shot upward and off his head and tumbled to the earth below. The head and arms hung down on one side of the tightened rope, and the legs and hindquarters on the other. The Marines in the patrol were fascinated by the spectacle and watched as all of these various objects flew magically around before the green background. The sniper rifle lay at Baker's feet. It had been tethered, as had the man, but its thinner strand had broken. Baker was among those hypnotized by all this, and quite pleased by the result of his shot.

Sergeant Hawk, however, was not hypnotized. When the next shot cracked and knocked the rifle from Baker's hand, Hawk was sufficiently aware and prepared to observe in which direction the M1 sailed. Looking in the opposite direction, he raised the Thompson toward the shadow in the top of the nearby tree and held back the trigger. A dancing red flash fluttered upward from the muzzle, keeping time with the staccato thumping of the .45 caliber burst. Without a scream, the second sniper launched himself from the top of the tree, his rope tether catching him only a few feet from the ground, and then snapping in two under the weight. The body pounded flat and heavily into the ground, the impact on the lung cavity creating a reverberating, hollow sound.

Again, everyone looked on in fascination at the dead enemy, as Hawk continued to scan the treetops. But no other shots followed. Either there were only two snipers, or the third had decided that now would be an excellent time to take a coffee break.

Hawk slung the Thompson. They made sure that the fatally stricken Marine was dead, and buried him there for the time being. The other man had been hit with the small caliber sniper round in the upper arm and was able to walk. The corpsman shook a sulfa pack over the wound, and slapped a bandage on it. Guards were posted in case the action had attracted unwelcome visitors from the nearby plantation house. The men, and Ranke, stood silently over the new grave, each thinking that they could be next, and that this hump of earth on a far-flung island was all they would be getting out of life.

"Let's get the hell outta here. They had to have heard all that racket. Maybe we can still get the radio back," Hawk announced over the grave. They wound through the forest, and Ranke was given an M1. In less than an hour, they were peering through the leaves at the edge of the forest toward the farmhouse, on the other side of the clearing. The area surrounding the structure was not perfectly clear, having patches of scrub brush scattered across it. The bushes were not substantial enough to give the attackers any degree of cover. The house remained suspiciously quiet.

"I imagine they're laying low. Waiting on us," said Hawk.

He had hoped someone would be walking around, so that he could confirm the Japanese presence, as well as kill them. He was slightly hesitant to fire a rifle grenade into the building, without knowing for certain who was in there. But only slightly.

"Do you think there could be any natives in there, or anybody?" Hawk asked Ranke. "I'm about ready to do business with them."

"They have all fled. If anyone is in there, they are Japanese. Are you going to ask them to surrender? It would prevent damage to the house," Ranke suggested.

"Nah. Japs don't surrender. I'm plannin' on blowin' the shit out of them."

"But the radio. You wanted the radio," Ranke protested. He didn't mind the Japanese getting "blown" as much as he did his home.

"Yeah." Hawk reconsidered. He *had* to have the damned radio. He had to use a little precision killing here, if he wanted to get the valuable equipment. Of course, if the situation deteriorated, and it proved too difficult, he was not above destroying the radio as well. He had to try, at least, to get it in one piece. Maybe the Japanese would flee or had already fled. Neither seemed very likely.

"We have to shoot it out with 'em, I reckon," Hawk said. "We can't use grenades."

"I don't see anybody," said Joe. "Maybe they ran off to their boat."

"That would be good. Baker!" Hawk called. Baker ran to his side. "Get around back, and see if you still see that barge down by the water." Baker nodded and moved back into the forest before flanking the house, and proceeding toward the beach. Within a few minutes, he had returned.

"It's still there," he told Hawk.

"That means the bastards have to be inside there. Waitin'."

"I don't know," said Baker. "It looked empty." He turned to check the forest behind him. It was one of those uneasy moments that would revisit him in nightmares. The enemy could be anywhere. If they were not in the house—they were somewhere.

"They might surrender," said Joe. "I wonder how many they have."

"No tellin'. That house can't hold too many. Damn sure is quiet," said Hawk. "I don't like it. I think I'll get a little closer, and see what I can see, or stir up. Watch the flanks, they might be hiding out there in the woods." Baker, growing increasingly nervous, had already been doing that on his own.

"We just stay here?" Canlon asked.

"Yeah. I'll come back, I hope." He studied the lay of the land in front of the house. A low circle of stones stood about a hundred feet from the front porch. He looked to Ranke. "What is that?"

"A cistern," the German answered.

"How high is that thing?" Hawk asked. Ranke held his hand two feet off the ground.

"I guess it would stop a bullet. Who wants to go with me? We'll split up when we get close, and check the place out." The men remained quiet for a moment.

"I'll go," said Turnage.

Hawk nodded. He noticed that neither Joe nor Baker volunteered. No one liked the looks of the place, the forest behind them, or the situation in general. It had all the earmarks of an ugly trap.

"Watch for mines or trip wires," Hawk told Turnage. "We'll run up to that bush over there, then I go right and you go left. We'll meet at the well, if nobody's shot at us yet. Everybody else, cover the doors and windows. Don't let the bastards pull a fast one on us."

Hawk jumped up and began running in a crouch toward the house. Turnage leaped to his feet and followed. They reached the bush that Hawk had indicated, without spotting any booby traps. As Lincoln might have warned, however, you can see some of the traps all of the time, and all of the traps some of the time, but you can't see all of the traps all of the time. As the two Marines stood before the bush, and prepared to split to the left and right, the clump of leaves burst from the earth, and a rifle bearing Japanese soldier popped up from beneath the ground directly in front of them. The bush had not been a living bush after all, but consisted of three or four tree branches lashed together, lying on top of an enemy spider hole. The soldier fired point blank into Turnage, who spun around and hit the ground.

Hawk, completely surprised, and as startled as he had ever been in his life, nevertheless had the advantage of seeing the lid snap open and the enemy soldier fire at Turnage. He had just enough time for his lightning reflexes to settle the Thompson on the attacker and fire repeatedly into him, catapulting him in a circle around the walls of the hole, to fall in a slashed heap at the bottom. The Japanese soldier had no opportunity to rechamber his rifle. A machine gun opened up from somewhere.

Hawk could no longer see the house. The spider hole's leafy lid remained stuck open and straight up, blocking his view. He heard the Marines behind him open up on the plantation house. He flung an arm under the arm of Turnage and wrapped it upward on his back. With the submachine gun in one hand, and Turnage under one arm, he dragged the man toward the hole. Shots whistled through the flimsy lid of leaves and all around them. Hawk rolled into the hole with his wounded burden. Hundreds of automatic, semiautomatic, and bolt action rifle rounds blazed over their heads.

"How is it, kid?" Hawk shouted, trying to find a wound on the boy.

"It's my...it's like my hip," said the Marine. Hawk looked down and saw the blood soaking the fatigues of Turnage's pelvis. "It hurts like hell, Sergeant."

"Yeah. We'll fix that. Hang on." Hawk pulled out a syringe from the pouch on his belt. He pulled the protective cover off the needle and jammed it into Turnage's hip. "Good as new in a few seconds. Stay down, kid. I gotta see what's going on."

Hawk tried to peer through the leaves of the upright lid. Several ricochets close by indicated that this was not the best idea. He ducked down again and waited for a better idea to come to him. The building was too far for him to hit with a grenade, even if it would have served any purpose.

"They hit one of them for sure!" Baker shouted to Canlon, as he poured BAR fire at the window hiding the machine gun. Canlon, now the corporal in charge, crawled behind Baker and toward Ranke. Steady enemy fire whistled, buzzed, and whirred just over their heads, tearing at the leaves and branches.

"Where's the radio?" Canlon shouted to Ranke. "Is it over by that machine gun?" Ranke raised his head from the dirt where he had buried his face.

"Where is the machine gun?" Ranke asked, in an almost unrecognizable high-pitched squeal.

"In that window, over here next to the door. On the right side of the door," Joe answered. A bullet exploded between them on the ground.

"No, no! The radio is in the back. On the left side." Ranke buried his face again.

"Osage! Hit that machine gun with a rifle grenade!" Joe ordered.

"You got it."

Osage prepared to fit the tubular grenade on the end of his M1. He crawled forward to the edge of the jungle to get a clear shot. He clicked the launcher into the slotted muzzle of his M1, ejected his clip, and inserted a blank. Propping himself on his elbows and lying flat, he took aim. He fired, and a pumping, vacuum snapping noise followed as the propellant sent the grenade spewing straight into the windowsill behind which the machine gun rested. The entire right side of the building disappeared in an angry black cloud that sprouted up as the missile exploded. Shrapnel belched all the way back to the Marine position.

"Shit! What a shot!" Joe Canlon shouted. "Got that bastard!" The firing from the farm house stopped. The Marines kept shooting. "Cease fire!" Joe called. He wanted to assess the situation. He didn't think they had killed everyone in the building, but the Japanese may have been dazed.

"Hey, Baker"--Joe gestured--"go back to the water, see if they're making a run for it. Pick off some, if they are. We'll back you, if we hear shooting."

"Right." Baker ran to the rear of their position and into the jungle, in order to safely circle behind the house. When he arrived at the rear of the house, he found half a dozen enemy troopers dashing down the path toward the beach and their landing craft. He opened up with the BAR.

Upon recognizing the sound of the BAR, Joe got to his feet. "Okay, take the house!" he shouted. "Baker's got some of them at the boat!"

Hawk looked up from his temporary shelter again. He saw the men slowly advancing on the house and joined them. Joe ran past him.

"I gotta go help Baker," Joe told Hawk, and turned toward the others. "Don't grenade nothing. We need the radio," Joe told the men. "Check it, room to room."

When Joe found Baker, the latter was still firing at the departing landing barge. Several of the enemy had made a clean get away.

"Good job," Joe told Baker. "Or good enough. Let's check the house. I think it's open."

"Was Hawk dead?" Baker asked as they walked back.

"Nah, shit, no. Are you serious?" Joe laughed. "Oh, shit! I didn't see the kid. Come on." Osage came to the back door of the building.

"Hey, you can come in this way," Osage informed them.

When they came in, Turnage was on the floor, unconscious. Several men kneeled around him. The corpsman was administering a transfusion. Hawk was at the radio and Blackwell was cranking a generator. Joe checked on Turnage first. No one seemed to know his condition. Joe turned to Hawk, and the radio. It was a large short wave with sets of blinking lights, taking up half a wall.

"Does it work?" Joe asked.

"Yeah. It's a good one. I got Martin," Hawk spoke, as he distractedly listened for something on the headset. "They're sending a boat here," Hawk relayed.

"You better tell 'em the Japs landed here. They're all over that strait out there. Maybe they oughta try somewhere else," said Joe.

"Nah, they know all that shit. I ain't sayin' nothin' that would slow 'em down. They said they'd send a destroyer if they have to. They're gonna get us out. It's all settled. They need this message we got from Ranke. We're high priority, buddy." Hawk rifled through his pockets in search of any form of tobacco. If he could find that, the world would be in order again.

"Oh, yeah? Then what are you still sittin' there at the radio for, if it's all settled?" Joe didn't like the looks of it. "Is Turnage okay?"

"They're sending him a doctor. I'm waiting on the colonel. Martin said they told him if I called in, the colonel wanted to talk to me. Relax, it's all over," said Hawk. He knew that Joe could get tense.

Joe turned away. "*All over*, my ass." He suspected the colonel wanted to talk to Hawk in order to get them into deeper crap. It certainly wasn't to discuss the Yankees' late season problems with the St. Louis Browns.

"Yessir. Yessir," Joe heard Hawk talking to Clark. He walked outside. He didn't want to hear any of this. "Yessir, we got the next name," Joe heard, in spite of himself.

"Very good. That's enough on that subject for now, but very good," said the colonel. "They are listening to everything you say. Say nothing more about that. Save all the reporting until you get back. Over."

"Yessir. They must have known we were coming. As

soon as we got off the boat, they sent a plane after us. We lost three men. Got shot off a mountain. Over."

"I know," Clark answered. "This means they know about the mission and are trying to stop us. The Navy let it leak, it must have been those bastards that brought you over to Caratu. It's hard to keep a lid on this thing. Somebody is going to get killed before this is over."

Hawk frowned. *Somebody?* That meant the four he had lost already were nobodies. He had a sudden desire to know what this almighty coded message was about. Was it worth all of these lives? The colonel continued talking.

"We're going to have to change the mode of transportation on this. The Navy is out, we're not dealing with them anymore. I'm not sure how we'll handle it, but you don't have to worry, none of those kind of errors is going to happen again. We can't be fighting battles every step of the way," the colonel sounded increasingly angry. "You're already three days late."

I'm three days late? What the hell? For what? First of all, Hawk knew that he wasn't late for anything, that he had been informed of. Everything was on time, in spite of the screw-ups that he had nothing to do with. Second, why was *he* three days late? Was this *his* coded message now? Was he in charge of this whole matter all of a sudden? Why was *he* getting a new *mode* of transportation? It didn't sound like this was anywhere near over. The Hoech message contained a line of words as long as hell, and there could be a lot of names and identifications in there, if only three or four words applied to each person's name. The colonel signed off, and Hawk was left puzzling over the comments he had heard. The little lights on the radio grew dim. The glowing tubes behind it still lit the dark wall of the farmhouse.

They made a stretcher for Turnage. He remained unconscious, which was probably better for him. As Hawk looked at the pale white face of the young man, who was quite possibly dying, he regretted ever taking on this endeavor. It was all too vague. Normally, his men had a purpose for fighting and dying. This time they were not invading enemy held islands to clear a pathway to Japan, and end the war. They didn't know exactly what they were doing. They were...tracking down a *code*? He had already lost a lot of men for an amorphous concept such as that. He didn't mind shooting it out with the Japanese for any reason, anytime, anywhere, at any odds; but he couldn't ask normal men to do the same. Men, who had left high school eight months ago. Their mothers had not turned them over to him for this sort of unexplained shenanigans.

Turnage returned to consciousness. His face was filled with pain. He asked to speak to Hawk.

"Hey, kid. How do you feel? You're looking *good*."

"Will I...make it?" Turnage asked with tears in his voice.

"Well, shit, yeah, you'll make it. Are you kiddin'? They got a doctor coming to pick us up. A surgeon. You ain't got nothing to worry about. Nothing. We're high priority."

"That...Jap...that scared the hell out of me."

"Yeah. Me, too. Popped outta the ground like old Beelzebub, didn't he? He gotta quick ticket back to where he came from, too."

"Did we...did we...is the mission done, I mean?"

"Oh, yeah. Don't worry about that. Yeah, we did the whole thing. They say this might win the war for us. You were a big part of it, kid. I think I see a medal here somewhere."

"Really?"

"Shit, yeah. Hell, yeah. You tired?? Rest a little. Don't wear yourself out talking to a bunch of dumb asses." Hawk stood. He looked at the circle of men standing over Turnage. "He's gonna be okay," Hawk told them. He nodded to affirm his words. "Shit. Give the kid some room. Bastards." Joe thought perhaps he saw concern on Hawk's face as they all stood motionless, looking down.

5

FLIGHT OF THE WASP

LATER IN THE NIGHT, THREE PT BOATS ARRIVED AT THE dock, armed with torpedoes and anti-aircraft guns. Under the cover of darkness, the patrol left Caratu and returned to Greater Helvedes. It was not until the afternoon of the next day that Hawk was told to meet with the colonel and deliver his report. The sergeant noted that time was of the essence in this matter of the code, only when it was his turn to do something. When it was the colonel's turn, however, the afternoon was soon enough. It gave Hawk time to pass by the field hospital and see how Turnage was doing. He learned the boy was being evacuated to a hospital ship. He was not allowed to see him.

"How is he doing?" Hawk asked the doctor, who came outside to answer his questions. The doctor was young and handsome, not the kind of doctor Hawk would have preferred for Turnage, or anyone else, for that matter. He would rather have seen some beat up, bald, old-looking wreck.

"Fifty-fifty," said the doctor.

"Fifty-fifty?" Hawk asked.

"Fifty-fifty."

"That ain't so good. He didn't look that bad," said Hawk.

"Fifty-fifty." The doctor put a hand on Hawk's shoulder, turned around and returned inside the big tent. Hawk stood there for a stunned moment. A beat up, bald, old-looking guy would have said more. He would have mumbled some folksy old saying with some sort of encouragement attached to it. *Fifty-fifty ain't worth a shit.*

The colonel met with Hawk soon after. Fresh from the visit with Turnage and his caretaker, Hawk had a growing number of unpleasant feelings about the code and his part in retrieving it. He and the colonel were alone.

"Listen, Sergeant," the colonel began, leaving Hawk standing, "we can't be discussing this matter on an open radio. I hope I've made that clear enough times. Do you realize that the enemy could pick up a transmission like that, and act upon it? The entire mission could be compromised."

"Yessir. I believe they done did that. They sent a plane to the mountain to stop us from getting off the shore, and they took over the German's plantation before we could even get there. We lost four, and maybe five men. There was a lot of compromising, the minute we landed on the island."

"I'm well aware of *all* of that. This is no time for crying in your beer. We are stuck with our hopes now. We can only hope that Hoech has not been detected by enemy intelligence, and hope for the same regarding his message. We can only hope that all the Japs have picked up pertaining to this matter are the Navy messages about delivering *you* to Caratu. If not, Hoech could be dead, and the message worthless. We are now risking the loss of a lot more men, for a compromised message. We have no idea how important this is. We won't know until reaching the end of that list of names, *if* we make it that far."

"Might be a good idea to forget the whole thing, sir," Hawk suggested. He thought the entire matter a little too tenuous for the investment of human capital. "If the message is that important, somebody in intelligence will figure it out somewhere else."

"What? *Forget the whole thing?* Are you *mad*? Don't ever say a thing like that again. The United States Marine Corps is not a bunch of quitters. We don't forget. We will complete the mission. We don't talk—and we don't *think*—that way."

"Yessir." There '*we*' were again. That meant it would *not* be Clark on the side of a cliff facing a Zero next time. Whenever someone started preaching heroics at you, you knew this was your baby. Hawk was now positive that he was still in on this search for God only knew what.

"Let's get down to business. You've wasted enough time as it is. We almost lost everything that time. What name did Ranke give you?" The colonel opened a folder with his copy of the message on the top page. "What was this '*green bottle soul*'? I was afraid of this one. It sounded like utter nonsense."

Hawk took out his torn, filthy, and bloodstained page with his printed copy of the code. He read the deeply scratched writings of Ranke, without worrying over pronunciation. "Vuniwai on Papanuca."

"What? What are you saying? Are those words? Let

me see that," said the colonel. He looked at the page and squinted. "I don't see any of that here." He turned the page ninety degrees.

"It's down at the bottom, sir. It's kind of light. The pencil needed sharpening."

"Oh. I still can hardly see it. Can you see that? Spell that out for me." Hawk did so. The colonel shook his fountain pen and wrote the names down. "You're sure that was the name he gave you, Hawk?"

"Yessir." The colonel shook his head as if this were the stupidest thing he had ever heard, rather than something twenty men had risked their lives for. "Ranke's here, sir. You can ask him yourself, if you want."

"Makes no sense. Is that a person?"

"Yessir. It's a witch doctor on that island. Sells potions and stuff like that. Like Marie Laveau or something."

"Like *who*? This island is in the Helvedes?"

"Marie Laveau was a voodoo queen in New Orleans. Yessir, it's a woman, I think. That island is supposed to be around here somewhere. Close by."

"If this isn't the damnedest thing." The colonel opened up his map and squinted at the tiny print in the key at the bottom. It listed the names of all of the islands portrayed above, in distinctive colors. "Damned, if it isn't. There it is. Not a big place. Not exactly around here. As a matter of fact, that's a *long* way from here. Across a lot of open water. Here, look at this." Hawk walked around the desk and leaned over. Distances were vast in the Pacific, even within the same island group.

"Mm hm. Sure, enough," Hawk replied in a Mississippi-toned affirmation. He hadn't really seen anything.

"I certainly hope the Japs don't know about this. They can cause a lot of problems between here and there. Look at the distance. I can tell you, this is a dangerous set up right here. I was not expecting the scope of this information-gathering assignment. I hope you can keep your lip buttoned this time. We certainly don't need any more of that."

As Hawk peered around the back of the colonel's balding head, he strongly considered giving the oddly shaped cranium a solid slap, one that would bounce the officer's face off the flat surface covered by the map. Instead, he walked calmly back around to the front of the desk, his heavy hands open and relaxed.

"I'm going to have to straighten out the matter of the transportation. That may take a little while. The Navy royally screwed this up. You'll need replacements, of course, and new equipment. I'll get you this map, a smaller version, and a larger one of that island, Papanuca, if we have it, or if there is such a place. You should be ready to go the day after tomorrow. I hope there is a way to communicate with this person in English. I better get an interpreter. No telling what kind of crap they speak over there."

Hawk didn't answer.

"And you *cannot* dilly dally this time, and run your mouth. Time is creeping up on us."

Hawk remained silent. It was going to take Clark two days to make a phone call to get a boat, and Hawk was the one causing delays? It was better to have the making of all of these high-level military decisions done at a distance.

Hawk was a little too close to the source of this operation. One likes to have a little faith in something when engaged in life and death matters. Seeing men like Clark at work was not conducive to such an end. The standard operating procedure in all such undertakings was first and foremost finding someone else to blame when plans imploded. Hawk did not have to wonder who was going to be at fault if the solution to the code arrived too late. And yet, he had a somewhat more intuitive grasp of the how the process worked than did Clark; that being that Hawk was too small a part of the equation to be blamed for anything. If Clark moved heaven and earth to shift the entire blame for the loss of World War II onto the shoulders of James Hawk, he would have accomplished little, for no one would care, including James Hawk.

Meanwhile, how was Turnage doing? That seemed more important to him than any of the rest of this.

* * *

BACK IN MIDDLE AMERICA, in the shady Maryland suburbs where the comfortable homes were built into the sides of hills, the fates of Turnage or James Hawk were of little consideration. There were no rosters of dying friends, deadlines, blame, fatal decisions, devastating explosions, nightmarish bayonets, smoke of war, madmen, horror, or terror. It was Sunday morning and the birds were singing. In the distance, church bells called the faithful to services. God was in his heaven, and James Hawk and all of that other nasty stuff, was somewhere else. The streets were virtually empty.

Ruth Nagle had reached eighty-one years of age, and had only recently stopped sitting on her front porch.

She used to enjoy her coffee out there, especially when her husband, Bert, was alive. She could spend hours in the cool breeze there, explaining to Bert what was wrong with him. But he had inconsiderately died earlier in the year and left her alone. She tried sitting on the porch for a while afterward, but had noticed that people looked at her, and she didn't like that. Especially unwelcome were the looks of the young students in the rooming house next door. Sometimes they would call greetings to her, or even worse, ask if they could be of some service. She had no desire for such condescension from the likes of them, and moved her chair and her coffee cup indoors, along with a small, needy houseplant.

There was a convenient kitchen window that she could look out, and see most of the world. At least, most of her world. It had room for a little table for her coffee and a saucer with toast. She could see the street and the rooming house, and be well forewarned if anyone approached her home with some unnecessary and intrusive offer of kindness. She could shut the blinds when she wanted to close the world off. That was usually around ten a.m., when the sunlight hit the window most aggressively.

Ruth tuned in the Sunday morning services on the radio. She had no interest in the war, or any of that. She was sick of hearing about it. She hadn't even liked the last war. Bert had bored her enough with his crap about that. There was a particularly graphic preacher on at ten that she liked to listen to. He told it like it was in the afterlife, with all the fire, brimstone and pitchforks, and without sugarcoating it with a bunch of stories about Jesus and the little children. This was fast becoming her favorite program, since the bastards had taken Ed Sullivan off earlier in the year. She had not closed the blinds yet. Suddenly, her hand shot out and she turned off the radio. She half closed the blinds. A 1939 tulip cream-colored Studebaker Champion had just pulled slowly up to the curb and parked, across the street from the rooming house.

She had seen the car before, and although the driver was endlessly fiddling around inside it, with something, Ruth knew who would eventually get out. She had seen the young Asian woman on several occasions over the last few weeks. Ruth assumed that she was Chinese. The house next door did not allow visitors before nine a.m. or after eight p.m. On the days when the car came, generally the Studebaker would remain at the curb from 8:55a.m. until 7:55 p.m. Only male students resided at the house, and Ruth did not like the looks of any of this. It could only mean one thing: funny business.

She did not like one of the boarders in particular, for he would come out on the porch and talk to the Asian girl. They put their chairs extremely close together, and Ruth knew that this was not just for the purpose of being able to hear one another, for Ruth's chair and Bert's chair had been twice that distance, and they had no trouble hearing one another, even though Bert pretended to be deaf. Ruth sipped her coffee as her eyes narrowed. Bert was an asshole. He was no more deaf than she was. She wished he could be here, if just for a minute.

One of the advantages of being indoors was that Ruth could talk to Bert out loud without anyone over-hearing. And she had a lot to tell him, things that he had missed out on by departing early, and damn well should have been told. She peered at the two young people with a disapproving sneer. She knew that they would stay on the porch and talk for about an hour, and then they would go inside, and do God knew what. How could they talk from nine a.m. to eight p.m.? Or ten a.m. on Sundays. It was unnatural. The young man, almost a boy, was rather sneaky looking, with his light-colored hair slicked back with oil so thick it almost looked black. Ruth suspected he was some sort of foreigner, because he always wore a suit and tie, and foreigners always did deceptive shit like that. He obviously didn't work, and that could not be good. How did he support himself? Even American students had at least some sort of part time job. Of course, most decent young men were in the military. The Chinese girl smiled frequently, she was clearly leading on the poker-faced dope beside her, with not only her feminine wiles, but also her Asian wiles. It kind of hurt to watch. But Ruth did. Until they went back inside, much later.

"There they go, Bert," she sighed. It was time to prepare Lenora, her dog, her morning bacon. Ruth stood and walked over to the stove. Lenora, her four legs sticking almost straight out from her round body due to obesity, diligently followed, causing the floor to shake.

Ruth was not looking when a 1937 black Plymouth Coupe pulled up behind the Studebaker, for she was busily turning over the sizzling bacon. She might not have thought anything of it. But had she seen the young Stefano Calvino get out of it, and stick his head curiously into the Studebaker's open window, before going up the steps to the rooming house, she would have thought a good deal of that. It would have to wait until another day for her to put these three individuals together.

* * *

JAMES HAWK WAS NOT much of a worrier, but he could be thorough. When Clark gave him an idle day to think about the upcoming mission, he recalled the colonel's comment about needing an interpreter. He did not have faith in Clark, and would not have been surprised if the patrol was assigned a Frenchman or something. Since some island somewhere had been owned by the French at some time, the U. S. military usually assumed a Frenchman solved all of your problems when it came to communication. That was not a huge obstacle, since the sergeant had gotten by with sign language in most situations anyway. The communication problem in general, however, made him think of Ranke. Not only did Ranke speak several languages, a talent common among Europeans, he had also met and knew this Vuniwai. He could be quite useful. Rather than mentioning it to the colonel, and having the German involuntarily drafted into some deadly undertaking against his will, Hawk decided to ask Ranke what he thought of the prospect. The farmer was being quartered in a tent, until he could be evacuated within the next few weeks. Hawk went to see him there.

"Yeah, they roped me into this deal to go see the voodoo queen on Papanuca," Hawk said. "I thought I was out of it. You can't never get outa this shit."

"My story is worse than yours," said Ranke. "Do you know where I am going? Only--because I was born in Germany?"

"Uh..." Hawk would hazard a guess, to be polite. "Germany?"

Ranke laughed. "Germany?" He laughed again. "My, that would be better, if it were even possible. They could throw me out of the bus at the front lines in Belgium." He shook his head. "No, they will *not* send me back to New Guinea. No, I am going to an internment camp, in Louisiana or some godforsaken place."

"Oh?" Hawk pretended to be interested. He wouldn't mind going to Louisiana. "Well, them places ain't so bad. We ain't like the Japs and Germans. They feed you ice cream and get up a baseball team for you. They call 'em internment camps, but it's more like the YMCA. You'll be weavin' baskets and shit like that. Listenin' to Jack Benny, and doing all kind of grab ass."

"No, no. You misunderstand. Not *that* kind of internment camp. A POW camp. I am not just an enemy alien, I am an enemy combatant. They do this to me, after three years of my fighting the Japanese for them. It doesn't seem to matter to them *who* I was combating."

"No, shit? That's the government, ain't it?" Hawk commented, his interest in Ranke's complicated problems fading fast. "Hey, listen. I was thinking about this Papanuca trip and all. The colonel is finding us a boat to get on over there pretty soon. It's some big deal since it can't be a Navy boat. It's a long way, right?"

"A very long way. You must be careful. I will bet they don't even know if the Japanese are there. They are still scattered all over the Helvedes, you know? That far? Ach, anything could be up there. These bastards will send you into anything." Ranke clicked his tongue. "Did you see the map of this place? It is hundreds of miles closer to Japan. You could be getting into...

anything. I wish Germany would surrender so I could go home."

"Yeah, the livin' must be really easy there about now. But listen, I been thinking, maybe if we had you along on this trip, you could talk to this crazy ass woman. You know her and all. We just need a few words out of her. You know all about how that works, too. Does she speak English?"

"I know *of* her. I am not her friend. As I recall, she does speak English. I don't know that I could help you at all." Ranke looked down thoughtfully. "But, I tell you. I would *definitely* like to go along with you. It is better than this prison they have for me in this Louisiana. Maybe this would make a stronger case for my loyalty. If they will let me go, that is. You have influence in this?"

"Me?" Upon reflection, Hawk suddenly changed the answer he was about to give. "Shit, yeah. I'll get you in. I don't want to sell you a load of shiny monkey shit here, though. There might be shootin', just like on that last deal. Clark made it sound like all I had to do was go shake hands with you and float on back here. You saw what happened."

"I know. I know. I tell you, I am afraid. People in the United States hate Germans. If I go to prison, I may be killed. I am too old for this kind of thing. I am too old for your kind of fighting, too, but I trust your abilities to get me back alive. *Louisiana*? Alligators?" He waved his hand in anger.

"Okay, yeah. I'll clear it with the colonel. He's my buddy," said Hawk, knowing full well that Clark would be just as willing to put *him* in a German POW camp as he would be to put Ranke in one.

The next day Hawk was summoned by Colonel

Clark. The arrangements for transportation had been made. Hawk listened patiently again to how they were behind schedule, or rather, *he* was behind schedule, and how he had gone less than halfway through the list of names. Along with Hawk, the US Navy received a good deal of criticism, and Hawk was assured that they would never be involved in this matter again. The sergeant was not as comfortable with this as Clark seemed to be. Ships had a lot of firepower. He had nothing against the U. S. Navy. He grew more than a little curious as to how the vast distance to Papanuca would be covered without the Navy. He soon had the answer.

Clark also informed him that reconnaissance had revealed no Japanese presence on the island. This did not mean that the enemy had never been there, or that they were unable to get there.

"Is this witch doctor person gonna be easy to get to, sir?" Hawk asked. "Like down on the beach or something, when we get there? Last time, they kind of dropped us off around the corner from Ranke's place. They might have done a better job. These places ain't as little as they look on a map."

"That was the Navy. I've taken care of that. No. Here is your map of the island. I would say her compound or village, or whatever she calls it, is about in the middle of Papanuca. I don't see any point on the coast any closer to her than any other. I was told that she moved her people inland for security purposes. They don't like visitors," said the colonel.

"Jap visitors—which ain't there—I guess," Hawk observed. "I wanted to ask you, sir. Was there any more on getting us an interpreter?"

"Oh, darn, I knew I forgot something."

"Yessir. I was thinking maybe we could take Ranke. He knows that woman, or something about her. He could make the introductions and all."

"You know, that's a good idea. I wonder if we could persuade him to accompany you?" Clark asked.

"I think we can. Yessir."

Clark restored the patrol to its former strength of twenty men. They assembled at the crowded beach on Greater Helvedes that afternoon, for immediate departure to the island of the voodoo queen. Clark came to the dock personally to wish them all well. Here, he revealed that they would be flying to Papanuca, rather than going on another ocean excursion. This was taken as a good omen. A great deal of the dread over this newest undertaking involved the distance that had to be crossed. An airplane would eliminate all of that.

The sun blazed bright on the lagoon as several ships passed in and out of Greater Helvedes. The men stood on a newly constructed wharf. From out of the distance, a plane soared toward the waiting Marines. The spectacle reminded several of them of the Zero on Caratu. That was soon forgotten as the graceful Catalina flying boat daintily touched down and slid along the calm surface of the water on its belly. It passed by the impressed watchers. The plane turned with great precision, and drifted back toward them. With some relief, they admired the skills of the pilot, as flying was not an everyday event for them. The whitish gray bottom of the two toned plane bobbed peacefully on the blue water, as the contrasting bluish gray of its top reflected the bright glare of the sun. The pilot, quite slender and in a jumpsuit, leaped with amazing, gymnastic agility from the plane to the pier and took long, confident strides toward Colonel Clark. Hawk closed one eye. He had seen that stride, and the swing of the arms, before. It couldn't be.

The pilot removed her cap and long blonde hair fell past her shoulders. She threw her arms around the colonel and hugged him warmly.

"Bennie! So good to see you again," she said, in her loudest, and phoniest, voice.

"Vera, you look absolutely stunning," said the colonel. "You are a sight for sore eyes. I wish you were staying here instead of getting mixed up in this gamble." He kissed her cheek, and she backed away a little.

"Let's not get into that all over again," she said. They faced Hawk simultaneously. Before the sergeant was brought into the discussion, however, Otto Ranke rushed up and hugged Vera.

"My dear, Vera! So good to see you. We had just been talking about you. With the...mission and the words...and that. I wanted to see you so, and here you are. Here you are!"

"Here I am," said Vera, holding out her arms. "It is good to see you, too, Otto. How have you been? Hiding out, there in New Guinea? What have you been up to? I bet it involves a native girl, or two." She shook a finger at him. "We will have to catch up later."

"Yes. No, no native girl." He giggled. "Yes, I am sorry to intrude. We will talk later," said Ranke bowing subserviently to the colonel, and backing away, still smiling at Vera.

"Sergeant Hawk, I believe you have met Vera Orr, Women's Auxiliary Service Pilots?" said the colonel. Vera smiled broadly and held out her hand.

"*Of course*, he has," said Vera. "Look at that big

smile!" She had to shout a little, because of the wind. Hawk reluctantly took her hand. He was not smiling.

"Yessir. We've met," Hawk admitted.

"She will be taking the patrol to Papanuca for us. I tried to talk her out of it. But, you know Vera!"

"Yessir. I do."

"At least you will have the most beautiful pilot in the South Pacific, right?" The colonel laughed heartily. "No question of that!"

"No, sir. No question of that."

"We discussed it." The colonel leaned over confidentially toward Hawk, who was still not smiling, "and decided that there would be very little danger on an unoccupied island. It's a good chance for her to run up a few of her flying hours, you understand."

"Yessir." Once again, Vera Orr was in on every discussion, if not leading it, on any stray matter, whether classified or not. Hawk seemed to recall from this morning that the island was a dangerous distance away, and there were no guarantees as to whether it was occupied or not. By this afternoon, it had become an acceptable place for Miss Emily's School of Girl Pilots to practice on.

"He is *so* excited, he doesn't know just what to say," Vera offered. "I hope that's not a tear of joy I see in that big blue eye?" She turned her dazzling smile on Hawk.

"Yeah. I was thinking that it might be kind of dangerous, to tell you the truth," said Hawk. He wanted to curse and scream at her at great length, making the best use of his limited vocabulary, but could not do so with the colonel present.

"Oh, I *know*. I *know* you were," she said. "Because of my extreme delicacy. You were always the most thoughtful knight in shining armor. He is *sooo* chivalrous! Such a little gentleman! But how else was I going to get a trip with *you*, dear boy? This is about the safest one you've ever been on, isn't it?" She laughed. Clark laughed. It was kind of like a company picnic.

"Yes, ma'am," said Hawk. She was having more than a little fun with him. He wanted to punch—someone—in the face.

"WASP pilots have no rank, Sergeant. Civil Service. No need for that 'ma'am' stuff," said the colonel.

"Yessir," Hawk said. "I was mostly being polite to the...*lady*."

"He is always *sooo* polite," said Vera. "It's those Southern manners. He's from this cute little town where everyone is so sweet. What was it again? Tobacco Road? I remember it was just past Dog Patch."

"Yeah. That's it. You got a memory, awright."

A messenger rushed up to the colonel, and the officer turned away to speak to him. "Excuse me a minute, you two," Clark said. Hawk walked closer to Vera.

"What the goddam hell are you doing here?" Hawk asked her in a low voice, the tone not as polite as before.

"Ah, this sounds more like the Tobacco Road I remember. Wish I was in the land of cotton. You boys are such charmers. Masters of the language. You're not going to start bringing my mother into this, are you?"

"I don't want you here, or anywhere near here. Tell him you changed your stupid ass mind and get the hell out of here. Are you nuts?"

"Nuts about you, baby."

"You ain't no pilot. You paid for like one lesson in

California, if that. You probably lied like a son of a bitch. What are you trying to pull?"

"Things change. I don't let grass grow under my tiny feet, like some people, with their *biiiig* strong feet. You're used to that slow lifestyle, south of the Mason-Dixon line. Riding Old Bessie, the mule, down to the jug band concert. The early bird gets the tobacco leaf, as we say up in the briar patch."

The colonel turned back to them. "Catching up on old times, I see," said the officer.

"Yessir. Lot to catch up on," Hawk replied. "I wanted to say, sir, it might be a little dangerous for Mrs. Orr. On this thing. On account of everything."

"Oh, believe me, I know what you mean. I know exactly. I talked to her until I was blue in the face. We're leaving in an hour. Get the men aboard, Sergeant." Hawk saluted. Clark saluted and left.

Hawk waited until the officer moved out of earshot before addressing his new pilot again. The men in the patrol stood a safe distance from the two of them, watching the discussion. Joe Canlon was especially amused at Hawk's discomfort. He, more than anyone, knew of their complicated relationship between the two of them. Watching Hawk's face made him want to burst out laughing. Everyone else was more focused on Vera Orr.

"So, a colonel talked to you until he was blue in the face and you're still here?" Hawk asked her.

"He's a true gentleman. *Emphasis*—on gentleman. And he already had a tinge of blue, as well. I didn't cause all of that."

"Yeah? Well, you must be Roosevelt's illegitimate kid

to get into this deal. *Emphasis*—on illegitimate. How do you keep doing all of this shit?"

"Don't you have enough secrets to deal with? Ask me no secrets and I'll tell you no lies."

"No, I bet you wouldn't. But I'll tell you one thing, though. And I don't care if you're damn Roosevelt himself in a bleached wig. You ain't going into this island with us. You're taking your little kite there, and your ass, and leaving as soon as we get there."

"Oh, believe me." Vera held up both hands. "I've been on island get-aways with you before. I have no desire to do *that* again. I would rather be a target in a shooting gallery. I'll drop you off, and I pick you up. You can leave me a tip at the end." She smiled and closed one eye. It made the open one look twice as green. "I might even give you a flying lesson, big boy. If you keep that sweet corn pone talk up."

Hawk glared at her for a moment. If she kept her word—and there were *no* guarantees on that score—it might not be too bad. She wouldn't be around long. He folded his upper lip against his teeth.

"Aw'ight," he said. "Good to see you, Vera." He nodded and picked up his pack. "Now, I got shit to do." He turned away from her and saw all of his men looking at them. "What are you son of a bitches looking at? Get on that goddam plane."

"Ain't you gonna introduce them to their pilot?" Joe called out. "Kinda rude."

"Yeah. This is Mrs. Vera Orr. Women's Auxiliary something. The pilot of that thing," Hawk shouted.

She curtsied. The men shouted, whistled and hooted. She twirled around on her toes, holding both arms straight above her head.

"Awright. That's enough of that shit."

As the men crowded around Vera and then filed aboard, Canlon approached Hawk. "Kinda giving her a rough time, weren't you?" Joe asked. "You better watch out. She ain't just a knockout. She's got hot connections, in more ways than one. You think she knows that Hoech guy?"

"I don't give a shit what she knows."

"She might be the one running this damn war. That woman is spooky."

"It's startin' to look like it, don't it?" Hawk said. "She's really aggravating. I know one thing: she's damn sure got something on the colonel."

"Yeah," said Joe. "I think I might know what it is."

6

THE WITCH OF THE FAR ISLAND

THE BLUE PACIFIC TOOK UP THE ENTIRE COCKPIT windshield of the Catalina as it sped northward. Its wings were situated high above the cabin, and two loud engines were perched upon the wings. The aircraft sailed beyond the farther islands of the Helvedes, toward the very last one out there. In fact, there was almost nothing left between Papanuca and Japan. Vera felt exhilarated as never before at the helm of the craft, with the heart of a key mission of the war in her hands, one of which still bore the massive diamond ring bestowed upon her by the late E. Wendell Orr. They soared over vast waters that angels would never bother to tread. Hawk leaned on the hatchway behind her, his arms over his head. He was not exhilarated.

"Lot of ocean out there," he said.

"Ah. Small talk. My specialty." She glanced over her shoulder at him. "I bet it's not the ocean on your mind, though. Right?" She turned back around. "You want to argue. Should I argue with you? Here goes. There is *not* a lot of ocean out there?"

"Do you always have to be a wiseass?"

"Spit it out. What do you hate about me now? I knew you wouldn't like the jumpsuit. I told them that in Sweetwater. They're made for men. They mistakenly rejected my designing expertise."

"Sweetwater, Texas?" Hawk rubbed his straight, narrow nose. "I been there."

"Have you? Why am I not surprised? Nice place. What were you stealing? So, what's the problem?"

"There ain't no problem. You know what you're doing, don't cha?"

"Yes. Look at it out there. It gives me chills. Nothing but water. It's like we're on the way to the North Pole."

"More like going to Tokyo—or the moon."

"The soul of a poet. I always knew the baboon costume was just a disguise."

"No, see, the moon is out over there. You can see it."

"Oh, yes. I never saw it so clearly in the daylight. Don't tell me you can't feel something out here? Or were you about to? That's why you came up here. You were overwhelmed by my ravishing beauty? I can understand, it's the standard reaction. Nothing to be ashamed of, you're only a man." She looked over her shoulder. He did not look at her. "No, I'm sure you came up here with some bit of wisdom for me. I so hope it's both patronizing and vulgar." She turned and smiled. "You don't much like flying, do you? Why not?"

"I hope you don't find out why not. This ain't Sweetwater. I was just gonna remind you: the Japs got airplanes, too. With guns. And they go about four times faster than this little toy."

"That just occurred to you?"

"Not very long ago, yeah."

"You have nothing to worry about. Fighter planes have flown this route a half dozen times to check it out for me."

"They ain't flying with you today, sweetheart."

"Relax. Don't be scared. Want to sit up here with mama? I'll hold your little hand. We can talk about what sissies girls are."

"No, thanks. I think I'll get a short nap back here. How much longer?"

She glanced at the gauges. "Two point six hours. Don't go scaring my passengers, or I'll have to throw you out. Lot of ocean out there. A lot of nothing—to fight over."

"Yeah, okay. I won't mention the pilot."

"Hey!" She stopped him as he was turning around.

"What?" he asked. "You never said anything. How do I look?"

"Pretty damn good."

"Now that's more like it. That makes my trip."

"Yeah? I hope so, Vera."

The sky's luster paled in two point six hours. Green Papanuca loomed up out of the blue nothingness below the Catalina. Vera circled it, looking for a sheltered cove on the western shore in which to land. Hawk again approached the front of the plane to have a look at the island. He could make out a brown patch in the center of the green, which he assumed must be a village. It resembled a dead spot in a lawn, where children played too often. Unfortunately, he saw no accompanying path to the dead spot.

Even from the air, the island had an eerie look to it, perhaps an odd shape to the bend of the trees, or a strange waving of the mystical leaves with their starry shapes. Weird outcroppings of stone leaped from odd places, for no reason, and there appeared to be a murky, half concealed, and smoky waterway through it all.

"I'll go around it a couple of times. I've found what I'm looking for," Vera told him. "See that little inlet? I'll have to watch the big rock in it." She pointed at a sort of human shaped formation.

"Looks like a mermaid oughta be sittin' on it."

Before she could answer, Joe Canlon came from the rear and slapped Hawk's arm.

"Hey, come see this. We got company," said Joe.

"*Shit.*" Hawk followed him to the rear, where the plane had a blister for a waist gunner with a fifty-caliber machine gun. The glass bubble presented a spectacular one hundred eighty degree view.

"Look out there," said Joe. "That can't be ours." Hawk ducked his head for a better view. He could tell only that it was a sleek fighter plane, but judging by where they were on the globe, he knew whose it had to be. Once again, the Japanese had tailed them. He felt angry, and a lot of other things.

"Have a seat." Hawk gestured at the machine gun. "At least we can fight back this time." Joe fell into the seat.

"Fight *that* thing? It's probably a Zero. It'll rip us a new ass."

"You think you got a choice? Get ready. I gotta go tell Amelia Earhart." Hawk swung rapidly back to the cockpit. "They're out there," he told her. "Right on schedule. Better pick your spot and pick it fast."

"You've got to be kidding."

"No, ma'am. Take it down fast."

"It's getting dark. Maybe they don't see us," she said. A machine gun rattled in the distance.

"They see us," said Hawk.

"I can't land with that going on, they'll shoot us full of holes," she said, her former cool demeanor had suddenly evaporated.

"What do you want me to do, ask them to stop? Take the son of a bitch down. We can't sit up here in the goddam air. You're the only pilot we got." The machine gun rattled again.

"This plane goes in slow and easy. They will tear us to pieces, I tell you," she insisted.

"What the hell? You ain't gonna outrun them. What else can you do?"

"I don't know. I'm scared."

"Son of a ...okay, go low over the island."

"Why? We have to land on water."

"Just do it." Joe opened up with the fifty-caliber machine gun, indicating that the enemy plane was getting closer. The loud gun expelled its huge bullets, and the noise reverberated through the cabin, blocking out the already deafening noise of the two engines on the wings over the fuselage. Vera skimmed the treetops, with the fighter plane swooping lower behind her.

"What are we doing?" she asked. "What's *that thing* doing?"

"I don't know. I wanna see if it's harder for them to see us against the dark trees." The Japanese plane stopped firing. Joe did not. "Hey, stupid! Cease firing until they do!" Hawk screamed.

"Now what?" she asked.

"Stay over the island. It gives us a darker background. Can you get lower?"

"I don't want to hit the trees."

"Lower and slower."

"This is really dangerous. What are you doing?" The fighter plane's machine cannon opened up. Joe Canlon immediately replied. There was an ominous thump in the area of the Catalina's tail. The Japanese pilot swerved in a lightning fast maneuver, appearing on the other side of the American plane, where Joe could not see him.

"We're gonna land in the treetops," said Hawk.

"We, *what*? I can't do that. We'll smash to smithereens."

"Nah, look at 'em. Level as a tabletop. And a lot darker. Just play like it's water. Go in real slow, slide along and set it down easy." They came to the edge of the island and water appeared beneath them again.

"I can't do that. We'll be killed."

"Yeah, well, here's the deal, little lady: we're gonna be killed anyway. You got to. Take it back over the island. He can see you too good, lit up over this damn water."

"This is horrible! *Horrible!*"

"Yeah. No shit. You're doin' great, kid. Lower. Slower." A tree branch viciously slapped the plane's underbelly, sounding like a gunshot.

"Oh, my god!" said Vera, involuntarily pulling up.

"That's awright. It's gonna sound a lot worse than that. Bring it down, and slower."

"It's not getting any slower, baby. You're looking at it," she said. "All we got left is lower. Into a tree trunk."

Dozens of branches explosively slapped the hull. The noise of all of them blended into a roar, and a screech, and then a groan as the plane finally slowed, scratched and skidded across the treetops. The Catalina bounced up and down, sinking into the limbs and then bursting back up, the foliage all but blocking the windshield. The forward motion slowed and the plane spun around on a wingtip, facing the opposite direction from which it had approached the trees. The nose drifted steadily lower than the rest of the craft and pointed toward the earth below. The people within were thrown roughly about until the plane finally stopped. Vera slumped with exhaustion into the seat. Hawk rushed back toward Joe Canlon.

The side of the plane with the machine gun bubble lay angled toward the sky. Joe's nose bled, where it had collided with a bulkhead brace. Hawk shook him.

"Hey, are you awake?" He shook him again. "Yeah. Yeah. Busted my head." Joe groaned.

"The Jap's coming in for a shot at us. Let him have it!" Hawk pointed upward at the sky. The Catalina lay dark and hard to see against the dusk background of the jungle, whereas the Zero was shining against the much lighter sky above.

"Son of a..." Joe shrieked in alarm upon seeing the massive plane streaking down at him with its guns blazing. The machine guns, mounted on its wings, lit a flaming pathway of fire on either side of the Catalina, completely missing the fuselage in the middle, as the Zero dove toward it. Joe pressed the trigger of the fifty-caliber machine gun. Its burst was focused into a single flashing spear, unlike that of the Zero's divided weapons. Joe steered the glowing spear directly into the face of the pilot in the cockpit. The giant rounds crashed into the enemy plane at a rate of sixty per second, with a stopping power that could not be denied. Smoke leaked from beneath the Zero as it shot over them, barrel rolled, and crashed with a giant roar somewhere off to the west.

"You got him!" Hawk slapped Joe's back. "Damn good shot! Not bad for a cross-eyed pile of shit!"

"Yeah!" Joe laughed with relief. "Did you see that?" Joe leaned forward, looking up at the sky, his smile fading. "Are there any more of them?"

"I don't think so," Hawk answered. "At least none shootin' at us. Let me check on our pilot."

Vera still sat slumped and strapped into her seat. Hawk raised her chin. "You okay, girl?"

"Yes." She gasped. "Do you love me now?"

"Damn right. Looks like you might've had at least one flyin' lesson. The one on how to land. Great job, Vera."

"Any landing you walk away from is a good one," Vera said. "Lesson one. Boy, were they right about that."

"Yeah. We ain't exactly walked away. I guess the fuel tank didn't blow up. Yet. We gotta get outa this thing." Canlon walked up behind them and tried to look out the cockpit windshield. He was looking up, and the windshield was looking down.

"Where do you think that Zero crashed?" Joe asked. "It might have landed on the old witch."

"Probably knocked her ass out of bed, that's for sure. I guess we ain't gonna be no surprise to anybody," said Hawk.

"Do you think it hit the ocean? I see smoke over there."

"There's a good chance. It's a lot more ocean than land," said Hawk. "Get the door open, we gotta climb outta this bastard. It might explode."

Joe threw the door open, and it fell heavily off the

plane and down into the tree limbs. "Shit!" Joe called back to them. "If it's gonna explode, it'll just have to explode. We ain't going nowhere anytime soon. We're stuck in a pack of...redwoods."

Hawk swung over to the doorway. Interlocking tree branches made it difficult to see anything, but he did manage to locate the much-desired ground, about four stories down. He shook his head and turned back toward his men.

"Get your shit and throw it out the door!" he ordered. "Get everything out. We gotta get outta here. Any tree climbers here?" Murdoch came forward. "I used to do a little tree cutting," he said.

"See if you can climb out there. Find us a way down." Hawk turned around. "Baker, is there a rope back there? We need a damn rope. Otherwise, it ain't gonna be nothing but monkey shines."

Baker answered a minute later. "I don't see nothing."

"There's one up here," said Vera. "In that door by the seat. Should I try the radio? We've had radio silence for an hour."

Hawk went back to her. "Better not screw with that. They expected you back at the base, didn't they?"

"Yes."

"I figure they'll send somebody for us, or you, when you don't come back. We'll just go ahead and do what we have to do."

"They might think we fell in the ocean," she said.

"Yeah, that's the thing about plane crashes. They'll leave you guessin'," Hawk said. He noticed she was still in the seat. "Can you walk?"

"Yes. Just gathering my wits."

Murdoch appeared in the open door. "I can get down all right," he announced.

"Can everybody else?" Joe asked.

"There's one tricky spot. I guess so. I can carry the lady, if I have to. Did you find a rope? We can probably rig up something."

Hawk stuck his head out the door and looked down. "Forget about her. She can climb down there faster than you can," Hawk said. He thrust a boot out onto a scaly limb and swung over to another one. Peering down, he leaped, more than stepped onto the next lower branch. He looked up at the underside of the plane. "Better hurry up," he called to Joe. "It's getting dark down there."

Within half an hour, everyone stood safely on the ground. The Catalina remained firmly perched in the treetops. It appeared intact, though no one had investigated it thoroughly. The wings had not been torn off. The engines were in place. It may have acquired a few bullet holes. There did not appear to be any logical way to extract it from its lofty position, however, in order to return it to use. At least, not in one functioning piece. The aircraft would have to be brought to the ground, and carried to the ocean, before any needed repairs could even be considered. It was the sort of problem to which one might devote some time and effort, if stranded for an indefinite stretch of time, with no hope of rescue. Hawk knew that the patrol would be missed almost immediately, and rescue efforts would soon be underway. Even if his mission were *not* of the utmost priority, as everyone had assured him that it was, Colonel Clark would not leave Vera Orr indefinitely in the wilds of Papanuca. She served that much of a purpose, if nothing else; and as it turned out, that was quite a lot.

Hawk harbored no blame for Vera because of the crash. Clark's efforts to redress the leak of information about the code, and its interpretation, had obviously failed. The US Navy had weathered his wrath quite well. The colonel's lack of attention to detail in the area of security was definitely causing complications. The Zero could easily have killed them all, including Vera Orr. It again raised the question as to whether this endless pursuit of the unknown solution to the code was worth it all.

"Where are we?" Canlon asked. "We must be close to the witch, since there ain't no coast around here." Hawk regretted filling Joe in on the details of the mission. Joe had an enormous and loose mouth.

"Stop talking about that?" Hawk told him. "What's the matter with you? What if the Japs catch one of us? They're gonna beat it out of him."

"Hell, everybody knows why we're here. And there ain't supposed to be any Japs."

"Yeah, well, our plane ain't supposed to have a pine tree jammed up its ass, either. Just shut up about it." Hawk took out the map. Joe spun the wheel of his lighter and held the wavering flame over the chart. "It looks like we're here," Hawk pointed to a location near the western shore. "We saw that cove here. If we go east, we shouldn't have to go too far. Looks like we'll have to wait until daylight, now."

"You're probably right," said Joe. "But the witch doctor knows we're here by now. I hope this is a friendly witch."

"I hope so, too. Because, if she ain't, she's in for trouble, and we might not get anything out of her."

"Whoa. Hang on," said Joe. "You can't go killing the witch. You gotta have whatever information she knows."

"I know what the hell I gotta do. Get a camp set up. Watch out for shit. They didn't tell us about snakes or any of that. We're supposed to be on our way back by now. There could even be Japs all over this place. Look, how damn dark it's getting in here."

"Can we have a fire? I don't think we can have fires, if there are Japs. Or, if this witch is gonna put a curse on us, being a witch and all."

"Yeah. Start a fire. Looks like the witch already put a curse on us." Hawk nodded toward Vera, who was talking to Ranke. "She and the colonel both swore she would *not* be on the island. And—*there* she is."

"I don't know, it ain't her fault. Nobody could have flown that little airplane any better. She don't *want* to be here," said Joe.

"Shee-it. She probably knew the Jap pilot and his grandma. Ain't nothin' about her no accident or coincidence or any of that crap."

Joe laughed. "You act like *she's* a witch. They'll send a new plane pretty soon. She won't be the pilot no more. It'll be better than before. Look on the bright side."

"Okay, Shirley Temple. I'll be lookin' for the Good Ship Lollipop."

Darkness closed around the camp, as if a door had shut it away from the rest of the world. Their spot on the island was like the darkest hideaway in a house, the part that had never contained a light: an old closet or pantry, or the spider webbed space under the stairway. In keeping with the feeling of isolation, it smelled like an unused place, forgotten by time. It had been exactly like this when Shakespeare was alive, and no different from that when Cleopatra lived. The men sat near their single fire. Two guards faced the forest. Amphibians trilled, and birds choked out uncanny night calls.

Vera looked across the fire at the brooding face of James Hawk. She could tell he did not like the situation. She had seen him face danger and death many times and could read his moods. It frightened her to realize that he was concerned. If *that* guy was concerned, there was reason for it. Whatever he was thinking, it did not radiate any outward optimism.

"Anyone know any good camp songs?" she said.

Several of the men laughed.

"No loud talking," Hawk growled. "I don't like this place." Everyone shuffled nervously. "We didn't get a chance to check it out right, and every stupid son of bitch on the face of the earth knows we're here."

"Yeah," said Joe Canlon, looking around, with the orange flame lighting the whites of his eyes. "*And* everywhere else we go. In case you ain't noticed."

"Might as well get some sleep. Can't do nothing else," Hawk said, tossing a stick into the fire. He turned to Joe. "Tell those two men to turn in. Set up a couple more watches." He raised his voice. "Better sleep light. We might get a welcoming committee with some bedtime stories."

"Keep the fire going?" Joe asked.

Hawk stared into it for a moment. "Yeah." He felt like daring...someone...to approach.

He sighed an obscenity, stood and walked a few paces away from the fire. He turned around like a dog, before lying down. Vera noticed the animal-like movement. She smiled, and held back a laugh. She put her head back and shook with silent laughter. He was truly more animal than human. It was a scary place, all right, but she had him, and that made it hard to be afraid of anything. Could anything in this horrible place be more horrible than him?

Canlon lay closer to the fire, rocking his head back inside his helmet liner. Above him, beyond the silhouette of the airplane, he could see the bright silver of a moon, its brilliance being kept away from the earth by the secretive island. It was the same moon that had risen in the daylight, when things did not seem so strange and threatening. He slowly closed his eyes, but they opened again when he replayed his glorious shot at the Zero, the moment that it disappeared behind an orange starburst upon being hit, bled black oily smoke that poured over him, and then crashed to the earth. He smiled. As his eyes slowly closed again, the sound of drums began to pound in the distance. His eyes opened.

"Of course," he said. "What else?"

* * *

RUTH NAGLE SETTLED into her kitchen window. She had finally put Stefano Calvino together with the other two students. It was puzzling at first, since he did not seem to fit with them. He was rather handsome and athletic, nothing like the other man. Calvino looked wholesome, whereas, Volmer appeared sickly and degenerate. Calvino was wholesome, but not exactly...American. He was too perfect. The three of them met regularly now, and it didn't seem like friendship. They were *doing* something. They were working on a plan. Perhaps it was her imagination, but Ruth felt that the girl preferred Volmer to Calvino for some reason. She couldn't imagine why. She didn't know any of their real names. One had to watch their faces closely to catch all of the finer points of the dynamics among the group. Volmer was the leader, but he did not push Calvino around. Whereas, he did order the girl about, a little. Ruth began writing down key observations in a little notebook. It had lain empty for years and was finally put to use. She had to write these things down to keep them straight. It began with their cars. She noticed Setsuko walking to a 1941 Hudson Business Coupe parked down the street, and only deduced that it must belong to Volmer about the third time the girl did so. Setsuko carried something to the car and came back empty-handed. Now Ruth had three cars to keep up with. All three of the young people went in and out of each other's cars as if they were owned in common. Ruth wondered if perhaps they were communists—not that there was anything wrong with that—as Mr. Roosevelt himself was quite fond of the Stalin fellow. She was thinking of buying a pair of binoculars, but she didn't know where you could get such things; and they were probably expensive. She didn't get out much. Binoculars were just the kind of useless thing people cheated you on at the store. She also wished she had listened to Bert when he encouraged her to take up lip reading. It would be nice to know what these three were saying. She had a feeling, though, that it would be in some strange language that no one could understand. Probably Armenian.

The students sat together on the porch. Ruth watched with clenched teeth. Setsuko inserted a flower on Volmer's lapel and they all three laughed, like the light-hearted youngsters that they were. *What the hell were these little bastards up to?*

* * *

HAWK LED the column toward the center of the island. Baker took up the rear with the BAR. There was no trail, and although the forest was thick, it was not impenetrable. The daylight hours were less charged with the electricity of shadowy threats, than the ghostly darkness of the night before had been. The passage of a peaceful night helped the general mood after the disorienting plane crash. When the drums stopped, around midnight, everyone had slept fairly well, other than the men on watch.

Within a short time, they came to a steep canyon, crossed by a rope bridge, floored with thick sticks. The sticks, lashed a few inches apart, allowed a dizzying view of the rushing stream beneath, filled with sharp boulders. A woven vine handrail extended to the other bank of the canyon, on only one side of the bridge. Hawk stopped and lit a cigar.

"Do you think that will hold us?" asked Joe.

"Maybe not all at once," Hawk answered. "Have to take it easy. It looks kind of old."

"It looks kind of *real* old. Looks rotten. Do we have to go that way?"

"No. I guess not. We could see where the river goes. Or go down there to the bottom and cross it. I think this is the way to the village, though. Why the hell else would it be here? There ain't nothing around." Hawk looked over and saw Vera staring at him. He winked at her.

"Why *else* would it be here? That's what the rat said about the trap," Joe answered. "Look on the other side. Skulls on poles. I'd say that's a message."

"I don't know. It don't look to me like somebody threw this up overnight to trap us. Looks more like it's been there since Hector was a pup." He looked at the skulls. "That kind of thing is just local hooey. Japs wouldn't do that ignorant crap."

"Yeah, but they could make a few changes to it overnight," said Joe. "Just for us."

"Tell you what. You don't have to be the first one to go over it." Hawk looked down at the green, boiling water below. "We'll go one at a time. It ought to hold that much."

"It would be a real good place to get shot."

"Sure enough. That's where your crack military trainin' comes in. If we go over one at a time, only one of us gets shot. We're a little smarter than rats. The rest of us will figure it out, see? That's what they got West Point for, to teach this kind of shit."

"Right. They got West Point to teach guys to send *us* to do shit like this so they don't have to," Joe replied.

"I guess I'll check it out."

"Hold on. When you fall through, I have to run this circus," said Joe. "Let somebody else do it."

"What is this? You trying to get out of doing *anything*?" He turned to the others. "Have a seat boys. Watch the fun."

Hawk took about three steps out onto the bridge. "This bastard really *is* old," he said. Upon taking the fourth step, the cross piece cracked dryly, and his boot shot through the floor of the swinging span. He drew back quickly, and walked back off the bridge. "Nope, that ain't gonna work. I guess we're climbing down to the bottom after all."

"I can't say I'm sorry," said Joe.

"I bet you could say 'I told you so,' though."

"Yeah, I could do that."

Baker walked up to them. "You want me to try it? It's probably just got a bad patch here and there," he said.

"Nah. That's awright. It ain't worth it. This place ain't all that big that we need this thing. One man could cross some old shit like that, and then all of a sudden the fourth or fifth man that tries it goes falling through. It ain't worth it."

"Climbing up that other side doesn't look so easy, either," said Baker. "I think this bridge is here for a good reason."

"I know, but we can follow the river a little ways. Where does it go? It's got to hit the shore pretty soon. We ain't in the middle of Asia or something." Hawk tossed down his cigar. "If we had to cross this bastard, that would be something else, but we don't. We ain't all that pressed for time."

"Hell, I've seen men drive trucks across stuff like that," said Baker.

"Yeah, well, one time I seen a man that said he was Peter Pan but turns out he could only fly in one direction," said Hawk.

Subject to the will of their surly leader, they climbed down the slope to the rock-strewn waterway below. The course of the stream ran circuitous, narrow, and deep, with a fast and troublesome current. The farther they walked, however, the narrower the waterway grew, until as they approached the ocean's shoreline, they were able to wade across. At that point, an opening in the stone coastal outcroppings led the way into a natural tunnel. The sea could be heard on the other side of the stone, and echoed within the tunnel itself.

"Baker, see where that goes," Hawk ordered, gesturing down the tunnel, as he rested the men. He could see nothing ahead of them but a stone wall, and behind them was the little stream, descending rapidly from the higher elevations where they had left the rope bridge.

"Hell, we came back toward the coast," said Joe. "We're going away from the village."

"You didn't want to cross the bridge. That's where the village was." Hawk answered. "We'll get there soon enough."

"All roads lead to Rome," said Vera Orr to Joe. Baker emerged from the tunnel.

"It winds back into the jungle again, it doesn't go to the beach. I guess the tunnel kind of walls off the ocean, because you can hear the waves the whole way," Baker informed them.

"I imagine it leads to the village. We'll take it," said Hawk. He raised his voice. "Off and on, let's get this over with. They might send a rescue plane, and we won't have nothing to show them for our visit."

The patrol wound through the cool, wet tunnel. Well-lit, with a sand-reflected glow at both the beginning and end, the passage turned completely dark in the central portion. The darkness lasted for a few short minutes. Upon coming out on the other side, they were in a jungle similar to the one in which the plane crashed. After turning his steps toward the middle of the island, and setting the course, Hawk paused to let the others pass. He started walking again, next to Vera.

"How are you holding up?"

"Great. Why? Did you think I wouldn't?"

"I never know what you'll do," he said, and stopped again, letting the others pass, and taking up the rear position. He sensed that someone was following them, or watching them, but there was no tangible evidence of it. It was not long before Joe came back to tell him that they had found the palisade of the village. Hawk proceeded to the front of the halted column.

Before him stood a row of timber, jutting from the ground like jagged teeth, carelessly sharpened at the top. The crude fence was studded with logs each a slightly different height from the others. It was designed for utilitarian purposes, rather than any architectural appeal. Hawk was curious as to what the big logs were protecting the inhabitants from, on this otherwise uninhabited little island. Adding to the oddity, and lack of master engineering, was the fact that the village lay somewhat lower than the surrounding terrain, so that during the inevitable island downpours, it had to turn into a mudhole. Skulls on the ends of long poles, similar to the ones near the rope bridge, stood at regular intervals along the walls. A high gate faced them and blocked the entrance. The local population gave all indications of being an unwelcoming one.

The strange hamlet spread silent before them. The backed-up water gave off a strong, sour odor, which hovered in a barely visible gray cloud over the wreckage of human habitation, like a soul escaping a corpse a bit too late.

"Closed for business," Hawk noted. He wondered if

perhaps the place had been designed to impress the visiting tourists, filled with religious zeal on their pilgrimages.

"Yeah, they had to have heard us coming, with our crash, *and* that Jap plane crash," said Joe. "They didn't exactly come running out with the ambulances and dancing girls."

Baker laughed. "They're hoping we died." His laugh faded. "If they're the only ones here, where did the skulls come from?"

"Otto, you think the voodoo queen speaks English?" Hawk asked Ranke. "How about the rest of them?"

"She does. I don't think the others would. They don't get many visitors now, since the war," said Ranke. "But I have heard that civilized people came here in the past, asking her for cures of various diseases and conditions. And for...spells...that sort of thing. Curses and love potions. I suppose she has picked up some English out of necessity, in order to make business dealings. Many rather wealthy people have made the journey here, I'm told."

"Yeah? I don't see what she spends her money on. It ain't carpenters," said Hawk. "I hope these bastards don't give us any shit. I don't want to be killing nobody, till they do some talking. Any word of 'em attacking the visitors?"

"I have never heard of that," said Ranke. "That would be bad for business."

"My, Lord! The smell!" said Vera.

"Poor folks, poor ways," said Hawk. "They probably seen better days, judging by the looks of it."

"It *looks* just horrible," said Vera. "This entire island, it's like we've been abandoned by God in some unkempt dump in hell. I wish we had the plane." Hawk refrained from the obvious *you asked for it,* a sentiment often shared among Marines.

Hawk's icy blue eyes narrowed as he surveyed the palisade and he made his hasty plans. He paced slowly. His hopes for a smooth meeting dimmed somewhat when confronted with the grossly primitive reality of the witch's stronghold. He had pictured something with more of a friendly ambiance. Everything about this place said: go away. As far as devotional pilgrimage sites went, the marketing was poorly done.

"Nah, when you deal with God, you just gotta be patient. He gets busy sometimes. He might not always hear the phone ring," Hawk said quietly, and stopped his pacing. She studied the wide, blue fire glowing and moving beneath Hawk's stubborn brow, seeming to light up half his face; and remembered why she came here, and how she had no regrets in doing it. Every unpredictable thing he said, every unpredictable thing he did, fascinated her—even now, on this looming edge of struggling existence. He was a crude poet of evil violence, unleashed on an unsuspecting world.

Hawk tightened his lips. It was time for action—his specialty. He walked toward the towering gate and looked up. "Hey, in there! Anybody home!" he shouted. "Open up! Some friends done come to pay you a visit!" Nothing happened for a minute or two, he shouted again, and then he heard rustling inside. The gate swung slowly inward, as if it had a life of its own. Hawk looked back at the men.

"Watch out for spears and stuff," he told them. "You gotta watch these ignorant shitheads. They do all kind of crazy shit, for no reason. We're going inside. Osage and Blackwell stay out here. I'll get 'em to leave the gate open."

Having given his advice, James Hawk, the best example of diplomacy the U. S. government had to offer the people of Papanuca, slouched through the open portal with a menacing glare, and a temperament to match.

He was met with equally menacing glares from the half- starved, poorly cared for residents of the island. They kept their distance, because their glares were not backed up with a Thompson submachine gun. They milled about, silent and watching—even the naked children had the same hateful glare. Exuberance had never visited this place. A single, spongy avenue led through the falling down huts to a large and well-maintained structure in the middle of the compound. A number of rivulets of sewage had to be stepped over. If this humble fortress was the capital of Papanuca, the tall edifice in the center of it had to be its capitol building. It was raised from the ground, as tall as a man stood, upon heavy poles, with sweeping steps leading up to a front portico. The circular thatched roof, sloping inward like a giant steeple, loomed three or four stories high over the entire village. The striking edifice was immediately visible upon entering the gate, and Hawk needed no guide to lead him there. His men followed, their weapons at the ready, although no immediate threat presented itself—at least, nothing to seriously threaten a contingent of armed Marines.

An elderly woman walked slowly from the dark interior of the building, matching their deliberate, approaching steps with her own pace, and stopped to stand on the porch at the top of the stairway. Her head resembled a battered coconut, in size, shape and condition. Two large yellow eyes shined from the wheatish, weathered face. They did not appear to be human eyes, though they were not exactly those of an animal, either. Hawk wondered if perhaps she was blind. Her white hair was pulled back by a band, and on top of the band perched a small stuffed bird of some sort. She wore brightly colored clothing, in contrast to that of the other poor villagers, who were dressed mostly in brown, or some sort of dead shrubbery.

She looked down from the greater height of the porch at Hawk. He took off his helmet. Neither of them spoke for a moment. They stared at one another with their vicious eyes, sizing one another up, neither caring much for what they saw.

"How do you do, ma'am?" he said. "Pleased to meet you. I'm Sergeant James Hawk, United States Marine Corps. I came here to speak with a Mrs. Vun-i-wai. If you be she?"

"You have come to make war on my people," she said in a small, cracked voice, and lifted a fragile hand to point at him. "You come with many weapons."

"No ma'am. We're all friends here. This ain't nothing. We got a lot worse weapons than this when we're attacking people." As he stared up at her, he knew the communications were going to be difficult. He could hardly understand her mean little voice, choking words out in something between a hiss and a squeal. How was he going to explain the code to her, or her part in it? It had been difficult enough to explain it to Ranke, or for that matter, to have it explained to himself. "We can spare y'all some food, if you don't mind C rations. They ain't overly tasty, but they're pretty substantial. I can get the colonel to drop some food in here, when we get back. Looks like y'all might have hit on a dry spell...or something."

"My people need no help from you, or anything dropped on us. They have me to care for them. They need only for you to go, and to take your war with you. I see your eyes. I know you are a demon. Your people, the English, the Australian, used to come here for my help, when they were afraid of the demon spirits, and I helped them. Now, they come only to harm us. This is how they repay us. They leave their damned with us. An army of the damned, left for me to drive into your hell."

"No, ma'am. We ain't leavin' nothin'. As a matter of fact, we came here this time for your help, again. We have a problem that only you can solve," he said. "It's a hundred percent demon-free thing. Guaranteed."

She took a step down from the porch and pointed at him. "You *lie*! Your soul does not need my help, because you have no soul. It has left you long ago. I can see this, and I know. Very few men can live and walk after losing their soul. They are powered only by demons. But *you* are one of them, and you have come to me. My fate is doomed now. I have no help to give your kind, nor do I want yours. Your words mean nothing, when you have no soul. You do not trick me, evil one. Return to your hell." She slung a stick-like arm at him. "Ask your Christian God for help and listen to his laugh!"

Hawk cleared his throat. "Uh...yes, ma'am. It ain't my soul that needs help. You're sort of right. It's the United States government that needs you. They wanted me to ask you a question. It's kind of important to them, for the war and all. But it doesn't mean much to you. It don't cost you nothin'. They just want an answer. See, they want you to give them a name."

She threw her head back, almost violently. "They want me to give them a *name!*" She looked back down at him, with her fiery yellow eyes. He knew that she was able to see him now. It was not a comforting realization. She seemed to be looking through him, from someplace other than the earthly plane. "They want one of my guarded souls! These have been entrusted to me. I cannot give away my souls to evil men." She shook her head. "Or to demons." She pointed. "To *you!*"

"No, ma'am." Hawk looked around at his patrol behind him. He was wondering if perhaps Ranke or Vera could do a better job with this progressively awkward conversation. When he saw their faces, he could tell that they wanted no part of it. No one especially wanted any ancient spells cast on them. While voodoo was amusing hokum in the parlor of the civilized, it had a different feel to it here. A good deal of tension hung in the air, primarily in the air between Hawk and the witch doctor.

"You can keep your souls, ma'am. What we want is a name. I'll give you some information that reminds you of somebody, and you tell me who it is. Just a name. It's somebody you know. It's a riddle, you might say. Like a... game." Hawk thought of other ways to rephrase this, as the unreceptive yellow eyes bored through him. It was a confusing concept to convey at best.

"This is *evil*," she said. "Such is this!" She waved an arm at her people, for them to behold this fork-tongued, two-legged serpent among them. "Why do you do such things, evil one? Why this restless evil, when you could rest? Why do you torment poor people with your weapons and foul words without meaning?"

"I'm telling you, ma'am...see...we ain't tormentin' nobody. We just want this one name and then we'll go. I got this paper here..." He put his helmet back on and pulled out the sheet with the code written on it. He held it up for her to see, still folded. "I'll read the words on it to you, and then you tell me who the little story is about. See? I know, it don't make a lot of sense. But it's important to us, just like your soul stuff is to you..."

"I *know* the words on your paper, and I *know* the name you want, you shell of a hellion. Did they not tell you *who* I am? I have spent many years fighting the trickery of demons like you. My people lived at peace with the spirits of the forest and ocean for thousands of years. We had no evil spirits here, only kind hearts. Then you came, the white Christians, with your devil and your evil spirits, leaving them here, and now they war against us and each other. I already know your evil magic words and your evil magic name. I see your black heart."

Hawk gave a small, polite laugh. "Well, see, you *can't* know the words until I read them to you, but then after I do, you'll know the name, too. We hope," he said. He was not surprised that the sorceress had no idea as to what he was talking about. The thought of placing his thick hand around her scrawny neck crossed his mind. But would that make her understand any better?

"I say to you again, I *know* the words on that paper. I will tell *you* the words. The words are, 'better that a millstone be hung.'"

Hawk frowned. He roughly opened the paper in his hand. After 'green soul bottle,' he read to himself:

'better that a millstone be hung.' He managed to keep the utter shock from his face, although he felt it course through him. He looked toward Ranke and Vera again. He turned away from the old woman and walked back to them.

"That's just what the damned thing says. How did she know that?" he asked them. They looked at him without answering. Vera's mouth was half open. Still, neither she nor Ranke volunteered to take over the dealings with the witch. Finally, getting zero response or support, he turned back around to face Vuniwai again, and took an additional step toward her.

"That was pretty damn good, ma'am. Have you read this before?" Hawk asked, raising the paper. He was not a believer in witchcraft, but for the moment, he had no better explanation.

"*Read*? I do not *read*. I saw it through your eyes. You have forgotten, demon. You have no soul, but you still have eyes. Even soulless animals have eyes. I do not fear you. Beware my power."

"Yeah. You're right, I did forget about that," Hawk admitted. Dumbfounded, he did not recall having read the passage until after she spoke the words. His eyes had probably scanned the entire page at some time in the past. Once or twice, even. He had no conscious memory of the "millstone" line. It had been just more nonsense to him. Had she heard his subconscious? "Do you think you could see your way clear to help us? We ain't quite as good at these mind reading scientifics as you are."

"You surrender to my power?" She laughed dryly.

"Yeah, kinda. In a way. I guess so. If you'll give me the name of who that millstone business is about." He figured he had to keep asking, keep humoring. What else was he going to do? Beat it out of an old lady?

"I will do better than that for those who serve me. I take care of them, as the earth takes care of us all." She turned around and walked into her majestic building. Hawk stood there, watching an empty porch. He turned around to face Vera.

"What the hell is this? Are you getting any of this?" he asked her.

"She's coming back. Be nice. She likes that. Don't be a jackass," Vera said. "Demon."

"I ain't being a jackass," he protested.

"You're always a Jackass. There she is, listen," said Vera.

Vuniwai had a green bottle in her gnarled hand. She held it up and swung it to the left and right for all to see. The light hit the half-filled bottle, and a thick liquid sloshed back and forth inside.

"Here *he* is!" the old chieftess shouted. "Here *he* is! This is *he*."

Joe Canlon nudged Baker. "I thought he would be taller," he whispered. Hawk watched the bottle going to and fro, without speaking. He was not sure who "he" was. He hoped it wasn't him.

"I have never let one of my subjects leave. I guard their souls forever. But this one, *yes*, this one I will give to *you*. I will let him speak to you, to tell you all you wish to know of him and about your war. And when you are done, you can have his wasted soul, and be soulless no more—for I know that is why you are here! I will be well rid of this terror. Take your evil and your devil and go!"

Hawk stood speechless for a moment. "That's damn

nice of you, ma'am. But...I don't need *all* of that. I just need his name. You could just ask him that for me"—he pointed at the bottle—"and I'll take your word for it. You can save the jug there, maybe wash it out and put something else in it."

"You speak the truth now. Because you cannot speak to him," she explained. "*Because you have no soul!*" she said. She smiled, showing a mouth only half filled with broken teeth. Hawk considered why someone with supreme power over souls and demons had no power over mundane dental procedures.

"That might be it, ma'am. I never was too good at talkin', probably even back when I had a soul. Everybody's good at different things."

"You speak the truth once more. You *are* good at something: *evil*. And you will help me, if you want to know these things that are hidden from you. You will use your powers of evil to do good for me. I harness you, demon. *Now!*" She snapped her empty hand shut at him.

Hawk looked blankly at the clenched fist. "Yes, ma'am. The fact is...I hate to admit it, but I really ain't no demon. I can't do no magic tricks. What is it you need done?"

"If you wish to speak with him"—she waved the green bottle at Hawk—"you will return my son to me." As the bottle shook in front of his face, Hawk noticed that it had a label of some sort, with writing on it. He probably would be unable to read the writing, but if he could get the bottle, perhaps someone at headquarters could figure it out. He considered grabbing it. But, it might only say some useless mumbo jumbo and he would have alienated the witch doctor. No, he had to play along. He had to somehow get her to tell him the name. She was definitely not making it easy. It was frustrating to realize that he could not outwit a backwoods moron.

"I don't reckon I got your son, ma'am. If I did, you could damn sure have him back. Is he in a flask or something, like that fella? I might be able to dig one up. Like what color bottle were you thinking of?"

"My son is here on our island. I do not permit him to leave. He is now with the Nippon. Only *you* can get him from them, with your loud weapons. Once you have killed one another with your war, my son will be returned to me."

Hawk thought about this. "Are you saying the Japs came here? And they took your son?"

She pointed off to the east. "They took my son and they are here. They wait for you. My son waits for you. When you return with my son, you will be given the man you seek." She held up the bottle. "*This* devil. You will no longer need to go find this terrible man with any more of your unending, soulless wanderings." She held up the bottle. "This man, in my hand, will tell you everything, even the *next* name on your devil's list. You will not have to go to his empty body, you can question his squirming soul, right here."

"Why do the Japs have your son?" Hawk asked, a bit unclear on nearly everything she had just told him.

"The Nippon tell me they will keep my son so that we do not attack them. They said they will kill him if we attack them. I know they will kill him, no matter what we do. You—must save him. Your evil powers can do this. I know these things. The good is not strong enough to save him from the bad Nippon. Only *you*, Devil, with your evil, can do this."

"Mm hmm. That's fair enough. It might not be easy. I'll grant you, they *are* pretty bad fellas. But, let's say it *is* easy. If I do that, deal with the Japs for you and all, you're saying this here bottle is going to tell me the next name, without me going to see the man himself? And I get *two* names?"

"Yes. I tell you this. My word is good, not like yours. And, if you do not get my son, you will never know this name, nor the other name, nor *any* name after that." She pointed toward the side of what was apparently her temple building. "You will bring me a Nippon in payment for their sin. Come with me, this way, and see what shall become of him. This is the price they must pay."

Hawk looked toward the side of the elaborate hut. Several men carrying spears approached him and pointed in the same direction. "Am I supposed to go with them?" Hawk asked her. His face showed no intimidation.

"Yes, and bring your three companions. Who are you, daughter? You are very beautiful," the old woman asked Vera. "You do not belong with such demons as these. Your soul is pure."

Vera looked up in surprise. "Yes, yes, I know. I'm Vera. Vera Orr. Nice to meet you. We just got on the same bus together. I came out of church and they came out of a bar. And here I am."

"You are welcome to stay here and live with us, where it is safe. You will be my daughter. I am growing old. You will follow in my ways and live for many hundred years. You are very fortunate that I have offered you this. And very fortunate to be rid of these evil demons hiding in the bodies of men. They will *all* live very short lives. Some will never leave this island."

"Wow, yeah. I'll say. That is quite an offer. I'll have to think about it. But I left my poodles back home, and they're *passionately* waiting on me to come back. I'm not sure if I can stay over, right now. But maybe another weekend, we could do it."

"You will think about this," said Vuniwai, ignoring the answer and not letting her confusion over it show. "You will come to understand the wisdom of staying with me, and being satisfied to the end of deathless time. Now, go with your evil one to see where the Nippon will pay for his sin. This man"--she pointed shakily at Ranke--"*you* will go, too. I remember you. You are bad." And then she pointed perfunctorily at Joe Canlon, almost as if she knew that he had some connection to Hawk, or some sort of rank. "And *you*, foul one."

Ranke smiled nervously and followed Hawk. He had decided that he should have opted for the POW camp, rather than joining this expedition. Joe followed mutely. He didn't like any of it, but it was far from the worst situation he had ever been in. The presence of Hawk gave him almost as much confidence as the loaded M1 in his hands.

"She don't care much for you," Joe muttered to Hawk.

"If I was you, I wouldn't be expectin' no flower necklaces, either," he replied. "Foul one."

"She liked me—a lot," said Vera.

7

ACROSS THE RIVER AND THROUGH THE TREES

AS HAWK, VERA, RANKE, AND JOE ROUNDED THE building, still within the fenced compound, Hawk noticed a deep natural well in the earth. He could hear water rushing, somewhere near the bottom of it. They stepped onto a bamboo walkway that ended in a balcony overhanging the opening. A clear pool lay far below the four of them, being refreshed by water running from under the rock to one side. The sides of the well were of a light-colored stone, with glistening white sand embedded into it, glaring to the point where it hurt the eyes, until just above the water level, where it took on a darker color.

"This is the home of Tu," said the witch. "Tu must be served in order to live, and in order for all of us to live. Except for you," she pointed at Hawk, "because you have no soul. Tu is a guardian of souls. He disposes of the body. It would serve him no purpose to dispose of you."

Hawk nodded, thinking that maybe being soulless was not all bad, depending upon what this Tu was. The water below churned violently, and it no longer looked as clear. Splashing and waves extended from one end of the pool to the other, under the force of some great agitation. A large, bronze, reptilian coil broke the water. Vera gasped. Ranke drew back.

"Son of a bitch! What is that?" asked Joe.

"Tu," Vuniwai answered, as if it were obvious. While they were entranced by the indescribable thing below, a railing on the balcony slid aside, and one of the spear carrying villagers pushed another one into the well. The victim did not scream until he surfaced in the pool below, and an enormous head with a massive eye rose from the deep. The body of the thing was as wide as the head, and stretched snake-like across the well. The head opened and dozens of little teeth latched onto the man's arm. The two of them thrashed about for half a minute before going under.

"That man was a thief," said the medicine woman. "We have no thieves here. You will bring me a Nippon. Tu will be much more angered by the sin of stealing my son."

"Right," Hawk sighed loudly. He wanted to get on with the task assigned to him, before it became any more complex. He was losing track of all of the witch's ramblings. "You just need one Jap for this...thing you got down there?"

"One is enough. One son for another son. I am not so arrogant as to think my love is greater than any others."

"Yep," Hawk agreed. "Sounds damn fair, if you ask me. Do you know where these Japs are camped? I'll see what I can do. If I can get your son back, I will. You see, the Japs and us don't talk to each other, or negotiate stuff out, like people do in other wars. All we do is kill each other. It's tough to come to understandings with them son of a...guns."

"This I know. Evil has met evil in my ocean. You deserve one another, but we do not deserve either of you."

"The Japs ain't got no other prisoners?"

"They took only my son, thinking to destroy me by breaking my heart. We will lead you to them. And now, you will destroy them. Do not fear. My magic protects you."

"Sure hope so," Hawk said, and looking at his companions, added in a low voice, "you never know." They returned to the front of the witch's palm-leaved temple. She assigned one of her servants, or bodyguards, to lead the Americans to the Japanese.

"My warriors will not help you in the killing. They will only show you the way. I will give you the name, and all that you seek from me, when you return. This is my word, trusted by your kind for many years." She turned and went inside her dwelling. The discussion appeared to be over.

Vera and Ranke stood in silence, unsure of who had outwitted whom, but with a pretty good idea. One party was returning to her leisure chair, and the other one was headed into the eerie world of odd-shaped leaves for a confrontation with a ruthless enemy.

Hawk turned slowly and returned to his men. "Get a guard out on the edge of the woods, there's goddam Japs out there, after all," he told Baker. He pulled out a block of tobacco.

"Did you get what you came for?" Baker asked.

"Shit, no. We gotta go get her son of a bitch son from

the goddam Japs before she'll tell me anything," said Hawk. "And we gotta get her a Nip prisoner, too, I guess. I didn't quite get all that. She's got this pet water snake or something that's gonna eat the Jap."

"You can't let her throw someone into that well with that thing," Vera said.

"A Jap? Why not? Are you in the SPCJ, too, now? What else am I gonna do? She's got us over a barrel. This is her country, they came here causing shit, they can live by her rules, just like we have to do. That ain't the worst part, the worst part is finding her son and bringing him back in one piece. The Japs probably already killed his ass. They ain't the best at lookin' out for prisoners. Then what happens? This has turned into a real crock of shit." From that point, his language became a bit ugly, and little content was added by the ugliness.

"What was that big thing swimming around in the hole?" Joe asked. "It looked like a sea monster."

"Some big ass fish or something. Who gives a shit?" said Hawk. "Just part of her sideshow. Some old stupid shit for the yokels."

"That was a giant eel," said Vera. "I saw one in the aquarium in Baltimore. The one in the aquarium was well fed, and still only half the size of that thing in the well. The well must be connected to the ocean. I think I saw water flowing in."

"You know, jumping a bunch of Japs wasn't in the deal when we took on this project," said Joe. "The whole mission was supposed to be asking some old lady for a name. We don't know how many of these Japs there are, or how they're fitted for weapons. We could take some serious casualties in this kind of thing. Something like that needs a bigger force. You need to contact the colonel. This detail had changed. You asked her and she wouldn't tell you, and that's that. The next move is up to the colonel."

Hawk's face immediately registered what he thought of that idea. "He don't do nothing but make shit worse. As far as the Japs go, why do you think they're here? They came here for us—to stop us. If you ain't noticed, it's not the first time. Wherever we go, there they are. Clark might have set us up. The Japs know more about this whole thing than we do. You heard what the old lady said," Hawk sighed. "What could I do? She's nutty as a peach orchard boar. I got to have that name to keep the code moving. She says she's going to give us *two* names, if we come back."

"She can't do that," said Joe. "That was bullshit. You believed that?" Hawk looked at Vera.

"I'm with Joe on that one. She can't do that," said Vera. "And Clark might have set *you* up, but not me. He wouldn't do that. I think you're going a little too far in your criticism. He's an idiot, but a harmless and well-meaning idiot. Where's your Marine loyalty to your leadership?" Hawk turned away from her. As far as he was concerned, there was nothing harmless about anybody with complete authority over you. He was in no mood for giving anyone the benefit of the doubt. Although, the appeal to Marine Corps loyalty was a little irritating. She could definitely be irritating.

"You're both wrong. The witch knew the words on the code sheet without me even reading it," said Hawk. "If she can do that, she can give me two names instead of one."

Joe laughed. "Yeah, she's gonna ask the guy in the green bottle for you."

Vera shook her head. "I don't think she can do it. You're talking about knowns and unknowns. A lot of people knew those code words, but no one knows who the next name refers to. It defies logic to..." Hawk spat and waved his hand to cut her off.

"It don't make a shit to me one way or the other. If she does, she does. If she don't, she don't. We got to get the first goddam name from her no matter what. Okay, look sharp, here comes her flunky."

The short warrior, wearing a loincloth, carried a spear and stood in front of Hawk. He tapped the haft of the spear on the ground, signifying a greeting of some sort. He motioned with his hand for the sergeant to follow him. Hawk nodded to the man.

"We're into it now," said Hawk. "No more conversation. Round 'em up, Joe."

Joe shook his head and began giving angry orders. He did not like any of the witch's assignment or promises. It seemed strange to the corporal that Hawk was willing to go along with her wishes. Based on past experience, Joe had expected only a violent confrontation with forcible extraction of the information from the shaman. Joe was certain that was exactly what Colonel Clark would have expected, and it was why Hawk had been chosen for this detail—to bulldoze any rough spots. Joe supposed Hawk may have deferred to Vuniwai because she was female. He also suspected, however, that Hawk, imbued in some sort of swampy Southern culture, really believed in the witch's horse shit. *"Stupid hill jack."*

The Japanese had chosen to retreat a safe distance

from the village. They had a heightened degree of respect for the trouble that the islanders could cause them. Whether they came here in pursuit of the code or for something else, however, was known only to them. There was no evidence of any other purpose, for clearly, Hawk was the one searching for them, and not the other way around.

The guide led the patrol to a small river located between the coast and the village. After following its course for a short while, he made several gestures, which no one quite understood, and spun around to return to his village.

"Whoa, whoa, podnuh!" Hawk called after the man. "Grab that bastard." Baker brought the guide back. The guide glared angrily at Hawk with a menacing glint in his eye. "Do that little song and dance again, we didn't catch all that." Hawk rotated his hand in the air, which was supposed to convey his meaning. Surprisingly, the man understood. He repeated the same gestures, slowly this time, ending with pointing down the river and jabbing a knife hand toward it, indicating a way to pass over the water. He then pounded his fist in his other hand.

"I see what he means," said Vera. "If you go down the river this way, there will be a bridge, or some kind of crossing. The Japanese will be on the other side."

"Okay, let the damn...thing...go." Hawk paced down the river bank a few feet and spat. "Take a break," he finally said. "I'll go down here and see what the hell he's talking about. We must be close to them, so no more noise."

Following the river proved increasingly difficult. The forest often grew down to the water's edge, and he had to wade in the murky eddies there. He was about to give up, thinking the guide had pulled a fast one, when he came to a straight part of the river, and saw the makings of a crude pontoon bridge in the distance. Bent at the waist now, which probably served no purpose, he approached the crossing to see it better.

The bridge consisted of nothing more than a half dozen log rafts lashed together with vines, and secured on both sides of the river, to keep them from floating away. The current of the water was of a moderate speed, and the rafts leaped and sank jerkily on top of it. The path across the juggernaut would be an unsteady one. The makeshift bridge had no guard rail. He saw a single Japanese guard on the opposite side, but because of the curve in the river, could not see where the bridge met the land on his own side of the stream.

The size and unsteadiness of the crossing told him that the enemy likely had no vehicles. He sat on the bank, among the reeds, rushes and cattails, watching the guard and spitting tobacco. The river would be difficult to cross, or the enemy would not have built this risky span, straining at its stakes. His patrol would save time and peril by crossing here, making use of the Japanese ingenuity and labor. Of course, that then added a degree of risk, by necessitating the elimination of the guard—or guards. Hawk had to know what was on his side of the river. It could be another guard—or a whole guard station. He spat, and entered the rainforest, to find a pathway circling around to the source of the bridge.

He stepped slowly to avoid any crashing noises in the crowded undergrowth. Finally, he found a cleared path that had to be the roadway to the bridge. He followed it, without getting on it, lest he collide with a passing party of the enemy. There were no travelers on the path, however, and when he reached the bridge, he found it unguarded on his side of the river. He took advantage of his position to look quickly across the bridge, with his head close to the ground, so as not to attract the attention of the man on the other side.

From this viewpoint, he could see the rafts madly rising and falling in the current. It was difficult to imagine walking across the perilous connection. The rafts thumped heavily against one another, creating even more danger. A user could lose his footing going from one of the rough platforms to another, and be crushed between them. The entire scene swam disjointedly before him, like a poorly assembled mosaic; so animated and so violent the view, he wondered why the rafts did not break loose from both one another and from the bank, due to all the punishment they were taking. One had to deduce that the stream had been a good deal more placid when this crossing was constructed. He noted the heavy concentration of interlaced lashings around two large trees, securing the first raft to his bank of the river. The outsized rope strained and creaked.

Seeing and understanding the nature of the bridge was an important part of his reconnaissance, but it was only a part. He still had no idea as to how large a force he was up against, its manner of deployment, or the location of the prisoner he was to liberate. He had been forming a vague and changing plan, since first being assigned this task by the witch doctor. He had settled upon a precisely executed rescue, rather than an all-out assault. He was certainly not above a bloodbath, but he had enough sense of purpose to know that all he needed was to get the all-important name out of the sorceress, and all that was required to accomplish that was the safe delivery of her son. The more chaos and killing he stirred up only raised the odds of losing the son, losing Marines, losing his mission, and losing himself.

He ran across the empty path like a rat from its hole. He had to achieve some sort of surveillance of the enemy camp. It was dangerous, but it had to be done; and he had to do it without using the bridge. His patrol could take out the guard, and commandeer the bridge, when the time came, but the element of surprise demanded that doing such a thing could not be accomplished more than once. He continued to follow the river, looking for shallows, logs, stepping stones, or anything to assist him in getting to the other side. He realized, of course, if it were all that easy, the Japanese would have chosen a different place for their crossing. As the river progressed, it grew narrower, but much deeper and with steeper banks. He paused at one particularly narrow spot, with the river rushing below in a deep canyon. The trees leaned across on both sides, almost interlocking over the middle of the canyon. He looked down at the river, far below. It was filled with sharp rocks. Should he try it? If he made it over, he would still have to come back this way, and maybe on the run.

"Shit." He spat.

He didn't like anything about it, but he had to see that camp. He could not just lead his patrol across the bridge, shooting their way down Main Street like cowboys at the end of a cattle drive. He may well have done such things in the past, but not blindly, as this would be. He slung a boot up against the tree trunk and hauled himself up into the branches. His submachine gun tangled periodically in the smaller twigs, almost every inch of the way up. He finally decided to leave it, hanging it on a sturdy knob, tightly against the trunk. The helmet came off next and it fell at the foot of the tree. The helmet was of little consequence. Removing the weapon, however, defined the nature of the rest of the expedition. He was virtually defenseless.

Unencumbered, he reached the branches that grew out over the gorge. The misgivings multiplied. The drop to the jagged river rocks was even greater from up here in the heights of the tree. The branch from the tree on the other side did not quite touch his branch. He edged out along the top of the limb, causing it to sink. He could not climb out on its extreme lengths because it was too thin and weak there.

He eyed the branch on the other side. He spat. He had made it this far, it would be a big loss of time and effort to go back now. He edged a little farther out. The water below boiled and hissed. The branch began to bend more insistently under his weight. The steady bending ended all planning and searching for options. If the branch bent too far, it would likely snap and take him with it onto the rocks below. He lashed a hand out for the branch of the tree on the other side, and missed. The branch on which he rested dropped lower.

"Uh oh." He lashed out again, this time throwing caution to the wind, and also pushing himself forward with his legs. He made the great leap of faith. His fingertips seized the leaves of the branch on the far side, and he swung off the limb of the tree on his side of the river.

He hung over the gorge for a dangerous minute or two, pulling himself hand over hand on the thinnest part of the new branch, until he reached the thicker portion that would support him. He raised his legs and latched them in a scissor hold around the limb, pulling himself forward, until he was over another branch, and dropped down onto it. He lay there gasping for air for a full three minutes. After that, he was able to, by comparison, race down lightly to the safety of the ground.

As he touched the earth, he noticed his opened utility jacket shimmering with a movement that looked like fractured light playing over a jewel. He dropped his chin to study the phenomenon and saw hundreds of small green caterpillars crawling all over the jacket. He raised his arm and saw them on his bare skin. A moment later, a buzz like an electrical shock jolted through his arm, leaving his entire body stunned with a poisonous vibration. The little green asps had a big bite. He had a large red knot on his forearm, where the worm had bitten him.

Hawk ripped off the jacket and kicked off his pants. He swiped the creatures off his body and shook them out of his clothing. He dressed again and sat on the ground to get his bearings. In the excitement, he had almost forgotten in which direction he was headed. On the ground around him, he saw the green asps milling about, and falling from the tree above him.

"Son of a bitch!" He dashed from beneath the tree, rubbing his hair and shoulders. Having spent enough time dealing with trees and insects, he proceeded back down the river toward the pontoon bridge. He had something of a new problem. He couldn't go back through the trees at this point, because of the asps. Had they attacked while he was hanging over the gorge, he likely would have been killed. There was no sense in abusing their hospitality by trying that again. A new plan churned in his mind, as he struck out, away from the river, and in a direction parallel to one that would lead from the bridge's exit. He had no firearm, but he had a grenade; and a seven-inch bladed jungle knife that was no stranger to confrontation.

He discovered the sought-after clearing containing the enemy not far from the river. He found that his patrol was actually much closer to the Japanese camp than he had expected. He crawled, flat on the ground to the end of the sharp-edged grass growing around the enemy bivouac. It was with relief that he noted the relatively small size of the camp. The enemy had a force about equal to his own.

Coincidence? He thought. He was convinced that the Japanese were going to dog him wherever he went in this quest for the answers to the code. There was a single tent, for an officer in charge, no doubt. The rest of the men had blankets on the ground. In one respect, the simplicity of the layout gave the American a distinct advantage. On the side of the camp upon which he had approached the Japanese, stood a barbed wire enclosure. It resembled an animal pen, except for the strands of wire across the top, to prevent the prisoner from climbing out. The wire was wrapped around four thick posts made of heavy tree trunks, some still with leafy little branches jutting out. Inside the pen sat an unhappy looking native of the island.

Hawk smiled. It couldn't have been simpler if someone handed him a diagram. He immediately formed his plan. There would be no attack on the enemy. His patrol would wait for dark, and liberate the prisoner as silently as possible, fleeing back across the pontoon bridge. Judging by the way the sun was dropping, he would not have to wait very long to put the plot into execution. If something went wrong and they were discovered, the American force was strong enough to make a fighting retreat, possibly destroying the surprised Japanese in the process.

He saw no reason to wait around. He swiveled back on the ground, like some big reptile, and crawled back through the grass, stood, and dashed into the deeper woods. There, he walked more slowly, and stopped. *What the hell do I do now?*

He had to get across the river. The way he came over, it was too much trouble. It had been a miracle that he made it across by means of the overhanging trees the first time. He wondered how long the sentry had been at the bridge. If it had been even a couple of hours, it could well be time for his relief to show up. The sergeant thought quickly as he advanced on the bridge. Would he recognize the man there? Had he gotten a good enough look at him, from across the river? He had no memory of him. He had just been a Japanese uniform to the American. If it was the same man, his relief sentry was probably due.

Hawk stopped on the river bank, whereby looking down the river, he could see the sentry. There was nothing distinctive about the soldier. He didn't know if it was the same man or not. He crawled closer in the river undergrowth, the sounds caused by rustling weeds and sucking mud covered by the rushing water. He slid out his knife.

As if God, or someone else, was on Hawk's side,

another Japanese soldier suddenly appeared behind the first. Hawk's knife went back into its scabbard. The two men exchanged greetings, spoke, and laughed. After a few minutes, the first man left, and the second began lazily pacing up and down before the bridge, kicking at an occasional stone. The timing was perfect. It should be two to four hours before another sentry showed up. The knife slid back out. As the man stopped and paused to stare down the river with his back toward Hawk, the American jumped to his feet and charged toward him. A large muscled arm struck the side of the small neck with tremendous force, dazing the man before ever wrapping around him. A knife was jammed upward into his kidney, lifting him off the ground with the powerful impact. The deed done, Hawk then thrust the knife into the ground, grabbed the soldier's boots and dragged him into the river. He gave him a kick, launching the body into the current. Turning, he scooped up the fallen rifle, sheathed the cleaned knife, and ran across the jostling pontoon bridge, toward the other side. Before his feet fell on the second raft, he realized how unsteady the floating span was. He almost slid off as the logs were tossed about. The bridge was not designed for running. He looked over his shoulder. The camp was out of sight. He proceeded more cautiously, trying to stagger along as quickly as possible, and made it to the other side.

Neither the danger nor the aggravation was entirely over. He still had to go back to the trees and retrieve his submachine gun. This took a little time, as it hung halfway up the tree. Climbing down with it, he dropped his helmet on his head and checked his clothes for bugs. He made his way back down the river toward his patrol. As he passed the pontoon bridge, he noticed with relief that it looked as if no one had been there yet to check on the missing guard.

Upon returning to the patrol, he gathered them together and told them what he had seen. Several of the men carried wire cutters in carriers on their belts. The sergeant believed that he could get the prisoner out of the camp without an open battle.

Hawk outlined his thoughts on the rescue. "If we get back before they post a new guard, we can cross the bridge and get the guy out of the stockade with the wire cutters. It'll be dark, and maybe they won't even know we been there, if we come up on the side where I was. We might have to jump one more guard, but that ought to do it."

"It'll be dark as hell out there," said Joe.

"That's good for us."

"Did you see any lights?" Joe asked. Hawk thought for a moment. It had been daylight at the time. But he had not seen a lot of any sort of equipment at the little camp, including lights.

"No." Hawk stood and slung his Thompson, muzzle down. "It'll be smooth as greased goose shit. Unless, they get another guard back on that bridge before we get there."

"Then what?" Joe asked.

"Well, shit. Then we gotta kill his ass. I guess somebody would have to swim the river and knife him. The water's too damn fast, so you'd probably have to hang onto the side of those goddam pontoons and sneak over in the dark. That'll be a major pain in the ass. You could get smashed in between them."

Joe shook his head. "If we get there fast enough, we won't have to worry about all that. Let's get on with it.

Do we put shit on our face so they can't see us in the dark?" Joe asked.

"What in the hell...? Git your goddam ass movin'."

"Uh...what about me?" Vera asked. "Am I in on all this swimming and stabbing and killing?"

"Oh, yeah. You can't stay here. We gotta leave a couple guys on our side of the bridge to watch it. You can stay with them, when we get there," said Hawk. "I told you not to come here, goddamit."

"Ah," she said. "Your wisdom is acknowledged. Feel better?"

"The witch took a shine to you. You could stay with her."

"I'll take the boys on the bridge," she said. The men filed down toward the river. "You know, you're a lot of fun to be around," she told Hawk.

"It's about time you figured that out. This ain't no vacation."

"I fell out of the sky, remember? A fallen angel. This wasn't my idea."

When they reached the bridge, it remained unguarded. Hawk rushed all but two of the men across the bouncing, slick, and perilous logs in the deep and damp darkness. From there, they passed through the forest to the side of the enemy camp where the prisoner's cage stood. It was dark when they began the raid, but the moon shone over the trees at about the time they arrived within sight of the camp. Peering from the cover of the leaves, they silently watched as a guard paced leisurely by the side of the barbed wire enclosure, turned a corner, and headed toward the longest side of the camp. Locusts sang out rhythmic love chants.

"We don't have to kill nobody. We can just run out

there and cut the wire," Joe whispered. Baker nudged him and nodded toward the other end of the pen. A second guard strolled before them, his rifle slung and his head pointed at the ground. "Shit," said Joe. "How do we get past *two* of them?"

"Ask Hawk," Baker whispered. "There ain't enough time and space between the two of them bitches to run out there without at least one of them seeing us."

"I say, throw the prisoner the cutters, and get the hell out of here," said Joe.

"Not a bad idea," Baker agreed. "It's a long throw, and it's dark, though. He might not see them. He might even be too goddam stupid to know what they are. These bastards don't even know what pants are." Hawk crawled up from behind them. The ghostly moonlight outlined the bone structure of their faces under the helmets, and little else.

"Sit tight. Wait and see what they do. One of 'em might go away," said the sergeant.

"How long do we lay here?" Joe whispered.

"As long as it takes," Hawk answered.

"They'll be posting a guard at the bridge before long and figuring out that the other one is missing. We better do something faster than that," Joe urged.

"I can't help that. We'll just have to deal with it," said Hawk. At about that time, instead of following their usual path around the camp, the guards stopped, faced each other, and walked toward each other. Hawk muttered an obscenity as the two came together and sat down on the ground in front of the stockade, facing the Americans in the forest. One lit a cigarette. Soon, they were talking rapidly, with an occasional laugh. Hawk rolled on his back, growling another obscenity.

"Now what?" Joe whispered. "They ain't followin' orders. They're doing some grab-ass shit."

"Number one, shut up. Number two, wait," Hawk answered.

The two Japanese guards talked slowly and blew smoke into the moonlight.

"They ain't supposed to be doing that," said Joe. "That ain't allowed."

"Report 'em to their lieutenant," said Baker. "Just hang on. One of them will have to get up eventually, to piss or something."

"Speaking of which," said Joe.

On the far side of the camp, they could see a man rise from his blanket, sling a rifle, and begin walking in the direction of the bridge.

"There goes the new bridge guard," said Joe. "The shit is gonna hit the fan now."

"Just take it easy. If they set up a howl, we won't go back by the bridge," said Hawk. Time passed, and the enemy did not set up an alarm over the missing guard, nor did the two guards in front of them ever stop talking. The latest bridge guard apparently thought that his predecessor had already left, presumably without authorization, and did not want to voice any complaint. The contingent of enemy troopers were obviously not on high alert. Yet.

An hour passed. Hawk's greatest fear was of someone coughing or otherwise giving them away. The distance between them and the two guards was less than a football field away. They could see the silhouettes of the Japanese caps bobbing as they spoke to one another.

Eventually, tiring of the conversation, one of the guards stood. The other remained seated. The one standing walked off. It would soon be time for their relief. Hawk considered rushing the seated man. The Japanese would be stunned by the charge for only a few seconds. The guard would still have time to fire a shot, or otherwise engage in some noisy activity to cause an alarm. The Americans continued waiting. Another guard relieved the first. Fresh from sleeping, this guard had no desire to rest. He paced around the fence as duty required.

The pattern went on endlessly. Tension mounted. The entire night was passing. At least the Americans knew the attack on the bridge guard had not been discovered, for he had been relieved more than once. He would not be missed until the morning roll call.

"I'm taking the shithead out next time he comes by," said Hawk. Joe had settled into the comfort of safely doing nothing.

"Why, what's different now?" Joe asked.

"Hell, it's gonna be daylight if we lie around here anymore. We gotta get *outta* here," said Hawk. Joe considered that. It was true. To be caught here in the daylight would result in major jeopardy. "I'm gonna crawl up there and find a spot where he's walking. When he steps past me, I jump up and club his ugly head in."

"I don't see no spot to hide in. He'll see you. You can't just lay out in the open."

"Well, I sure as hell can't rush him from this far away. I just have to crawl up there and see what I can find. It ain't like he'll be looking for me."

"I still say, just throw the guy the wire cutters and

run for it," said Joe, holding up a pair of cutters. Hawk took them from him.

"I might have to," said Hawk, crawling forward without another word. The sentry was located on the far side of the stockade. It would take a minute or two for him to round the corner and walk to Hawk's position.

Hawk crawled to within ten feet of the barbed wire. There was nothing but open ground before the fence, nowhere to lie in concealment, including the spot where he was lying now. He had nonetheless found the place he was looking for. The post at the corner cast a long and deep shadow. He crouched against it, pulled back, and unslung the Thompson.

"What the hell? He's standing out in the open," said Joe to Baker. "What's he gonna do, shoot the guy?"

Baker's chin was lying on the ground. "Don't ask me. That's the craziest thing I ever saw. Maybe he thinks it's too dark for the guy to see him from that angle."

"Shit, we see him and he's a hundred miles away," said Joe. They didn't have long to wait. The guard walked right past both the post, and Hawk, as if no one were there. Hawk stepped out, reared back in a batter's pose, and swung the Thompson as if he were swinging for the fences. The stock connected with the man's head, sounding like wood on wood. The field cap flew off. The man's feet came off the ground and he was launched into the barbed wire. In a single motion, Hawk slung the submachine gun strap over his shoulder and brought up his hand with a set of wire cutters in it. He spun to face the moonlit wire, and with snake-like speed snipped three parallel wires, one after the other. He dropped to the ground.

"He did it!" said Joe. "It's open! Where's our native guy?"

"Is he asleep?" asked Baker. "Where is Hawk?"

"He's still layin' there where he was, like a dumb ass," said Joe.

Hawk lay flat, straining his eyes to see into the enclosure. Most of it was covered in darkness. *Where is the bastard?* Sweat poured down Hawk's face. "Shit," he grumbled, rising to one knee and running through the severed wires.

"Oh, goddam! Now he's done it!" said Joe. "That crazy son of a bitch! He went inside!" Joe leveled his rifle at the stockade, prepared for the worst. Hawk ran through the utter darkness and into a patch of moonlight, from there, he could see the prisoner lying in another pool of darkness. Bent at the waist, he ran over and kicked him. The man looked up with a start. Hawk waved his hand violently at the captive and pointed at the open fence. The man sprang to his feet and ran for the opening, leaving Hawk alone in the dark.

Having done what he set out to do, Hawk ran back outside the wire and tossed himself down on the ground. Unlike the witch's son, he was not going to go off running upright, to give the Japanese a target. He crawled back to the forest, the same way he had crawled to the stockade.

"The crazy fool is out," Hawk gasped to Joe and Baker. "Did you see where he went?"

"He went that way," said Joe, pointing into the forest, in a direction opposite from the way in which the Marines had come, and away from the pontoon bridge. "The wrong way."

"I was trying to get the bastard to come with me,"

said Hawk, "but he went zooming off like a striped ass ape before I knew it."

"Now what? We'll never find that son of a bitch," said Baker.

"It don't matter. He knows this place better than we do," said Hawk. "He was born here. He knows the way home like a horse. We just gotta get *us* outta here now." He motioned them deeper into the forest and they quickly turned back for the bridge. They paused upon seeing the most recent of the posted bridge guards. Hawk described a plan in which Baker would stab the man, as Hawk had stabbed the first guard, but before the plan could be executed, shouting erupted in the camp behind them.

"Sounds like they found the sentry," said Joe Canlon. "We gotta get a move on."

"Yeah, that ain't good," Hawk said. He turned his submachine gun on the bridge guard, and unhesitatingly cut him down with a short burst. "Get across! Run for it! I'll cover you!" Stunned by the sudden burst of fire, after the night of tense silence, the men quickly recovered and followed his instructions. Hawk waited at the head of the bridge, as each of the Marines ran past him. He faced the pathway the alarmed Japanese would use when leaving the camp and approaching the bridge. After every Marine had bounded upon the wildly gyrating raft pontoons, he backed slowly down the bucking bridge, waiting for the enemy to appear. He could hear the thundering footsteps of charging Japanese. He knew for certain that he would not have time to make it across with the others. Time for a new plan. Less than halfway across, he flattened out on the rough logs. The night waned, and the low light of dawn shed an eerie glow at the head of the bridge, where the Japanese would appear at any moment.

"Shit, what's he doing?" Baker asked. "Why didn't he keep running?" The men made it across and were bunched on the land at the other side of the bridge. The Japanese appeared on the far side with angry shouts and began firing at the Marines opposite them. They did not yet see the sergeant on the bridge, lodged between the two groups. The Marines ducked for cover and returned fire. One enemy soldier fell and rolled into the river. Another ran onto the bridge, and he also fell into the water after being shot. As the Japanese gathered in mass to rush the bridge, Hawk came to life. He rose on his elbows and fired a burst into them. The raft upon which he lay rose and fell wildly, dropping him beneath the level of the raft in front of him, and ending his ability to see or fire.

"We have to get him off there," said Joe.

"I don't see how," said Baker, firing the BAR at the Japanese. "We'll just have to shoot it out with them until they're all dead." A Marine screamed and fell. His silence indicated that he would not be getting up again. "Or, until we're all dead," Baker whispered under his breath. Hawk rose to his knees, turned, and began crawling back toward his men. He had not made it far before dozens of shots sank into the soaked wood all around him. He quickly faced the enemy again, and flattened out as much as possible. Using his own strategy against him, the enemy began crawling out on the rafts toward him. He could seldom see them on the rising and falling logs, and never had a decent shot.

"Cut the rope!" Hawk shouted over his shoulder. He and the enemy tried to exchange fire.

"What'd he say?" Joe asked. "Cut the rope? What's that mean?"

Hawk shouted again, "Cut the bridge loose!"

"He wants to cut the ropes on our side of the bridge," said Baker. "How's he gonna get back here if we do that?"

"Cut the *gotdam* rope!" Hawk screamed.

Joe pulled out his knife and began hacking at the heavy hawsers mooring the bridge to the shore. Baker shook his head. He aimed the BAR at the rope on the side opposite that of Joe and fired a long burst into it, severing the burned strand. Both sides of the rope let go of the anchoring stakes at once. This allowed the first of the heavy rafts to be seized by the current and pulled away from the bank. The entire line of rafts quickly followed, drifting down the river. The raft next to the first one twisted in the water and snapped its lashings, then rocketed off by itself down the raging stream. The half dozen Japanese on the two rafts closest to their side of the river found themselves afloat. The moorings on that side of the river gave way under the tremendous weight.

Hawk's portion of the floating logs broke free from the others, and he spun around, caught up by the swirling current. His raft struck the neighboring vacant one, and as the collision slowed and steadied his progress, he half rose and fired across the open water into the Japanese soldiers clinging to two other rafts, loosely fastened together. One fell, and the others flattened out on the logs for cover as they shrieked in terror. One of the enemy finally recovered his sense of direction, and rose from the slick surface enough to fire back at Hawk. This forced the American to in turn flatten out.

The rafts of the Japanese split apart, and one fell behind, while one kept abreast of the American. The men from both banks were firing at the rafts, as well as each other, but it was almost impossible to hit the disappearing targets in the bouncing surf.

The rafts of Hawk and the Japanese raced next to one another, only a few feet apart. Three soldiers clung desperately to the float, and one tried to lift himself and fire at the American. With the Thompson lying steady on its side against the logs, Hawk squeezed off a short burst, just as the raft rose to the perfect height for a clear trajectory. He thus eliminated the man aiming at him by sheer chance. The other two stretched out again in terror at the sight of the slashing automatic fire, as the dead body rolled off into the river.

Hawk felt his raft thump heavily into something. With a jolt of adrenaline injected into his already overloaded bloodstream, he realized that he was rubbing against the raft of the two remaining Japanese troopers. They were facing down river, and appeared unaware of what had happened. Without thinking, the Marine rolled with a speed defying the ability of sight to capture, over onto their logs, and fired point blank into the side of one of them. Within a moment, Hawk and his last opponent were on their knees, struggling to push one another off the raft. As the logs struck a rock and lurched abruptly, the Japanese soldier lost his balance and fell into the water.

Alone now, Hawk was better able to survey his surroundings. It occurred to him that he had been hearing shots all throughout his altercation with the men on the raft. That meant someone close by had targeted him. He now saw that they were coming from yet another raft behind him. There were still another two Japanese soldiers clinging to it, and occasionally aiming for his back at their leisure. Exhausted and desperate, he sat upright and fired back at them, striking one due to the advantage his automatic weapon afforded. It was Hawk's turn to flatten out as the other man used the lack of attention directed his way to return fire.

Amazingly, the current only grew faster, the mud banks that had been covered with greenery turned to bare, blurred stone. The stone rose higher and higher on either side. Hawk and his involuntary pursuer were being rushed blindly into some downward region of possibly deadly rapids or waterfalls. They swirled around a long curve and suddenly shot out into a relatively calm pool. Hawk looked up.

He immediately recognized what now looked like stained and streaked, red-orange stone around him, and the lighter colors of stone stretching far above on all sides. He and his unwelcome guest had emptied out into the well of Tu. Hawk had not noticed all of the contrasting hues on the well wall from his panoramic view of the pit from above. Things looked different, and extremely life-threatening from down here. The world was hard, close, humid and claustrophobic. The small circle of sky above was fringed with angry faces. The two rafts bumped heavily together. Both men rose simultaneously and groggily fired at one another. But they were firing empty weapons. The Japanese thrust his rifle and bayonet at Hawk, who backed away. Japanese soldiers practiced a great deal with the bayonet. Hawk knew all about that and had a healthy respect for the honed razor pointed at him. The soldier swung his arms forward again, leaping onto Hawk's raft. Hawk backed to the edge, awkwardly and narrowly avoiding the sharp blade swinging at him.

A huge, yellow-grayish head, with an open mouth full of teeth, rose from the water. It landed on the empty raft and its massive body slithered forward, pushing the snapping teeth toward the men on the other raft. The Japanese soldier had his back to the sea creature and had no idea what seized his leg. He squealed in horror. Hawk wrenched the rifle from him as the soldier flailed about. He turned the blade toward the monster, poised to stab it to death. The Japanese victim lay clinging to the raft. The giant animal's great red eye seemed hypnotized by the threat of its imminent death and lay there defiantly gripping the man's leg. The raft spun in a slow circle.

"Stop!" a raised, but ancient, voice ordered from above, cutting through the chaos. "You must not injure Tu!" Hawk looked up to see the witch high overhead, raising a commanding arm. The Japanese soldier continued to shriek and cling to the raft as the monster wagged its head vigorously back and forth, the teeth buried deep into its prey. Hawk held the bayonet an inch from the eye of Tu and was not well disposed toward stopping it there. "Tu holds the souls of many of our people. He must live!" Vuniwai shouted. Dimly, it occurred to the sergeant that this fish creature had something to do with her spiritual beliefs, which he currently had a minor stake in. More immediately, however, he noticed a dozen spear arms drawn back and aimed downward at him.

"Then you goddam bastards throw down a rope," he gasped at her. "Or you got a dead ass lizard on your hands." A woven vine ladder tumbled down the side of the well. He did not know if he had the strength to climb it. He stuck the rifle upright in the wooden raft and slung the Thompson. Hawk stepped onto the bottom rung of the ladder. "Pull me up, goddammit," he shouted. Slowly, the ladder rose. Hawk hung onto the ladder by one hand, with one foot on a rung, and one dangling out over the pool. When he reached about halfway up, he looked down and saw the massive eel still holding the bloody leg of the moaning soldier as the raft circled with both of them. The logs sank half under the churning water, with the raft sticking upright in the foam. The creature then dove, pulling the man with him into the water. The leviathan threw half the length of his enormous, coiled body from the depths of the clouded pool, and slammed the man down like a hammer onto the raft. The vicious blow stopped the cries and the movement of the Japanese. Tu dragged him under the blood-clouded water.

8

DECODING BY VOODOO

Hawk stepped off the ladder. "Thanks, folks," he told the men manning the ropes. "Appreciate it," he said as he stood next to the old woman. "That was the Nip you wanted. Signed, sealed, and delivered. I had a few more for you, but I lost them in the river on the trip down here."

"You have done well, spawn of evil. My son has returned. Our only fear is the revenge of the Nippon."

"I don't know what to tell you about that. That leaves you with the rest of the world, lady. Fighting Japs for you, till hell freezes over, wasn't part of our deal. You owe me some answers." Hawk, with his chest still heaving from the exertion, was not disposed toward any further bizarre negotiations.

"You speak the truth, most ugly false one. Come to my home. All will be answered as promised. Your servants must defend us from the Nippon while we talk, must they not?"

Hawk squinted in the sunlight striking his eyes. He had lost his helmet. His sandy hair stuck up in several directions. She was playing him like a fiddle. He didn't give her an answer. She knew that the Japanese were likely on their way to her village, and that they were not in the best of moods. She had only to keep Hawk's men there long enough to engage the Japanese, until the two warring sides thinned one another out to the point where a superior number of men with spears could master them. Then, maybe Tu could have his own little celebration with the vanquished. Hawk silently followed her around to the porch at the front of the grassy temple. There he saw his men gathered, and recognized the shapeless son of the voodoo queen, who was not as young as he had appeared in the darkness.

"You got lookouts posted?" Hawk called to Canlon from the veranda. "Those Japs might be headed here!"

"Yeah, I'm surprised you're here! It didn't look so good, last time I seen you," said Joe. "It looked like you were tied to the back of a truck, when that river took off with you."

"Ah." Hawk waved his hand dismissively. "I coulda got away any time by jumpin' in the water. I just wanted to knock off a few of the shitbags."

"Yeah, okay," said Joe. The prospect of jumping in the rapid water might sound feasible in the abstract, but it looked rather deadly at the time. "You think they're coming here?"

"That's what they do, ain't it? Just watch out. She's expecting them. We can hold this shitty old fence if we have to. There ain't that many of them. Have to watch out for 'em bringing in reinforcements." He followed the medicine woman inside. She motioned for him to sit on a finely made mat on the floor opposite her. A torch burned over them, casting leaping shadows.

Feeling tired and mentally drained, it was a relief for Hawk to sit down. He looked up at the flame on the torch, shooting out over him like a giant tongue. The rhythmic motion was somewhat hypnotic.

"You really need that thing?" He gestured at the large fire periodically whipping over his head. "Kinda warm in here. Might play hell with the drapes, too."

"I need the light to see. I am not as young as you, demon," she said.

"Yeah, okay. That's fine. What's the name you were gonna give me?"

"I am forced to thank you for what you have done for us, regardless of your evilness, and bad intentions."

"At your service. We fight Japs for a living. But I tell you what, we lost a man, and I didn't like that. That was because of your idea. It wasn't part of the deal when we came here. Shootin' Japs ain't against my religion, but I still ain't exactly celebrating right now. I can't be losing anybody else. I need that name right now, and no more funny business." He noticed a few aches and pains, and shifted about. "Before we get into any other...thing."

She slid the green bottle between them. "This is the man," she said. "He is yours. I release any interest in him."

Hawk picked up the bottle. He tried to read the writing on it. As he had earlier suspected, it was unintelligible. "That's mighty nice of you," he said, pointing the bottle at her, "and I'll take real good care of him. But me and him don't seem to speak the same language. I still need for you to tell me his name. That was the deal we made. You were gonna give me *two* names. I got people waitin' on this. Some of 'em ain't as nice as I am."

"If you speak to this soul, he will tell you the next

name," she said with her eyes closed. "He understands why you are here. He is as evil as you."

"He does, huh?" Hawk said, glancing at the dirt encrusted bottle. "Then he's way ahead of me. I'm afraid I'm just going to have to take your word on what he says. I ain't real good at speaking hoo doo. The name?"

"His name is English, like yours. He is Christian, like you. His name is Edmund Latham. Do you know this name?" She asked.

Hawk registered surprise upon the sudden hearing of a name and shook his head. "No, I don't know him. I've heard names like those before: Edmund and Latham. They're English names, you hear of people with those names in our country. Where is he, where did you see him last? I'll probably end up having to pay him a visit, like I did here."

"He is in the Helvedes Islands. He is a missionary. He is a white Christian, like you. I last saw him here. He came to me for help, as you came to me for help. You white Christian men are much advanced in knowledge over my people—*you* say—and yet, one day, you all come here for my help. I say you are *not* advanced, other than in evil weapons."

"Ain't that the truth. I'll tell you what, the white and Christian part didn't have a whole lot to do with me coming here. It had more to do with the government. Ain't no sense in us bringing Christ into it. This fella, Latham, why did he come here?"

"For the return of his soul," she said, pointing at the bottle. "I could not give it to him. He freely gave it to your devil, who freely gave it to me. I did not ask for it. I only wanted to be rid of it. And now I am. You wanted it. The only way you can get rid of it, is if someone else wants it, and you freely give it to them. Someone other than the body of Edmund Latham must ask for it. I thought I would die with this cursed thing, and yet, now it is your burden. I expect you to die with it. But I will not look at the future to find out."

Hawk tossed the bottle up and down lightly in his hand. "Oh, I can get rid of it pretty goddam quick. I don't mind taking the...little fella...off your hands. How did he get in the bottle? What do you have to do to get put into one of these?"

"He is a Christian missionary. He abused the children of the islands. He repented, but your god would not grant him forgiveness. This has something to do with the millstone of the holy book in the passage you read to me. The sin cannot be forgiven. You are familiar with your own religion and its holy book? Your god sent you here to take possession of this soul, but you did not know it? You, too, will not forgive this man. And be not mistaken—no one shall forgive you."

"Yeah. Well, probably not. So, the rest of this guy, his body and all, is still back in the Helvedes—preaching? He's alive?"

"The body is there. But it will speak no truth. It's life is a falsehood. You can only get the truth from his soul." She pointed at the bottle. "There."

"Oh, sure enough. No doubt about that. That's a real streak of luck for me. You said you could tell me the next name, though. Just in case this lyin' bastard won't talk." He twisted the bottle.

"I would that you speak with him, as I do not like conversing with the souls in your hell. As you have no soul, no harm will come to you. I can speak with you as with a rock or sand. You are a harmless being to any person intending only good."

Hawk came close to audibly growling, but he held his temper. He had some background in reasoning with idiots. "Well, let's just say it's *like* me asking the soul, and you just being the interpreter, since my magic is a little weak. See, when I lost my soul, I kind of lost my voice, too."

She closed her eyes. "I should speak no more to you. You are mocking and false. But you have tricked me. I have already promised to tell you the name. Now I am indebted to a devil. You play stupid, but are a prankster."

"You don't owe me nothing, lady. Just—give me— the goddam—name." Hawk said slowly. "And let me get outta here." She kept her eyes closed and wrestled with some great theological dilemma. It finally dawned on him that he was demanding she tell him something that she had no way in hell of knowing. He had somehow believed all of this crap, in spite of himself. No matter what nonsense she told him, Hawk would still have to find Latham, in order to know the truth. Even knowing *all* of that, he was *not* letting it go; since she had promised him she would give him two names, he was getting two names.

"Melvin Singer," she said suddenly.

"What?" Hawk leaned forward. He had heard another relatively normal name come from her lips. And yet, it was not something so common, that she could have just made it up. "What was that again?" He had heard it well, but he had to confirm it, and remember it.

"Edmund Latham tells you that the next name is

Melvin Singer. I may not say it again. I will not remember it. It was not spoken to me. It was from the condemned and for your condemned hearing."

"Melvin Singer." Hawk repeated it. He supposed he could remember the two names easily enough, although he would have preferred a Bob Smith or two. He would have to write them down at the first opportunity. "And where is Singer?" Hawk asked, envisioning people paging through phone books from San Francisco to New York trying to find this character.

"Everyone knows where he is. Your people in the war, your evil owners, they will know where he is. You will not have to look for this one," she said. "He is well known."

"Yeah? He's famous? Everyone knows him—including you?"

"Not I. I do not know. The white Christians will know. I have no use for him or his nonsense." Hawk nodded. He had this in common with the witch. Having lost his soul, he supposed he was out of the Christian club, and thus, he had never heard of Melvin Singer.

"Okay. That's fine—good enough. It's been a pleasure, ma'am." Hawk got to his feet. "Y'all better watch out for them damn Japs when we leave. Ain't no tellin' what them son of a bitches will do."

"They have not come here yet, though they must know you are here. This makes me feel good that they will not come. They fear your evil. When you leave, they have even less reason to come to me. You brought the curse of their presence down on us. We have hope the curse leaves with you."

"Yeah, well. I wish you luck with that. I'd still

sharpen up a few sticks. We gotta be movin' on. This island is way out of our neck of the woods."

Hawk conferred with Canlon, Baker, and Vera. They concluded first of all, that Clark had sent a rescue mission by now, and second, that it was probably a plane, in order for the rescue to be a swift one. It was Vera's opinion that the plane would try to land in the same cove in which she had attempted to make her landing. The patrol would have to travel to the cove, and wait for a rescue. This plan had the advantage of taking them in a direction away from both the village of the witch doctor, and the Japanese. If none of this worked out, they had the options of doing nothing, and waiting to be found, or returning to the airplane and trying to get the radio in operation. None of the possibilities inspired a good deal of confidence, and capture by the Japanese remained an imminent threat. The enemy contingent was still on the island, and its reinforcement was certainly on the table, with Japan lying virtually the same distance away from Papanuca as Papanuca lay from the rest of the Helvedes.

Hawk was of the opinion that his patrol could handle the number of Japanese he had seen, at least until there was a rescue. Problems would arise if he had not seen all of them, or if the rescue were delayed. Equal forces, trapped together on an island like this, would eventually wear one another down. In all of the possibilities as to what the future held, none included a truce with the uncompromising enemy. The Marines knew that in the one in a million chance that the enemy *were* willing to compromise, Hawk would not. It was kill or be killed until the two forces were somehow separated, or all dead.

In spite of all of that, there was yet the chance of the status quo remaining undisturbed, that is, a default consisting of the two sides leaving one another alone. Hoping for this, at least for the time being, Hawk decided to take the quickest way out of the village.

He had been told by the sorceress that the rope bridge was serviceable, regardless of what he thought, or how it looked. The villagers used it on occasion, although not having any reason to frequently go in that direction. The patrol stopped before the old span, surveying it from the opposite side of the canyon where they had first encountered it. It swung freely in the wind, looking as frayed and feeble as ever.

Hawk addressed Baker. "You said you could drive a truck over that bastard. Here's your chance," Hawk told him. "Still think so?" Baker looked it over. He tested a cross tie with his boot.

"Yeah." Baker nodded. "I think it's even in better shape on this side. It gets kind of rickety close to the other side."

"No, shit. The thing about bridges," Hawk noted, "is that they're all or nothing. Give it a shot. Hang onto the hand rope, it looks a little newer than the rest of the damned thing."

Baker walked out onto it. The sticks lashed across the underlying vine ropes of the base were well spaced, giving a breathtaking view of the drop below. Baker grabbed the rope handrail and glanced down at the winding little waterway beneath him.

"I ain't gonna shit ya," Baker called back. "This looks like hell."

"I kinda figured that," said Hawk, spitting down into the gorge. "Get on with it. Okay, who's next?"

"Hell, let him get over, first," said Joe.

Hawk shrugged, nodded, and sat down on the edge of the drop. He searched for part of cigar. One of the sticks cracked sharply, and Baker drew back a step.

"I wouldn't step on that one," Hawk called out.

"Right," said Baker. It was a long step to the next cross tie. He hung onto the rope handrail, and stepped only on the very end of the broken stick, where it was tied. In this way, he was able to edge past the broken segment, and onto the next cross tie. Two more of the sticks broke before he reached the other side, and he had to cling to the handrail and edge past them in the same manner.

"That wasn't too bad," said Hawk, when Baker was safely across.

"It took forever," Joe observed.

"Want to try it? It ain't gettin' any stronger," Hawk advised.

Joe considered. "Yeah, okay." He decided that he could follow Baker's strategy and make it across relatively easily. He was able to skirt the three broken cross ties, and broke a fourth one on his own. He shrieked in horror and pulled himself back in time to avert a precipitous dive onto the rocks below.

Half suppressing a laugh, Hawk called out. "Hang onto that side rope on all of them. Don't go bustin' the damn thing to pieces." Joe responded with a few obscenities. His progress grew slower. He broke yet another rung before getting to the far bank.

"Well, this ain't worth a shit," Hawk said at last, shaking his head and standing. "They ain't gonna be nothing left of the shitass thing. We're gonna have to climb down to the bottom, and it'll take forever."

"What?" Joe Canlon called from the other side, "after I risked my ass?"

"After you broke the son of bitch to pieces, so nobody else could use it," Hawk answered. He believed it might be tricky for Vera to cross this wreck now, among others, and if someone had to take her across by climbing down to the river, everyone might as well go down there. He did not voice this opinion, as she was just as agile as many of the men, and it was not entirely logical. He just didn't want her doing it. If the bridge fell to pieces, reduced to remnants, the men had some training in rope climbing, and she did not. He thought.

"What was the point?" Joe shouted. "That was a waste of time."

"Wastin' time—that's my business," Hawk shouted, muttering a parting "shithead," under his breath. He motioned Osage down the slope. "Blame the witch," Hawk called to Joe. "She lied. She said they use it all the time. Are you watching for Japs over there, or just bitching at the top of your stupid lungs?" Hawk waited as the men climbed down into the canyon. Joe cursed at him occasionally from the other side, but Hawk never answered, other than with a dismissive wave of his hand, as he contentedly finished the cigar.

* * *

COLONEL CLARK GREW concerned about Vera Orr after losing contact with her plane. She was a personal friend of his, and he had only granted her permission to ferry the patrol because she requested to do so; and because General Dennison had also persuasively suggested it. He had never been clear on her relationship with the general. The colonel had made it a practice not to investigate the background of Mrs. Orr very closely. He adopted the practice after a letter from the office of a cabinet member in Washington questioned why Clark was making so many inquiries as to the background of Mrs. Orr.

Of secondary interest to the colonel was the fate of Sergeant James Hawk, although there was the complicating factor of his twenty men. They were definitely of interest, both professionally and as fellow Marines. They were involved in a highly classified mission that had to be completed soon. They could all be replaced, but it would be inconvenient to have to select a new leading agent to finish things up at this point. The mission had turned out to be considerably more dangerous than first anticipated. Anyone recruited to finish the project would have to be a skilled and expendable operator, similar to Sergeant Hawk. That would take time. The timeless Vera Orr, on the other hand, was irreplaceable.

Reconnaissance planes were sent to Papanuca, to do a quick flyover. Clark had no desire to draw Japanese attention to the island, lest the integrity of the mission be compromised, or Mrs. Orr endangered. Clark was considerably more astute than Hawk gave him credit for, just as the reverse was true. The first recon plane returned with a report of having sighted the Catalina, crashed in the treetops, with no sighting of its former occupants. The second plane, however, sighted Marines in a canyon, as well as a small Japanese presence elsewhere on the island.

Clark enlisted another Catalina. With a Marine pilot this time, he sent a platoon of Marines to recover the lost patrol. He was so concerned, in fact, that he had decided to accompany the men himself to Papanuca. This was adventurous for the colonel, and obviously dangerous, considering the history of the previous patrol. The thought did cross his mind, however, that he might be given a medal for the effort, due to the importance of this code, and it might be the best opportunity and the safest way to get such a medal. Unlike Vera Orr, and the foolhardy Sergeant Hawk, the colonel wisely included a fighter plane escort.

* * *

Setsuko Takemitsu sat on the porch of Wilhelm Volmer's boarding house, where they awaited Stefano Calvino. She reached through the railing and toyed with the white flowers growing in the bed there. Volmer rocked back on two legs of his chair, letting it prop against the shiplap covered wall. During all of their meetings, they had never noticed their inquisitive neighbor peering through the blinds next door.

"I have about convinced her," said Setsuko. "It should not take much longer. It is such a simple matter, I do not understand her reservations."

"People are very reserved in medical matters," said Wilhelm. "But you are correct, she is a nurse, it should not seem all that unusual to her. I suppose she is in awe of the patient. These things sometimes happen. I have the drug ready to go. I altered the log and no one will ever know that I have taken some from the lab. I am anticipating the end of this, so that I can be done with this awful job. It is so dull and boring, and yet when you think about it too much, it seems immoral, as well."

Calvino's car pulled up. They stopped talking until he climbed up the steps. He held a handful of envelopes. Ruth had been dozing, until Calvino arrived. She had been up late the night before thinking of the insults she missed out on handing Bert in his living years, and now she was out of sorts. But the newcomer served to renew her interest.

"Papers for everyone!" Calvino announced, tossing them down on the wicker table between Setsuko and Wilhelm. "We will have no trouble leaving. They are from the exact same printing house that does the identical legitimate government documents."

"Incredible," Wilhelm smiled as he picked up the envelopes. "We are almost there. I don't want to seem overconfident, however. From the beginning, we were given very little chance of success. We must still be willing to accept failure." His smile faded.

"Ah." Calvino laughed. "We must be willing to accept success, too!" He slapped Wilhelm's shoulder. Even Setsuko smiled, but only slightly, as she did not want Wilhelm to think that she was being disloyal to him.

Ruth Nagle dropped the slat shut in her blinds. She didn't like Setsuko, or Volmer. She hated to see Calvino mixed up with them. The nice young man reminded her of Rudolph Valentino. He was probably giving the other deadbeats free tickets to some sort of affair, as they had no visible means of support. They were probably going to go drinking alcohol, or something similarly destructive. Well, Calvino would learn to pick his friends more wisely soon enough. It was just part of growing up, she supposed. Still, it was a shame. Such a nice young fellow. She thought of talking to him. How would she explain that? Lenora whined.

"I know," she told the dog. "I would never do anything like that. I don't give out advice. But I should. I've always said, keep your mouth shut. Silence is golden, and it's never steered me wrong. Still, when something is so obvious, you want to guide a foolish young person like that." Lenora turned suddenly with the intention of chewing an itch on her hindquarters, but her neck would not extend that far. Instead, she energetically rotated like a shuddering globe in the middle of the floor, until the kitchen shook.

* * *

WHEN HAWK's patrol reached the cove, they found that Colonel Clark had landed only an hour before, and the esteemed personage was now ashore on Papanuca. Behind him, two Catalina's bobbed calmly in the protected waters of the bay. The officer was dressed in his newly starched combat fatigues and shiny helmet, looking somewhat out of place, like a Boy Scout, only with an old head. His large pants were hitched up high across his midsection. He was all smiles at the sight of Vera Orr and rushed to greet her. She held him back with a hand.

"Oh, no," she said. "I haven't bathed since we got here. It's a policy of our fearless leader. Very strict." She glanced at Hawk. The sergeant looked at the ground, prepared for an onslaught of verbal abuse, now that she had the colonel backing her. Vera was not above dishing it out when they were alone, but she was also not above dishing it out twice as much with the colonel around.

"We were worried to death, Vera," said the colonel. "Anything could have happened to you. Did you know that there are Japs on this island?"

"We have heard rumors." She laughed. "In fact, if I were you, Bennie, I would cut this short, and get back on the plane."

"Yes, of course, we only disembarked to find you. But by all means, let's return. Did you accomplish the mission?" The colonel asked. She noticed that he asked her, and not Hawk. Hawk rubbed his nose, looking at neither of them.

"I think we can discuss that on the plane," she said. "And perhaps you should debrief our fearless leader. He probably knows more of the details on that than I do."

The colonel laughed. "I doubt that. I doubt that." He put a hand in the middle of her back, and steered her toward a rubber raft, turning his back to Hawk. Joe Canlon leaned over to the sergeant.

"I doubt that. I doubt that," said Joe, with a blustery voice. Hawk was forced to smile at the well-done imitation. Meanwhile, Baker and the others had their weapons trained on the jungle behind them. They were not as prone to considering the Japanese a part of the long ago and far away. A bullet through the inflatable raft, or any number of other things, would not have been all that surprising; and could well have ruined the jolly reunion.

The two Catalinas drifted closer to the shore, pointing their fifty caliber machine guns toward the jungle as the last of the men boarded. But the Japanese had not followed them. Perhaps they knew nothing of the code, or did not think they had sufficient strength to engage the Americans. It was the sort of luck that Clark brought with him, because it was certainly not the luck of Sergeant Hawk.

Sparked by a comment from Joe Canlon, a discussion arose about using the fifty-caliber gun in the other plane, containing Clark's Marine escort, to strafe the enemy camp at the far end of the island. Clark radioed his approval to the other plane. They heard some time later that the camp had been scattered by the machine gun fire, and only a couple of the enemy escaped into the jungle. Hawk was somewhat pleased with that result, as he figured the natives, or perhaps their pet eel, could now handle the stragglers.

Clark decided to debrief the sergeant—and Vera—aboard the plane. Upon hearing that the mission had been accomplished, the thought crossed his mind that there might be yet another medal in this thing for him. In all honesty, even to himself, he had to admit that he really handled the matter well. He remained rather subdued during the loading of the casualties.

"It went well, you were able to get all of the information?" the colonel asked Hawk, his voice rising above the noise of the engines.

"Yessir. The witch doctor answered the question. Whether any of it's true or not, you know, has to be checked out. She was kind of...unreliable. She was into that voodoo and all. Rambling...crazy talk," Hawk explained. Vera and Clark were strapped into their seats, and Hawk sat on the floor next to them, being jostled this way and that, with the motion of the plane. "She said the name that goes with the 'millstone around the neck' line is Edmund Latham, a missionary in the Helvedes."

Clark nodded. "I've heard there's a missionary out

there, who had refused evacuation. Getting to him might not be a problem. I don't think the Japanese have occupied the island he is on. We can just pay that gentleman a little visit."

Another unoccupied island. This has a familiar ring. Hawk thought.

"Tell him the rest of it." Vera kicked his leg, and none too lightly. Hawk scowled up at her.

"There's more?" Clark asked. "By all means. What are you holding back on us. It's a good thing I had someone in the know there." He smiled warmly at Vera, who raised her eyebrows at Hawk.

"Yessir, that's a little harder to explain," Hawk said. He had hoped Vera would continue to run with the ball, and explain the rest of it to the colonel, since she had inserted herself into the debriefing. But she sat smiling, and silent, looking down her tiny, perfectly shaped nose at him.

"Try," she encouraged with another kick. Clark frowned at him.

"This Vuniwai says that she can talk to Edmund Latham's soul." Hawk paused, feeling rather ridiculous, and pulled the green bottle out of his pocket. "This here thing is his soul. I believe I'm supposed to give it back to him. Anyway, she says this soul here told her the next name on the code list, and we don't even have to go to Latham to ask him about it."

Clark stared at Hawk as if the pathetic underling were a farm animal. "You realize, Sergeant, that is preposterous."

"I thought so, too, sir. Except she knew more than names. She knew what the next line of the code was, without me telling her. I think she really knew the next person. I don't know how. When you think on it, how do any of these people know the next name? How did any of that come about?"

Clark continued frowning down on Hawk. He didn't like the idea of Hawk *thinking* about this. Vera smiled at the colonel's puzzled expression, holding back a laugh. She did not believe that the witch knew the next name, but she also knew that Hawk, master of a somewhat more primitive level of thought processes, *did* believe that the witch knew the next name.

"I'm sure I don't know, unless you let her read it," Clark said. "But I do know that there is no way in hell she knew the next name. I don't think you realize the complexity of that code, Sergeant. Those words you are reading on that page were encrypted to begin with. You would not have understood any of it in the original version we received. What you are claiming now is impossible on several levels. You have no idea how impossible." The colonel sighed with disdain at such naivete. "This is how magicians entertain the gullible."

Hawk ignored all the supercilious skepticism and went to the point. "Maybe. But it would save a lot of time. And lives. It's a big shortcut. Someone could still check out Latham, but in the meantime, someone else could be moving on to this next person. It would save a step." *And lives,* he thought to himself.

Clark considered this, as did Vera. Hawk's intuitive craftiness had seized upon a point they had missed. He was an expert at staying alive and did not miss many of the most vital points in that art. Being thrown repeatedly into life-threatening situations bestowed a unique sort of wisdom upon him.

"Perhaps," Clark conceded. "What is this name?"

"Melvin Singer."

"Melvin Singer? The anthropologist?"

"I don't know. The witch said everybody would know where he was."

"Well, yes, he's in Tahiti," said Clark, looking at Vera. She shrugged. "That's well known, and also thousands of miles from here. That's not in the war zone."

"Maybe not," said Hawk. "I don't think being in the war zone was required by the code, the way it was explained to me." Hawk offered. "I think that was just a requirement for me to be in on the deal. Fact is, these people could be anywhere in the world. They put some close together on account of the time it would take to find them. But they didn't have to be. Mrs. Orr was in Hawaii at the time, as I recall."

"You're right. That's absolutely right," said Clark, sounding suspiciously unconvinced. "Maybe there was a slipup, and this medicine woman found out something. Very well, I will go to Tahiti and resolve this. It would definitely save an enormous amount of time. But just in case, you must go check out Latham as well. We have to be sure he confirms that the next name is Singer's."

"Yessir," Hawk replied, thinking: *how about me going to Tahiti, and you going to Latham?*

"And Vera, you will love Tahiti. I'm taking you along," said the colonel. "It'll be like a grand excursion."

"Oh...goody," said Vera. "But, no, I've had enough adventure for a while. And I've been to Tahiti. It's very nice. Once."

"Nonsense, you owe it to the war effort." The colonel wasn't taking no for an answer. It was such a good idea.

"I *was* thinking of the war effort," Vera countered.

"I was thinking the sergeant would need a pilot to reach Latham, and I could add a few hours to my score."

"Precisely. You can add ten times those hours by taking me to Tahiti. I can tell you this, it will be a whole lot safer," said Clark, winking.

No, shit, thought Sergeant Hawk, with a smile. When he looked up, with the smile, Vera was glaring at him. What was he supposed to do about any of it? The glare made Hawk decide to try to bail her out.

"Mrs. Orr is probably kind of...tired, sir. We had a little more excitement than we bargained for on the last island. It wasn't all smooth." It was the best he could do, and probably all he could do.

"But not too tired to go to another island with the same risk? I don't think so. She's coming to Tahiti with someone who knows what he's doing." Everyone fell silent after that. Hawk eventually drifted toward the back of the plane with the rest of the men. Most were sleeping. He thought of Turnage and wondered how he was doing.

"Are we getting some time off now?" Marchand asked him.

"I don't think so," Hawk answered. "He's got one more detail for us. It might not be as bad."

"That's what they said last time," Marchand replied.

"You think they lied to us?" Joe Canlon asked with a serious expression. He liked to needle Marchand. Marchand did not take the bait. Sensing the tension, Murdoch spoke up.

"You know what I think? I think everybody goes to all this trouble, to do all this stuff...like we're doing...for nothing. And, just like planning all these battles on how to kill thousands of Japs and all that. What does any of that do?"

"Kills thousands of Japs?" Marchand answered.

"No, it doesn't do anything," said Murdoch. "We just have to do it over and over. They should be spending their time figuring out how to kill the leaders. Nobody else cares about the war, right? It's only the head guy that started it all that cares about any of this. What do we care? What do regular people care? Nothing. But— the head guy..."

"My grandma used to say that," said Joe. "In a way. She'd say, if they just killed Hitler, there wouldn't be no wars." He shook his head. "She didn't like Hitler." He laughed, and shook his head again. "Hitler."

"That's true," said Blackwell, joining in. "Where would Germany be without Hitler? Why hasn't some-body killed that bastard?"

"And, with the Japs," said Murdoch, "if you killed Tojo or the Emperor, that'd be the end of them. It's always one man that wants to take over the world. Most people don't care about that kind of crap. They have too much other stuff to do. But this one crackpot stirs all this up. Like Napoleon."

"I don't know if that applies to the Japs," said Marchand, seeing what he perceived as a flaw in the theory. "They're all crazy as hell. We're gonna have to kill every damned one of them."

"No, I think he's right," said Blackwell. "It's kind of like in the Bible, the Adam and Eve thing. Everybody gets the blame because of the headman. Everybody's got to go to hell because Adam bit the apple."

"So, you wouldn't have bit the apple? You know what I think? I think the guy bit Eve." Joe Canlon laughed.

"The Germans and the Japs all bit the apple. They followed the head guys, didn't they? That wasn't the Emperor bombing Pearl Harbor, was it? He was getting his foot rubs at the time." Joe nudged Hawk, who had yet to say anything about any of it.

"Like we ain't following some head guy?" Hawk said, in his contrarian way. He thought of Clark. What a head guy.

"That's different. We want to," said Murdoch. "We volunteered for this."

"That's probably the same shit that they're sayin'," said Hawk. He looked up. Vera was looking down at him. She motioned for him to follow her to the opposite side of the plane. She sat down there, and he sat beside her. He waited for her to begin the conversation.

"I don't want to go to Tahiti. I want to go anywhere else," she said.

"People in hell want ice water," Hawk answered.

"What's that? The Marine Corps philosophy?"

"You're used to doing what you want. Some people never do what they want. They probably don't all join the Marine Corps. Some might even be in the Women's Auxiliary...something."

"Don't you want me to fly you to Latham?" she asked. He didn't answer. Their legs were stretched out on the deck. She kicked sideways at him. "Answer, please."

"In case you ain't noticed, it don't much matter what I want," he finally said. "I told the guy you didn't want to go. He didn't want to hear that. Especially, from me."

"You didn't answer the question?"

"I don't know, Vera. It'll probably be dangerous, just like the last two deals. It's all rosy when they're roping you into it, then it turns to shit. You're gonna end up gettin' killed, if you don't slow down. Followin' *us* around is about the worst idea anybody ever got into their head. Why are you doing all this?"

"Why are you?" she asked. "If anybody is going to get killed, it's you. You act like an absolute maniac. Do you think anybody would care? Do you think Colonel Clark would give it a second thought?"

Hawk laughed. "Sure, he would. He'd cry his beady little eyes out. Don't worry about me. I'll be awright." She stood up quickly, saying no more, and returned to the seat at the front of the plane. "Guess that was the wrong answer," he muttered.

Hawk sat there alone and closed his eyes. He had no interest in returning to the others, and the theoretical conversation about killing the Emperor. Although, for just a moment, he did wonder why he was flying all over the world surreptitiously killing people, and yet the Emperor was off limits in his rose garden. Airplanes flew over Japan daily, now, killing thousands of people, but the Emperor was invisible to them. Why was that? Had that ever occurred to anybody? *Oh, yeah, it occurred to Murdoch. Nobody listens to him.* Hawk opened his eyes. *Nobody listens?* The plane droned on. He stood and went up front to find Vera. He motioned for her to follow him to the back. Clark slept in his seat, looking as peaceful as a wicked baby.

"I just thought of something," Hawk said.

"How much you loathed me?"

"And something else." He looked down and kicked Joe Canlon's hip. "Come here a second, shithead," he told him. The three of them sat against the bulkhead.

"You remember how y'all said nobody could know

two of the sets of words in the code? It was impossible for the witch to do it?" Hawk asked them.

"Yeah, I meant with magic," said Joe. "It *is* impossible."

"No, it ain't. I knew two sets, the one before me and my own. Everybody knows two sets," Hawk said. "Or *at least* two sets. See?"

Joe nodded dimly. "Yeah. I guess that's true. And, so?"

"There's a way to do this code. I think that Hoech built in a way to do it without all this trouble, or at least, a way to do it two different ways," Hawk said. "And faster. There's more to this. Maybe it's a way to double check it."

"Sweetheart, the witch didn't know two sets of word clues," said Vera. "She knew two *names*."

"She knew two sets of words. The green bottle thing and the millstone thing," Hawk replied. "And then, she knew *three* names." Vera frowned, but not for long.

"Right, she knew another name. Get it? It's a completely different step from everybody else," said Vera. "And on top of that, she knew it without having the words to identify the name."

"Yeah. Nobody can do that," said Joe.

"She did it, dumb ass," said Hawk. "You were right there."

"You don't know that yet. She gave you a name, you don't know if it's right," said Joe. "She could have said Bob Hope."

"And she did *not* give you the clue to that third name," Vera added, "the next clue that you had written on your little paper? *That* you could have double checked her on—but—you didn't. She just came up with a name out of nowhere. It can't be done."

"I didn't hear nobody else buttin' in on the conversation at the time. I'll bet you my place in hell she is right about the next name," said Hawk. "This Singer fella will be next. Remember that."

"I'll take that bet," said Joe. "You can keep your place in hell. Let's put some cash on it."

"Don't waste your money. If you'll notice, she picked the name of a famous person. It wasn't like all these other names. She heard that name somewhere," said Vera. "Sugar plum, there's no such thing as voodoo, magic, or the Easter Rabbit."

"Yeah, she heard it somewhere, awright," said Hawk. "She knew the line before I read it. Rattled it right off. That didn't strike you as funny?" Hawk asked.

"Odd. Not supernatural," said Vera.

"Oh, it's supernatural, awright. A supernatural Jap had just read it to her. They got this code, too, and they had some kind of falling out over it. The Japs didn't just walk in there and take her son off because of his good looks. Everywhere we go, a ton of Japs hop up on these 'deserted' islands, doing crazy shit. To us."

"That *is* funny," said Joe. "I'm kinda sick of that."

Vera shook her head and stood. "The Japs didn't do any of that. If they did that, they're the ones that had to tell the witch doctor the name of Melvin Singer, and they would have no reason to be there in the first place, if they knew that. The Hoech code may be a *little* over your head, gum drop. There's no way you're going to figure it out. Better stick to what you're good at, ruining people's lives." She walked toward her seat, but turned around and added: "Mr. Moto."

Joe laughed. "I guess she told you. I noticed a chill in the air. You two having a disagreement?"

"Ah, she can go to hell. Two hundred bucks says it's Singer."

"Did you ever ask her if she knew Hoech?" Joe asked.

"To hell with her. Two hundred bucks."

"I ain't got two hundred bucks."

"Looks like you get my place in hell, then."

9

THE SEARCH IN OTHER LANDS

Colonel Clark flew east from the Helvedes aboard a Boeing 314 Clipper, an adventurous fifty-four hundred kilometers, across Melanesia and Polynesia, south of the equator. Beside him sat the unusually quiet Vera Orr. She was not being her entertaining self, and it annoyed him. She looked out the window at the blue eternity below. Behind them, the luxurious dining room was being set for the evening meal. They had an expert pilot and co-pilot conducting the journey, neither of which was Vera Orr. She would not gain any flying hours from the junket.

"Why so solemn? Miss that sergeant?" Clark asked suddenly. Vera sat stunned for a moment, but she was never stunned for long.

"Bennie. Whatever made you say a thing like that?" She turned toward him with a feigned expression of shock, and he felt a little foolish. Her eyes were accusing and reprimanding him for his boldness.

"I don't know. You seem to have an interest in him. God knows why. You turn up wherever he is. I mean, really Vera, he is as about as low class as a man can get. He sounds so...white trash."

"Bennie, a person can find another person interesting, without 'having an interest' in them. Don't be crude. He is very unusual. He is not afraid of anything. And I mean, anything. I can't even describe some of the things I've seen the man do. I've never known anyone like him."

"Well, I have. They're a dime a dozen. I have a regiment full of them. You know, I think you need to get back into normal society, around normal people. It's a shame losing Wendell, and your accustomed social circle. A war zone is no place for a young lady, with all this frontline riff raff. Next thing I know you'll be pen pals with some death row inmate." Glasses and silverware clinked in the next room. The pilot leaned out of the cockpit and winked at her. It was her seven thousandth wink since coming to the Pacific.

She turned back toward the window, her mood unimproved. She wondered if Tahiti might not be on another planet. The earth could not possibly be this large. She found the subject of James Hawk, as shared with Clark, infuriating to her.

"I seriously doubt that," she muttered.

* * *

WHILE HOPING that his role in the solution of the Hoech code had ended, Hawk returned to Greater Helvedes. Captain Macintosh and Lieutenant Kirk had both informed him that he was to return to the campaign, with the goal of capturing the remainder of the archipelago. Before this actually happened, however, the orders came down that he was to proceed to Salvation Island and contact the Reverend Edmund Latham regarding a highly classified matter. Although the orders contained no details, he well knew the purpose of the journey this time. It held no mystery. The briefing by Lieutenant Kirk was no more than a formality.

After leaving Papanuca, Hawk had been filled with curiosity as to whether Latham could be bypassed in the search for the next person of interest. A day or two later, however, that interest had evaporated. He was relieved to be done with the code. When he was dragged back into the search, his curiosity only grudgingly returned. He would travel to Salvation Island and do his job, but it held no fascination. Turnage was still in critical condition, and Hawk had not forgotten the others lost in this much too vaguely defined mission.

The disagreement with the Navy had been left behind, as is the way with inconsequential squabbles, and Hawk's patrol was conveyed to Salvation Island by landing craft, just as it had been on the first of the landings on Caratu. Once again, he was assured there would be no contact with the Japanese. Salvation Island was securely within the American held portion of the Helvedes, and compared to his other recent destinations, it was nearby. The men took note, however, of the extra supply of ammunition supplied to them this time. Several crates of bullets and grenades accompanied the party. One had to wonder to what purpose such weighty luggage could be put to, without contacting Japanese traveling companions.

"Probably target practice," Hawk assured the men, as the cargo was loaded. "Gotta keep on your toes." Hawk had no objections to the additional equipment, mainly because, among the items requisitioned to him this time, was a serviceable radio, and permission to use it. This was an improvement over his last few assignments, which required suffering in silence as a part of the requirements.

Bounding across the heady waves in the lunging Higgins boat, Hawk thought of Clark and his trip to Tahiti. It would have made sense for Hawk to wait to contact Latham until after Clark had found Melvin Singer. Clark had seemed pleased with the time and effort that could be saved by skipping Latham, and yet, here they were, on the bounding main, shipping off to Salvation Island. Hawk suspected that Clark did not have the same degree of faith in the witch that Hawk had held. He noticed that people didn't seem to care much for the witch, or her skills. As a student of human nature at the platoon level, he did not so easily dispense with the worth of human resources.

The only satisfaction that Hawk could derive from any of this, therefore, was to prove Clark, Vera, and the idiot Joe Canlon wrong, by having his mission to Latham prove useless. He hoped to confirm that the next name in the code was in fact that of Melvin Singer. In the throes of all the effort, travel, and danger, this did not seem like a lot of satisfaction. It *was* amusing, however, to think of Vera Orr stuck with Clark, thousands of miles away on Tahiti. He would know if they had been wrong about the code, long before they would know.

Once again, just as on Caratu, after landing on Salvation Island and unloading his cargo, the Higgins boat pilot beat a hasty retreat.

As Canlon watched this with recurring uneasiness,

he expressed his misgivings to Hawk. "You know, it seems to me he could hang around. All we have to do is ask this Latham a question. I mean, how long can that take? Now, we have to wait for another boat to pick us up, and all that shit? A man could get killed. And, it ain't like we haven't already had a couple of close shaves."

Hawk nodded and closed one eye. He kicked one of the many crates of thirty caliber ammunition resting on the sand. "Yep." He nodded again. "No—you're right."

Of all the herculean tasks encountered thus far, in this Odyssey, the assignment to visit Salvation Island appeared to be the simplest. The patrol had been set ashore within a short distance of the Reverend Latham's church and schoolhouse. The few natives living here seemed well fed, well kempt, and friendly, unlike those on Papanuca. There was no brooding jungle, or atmosphere of lurking disease as on the witch's grimy little island. The earth was cleared and raked. The men filed off the beach and proceeded without incident to the church grounds, where they were met by none other than the renowned missionary himself, Edmund Latham.

Latham was still young, but tall, thin, and rather bent over, giving him a sickly appearance. He wore a long black cassock and a straw hat, giving him a Puritanical, or at least, a nineteenth-century "look." His skin was more the red color of a boiled crab, than white. When the patrol approached the front of the church, he appeared to be engaged with a group of children, constructing a May Pole, or some similar decoration. Hawk recalled the witch's pronouncement on how she came to possess the missionary's soul. "Mm hmm," Hawk muttered under his breath.

"How do you do, sir? I'm Sergeant James Hawk, US Marine Corps, here on official business." Hawk cocked one shoulder at the pastor, in his customary manner, looking a little unsociable, and more like a street corner tough than a government emissary.

"Oh, dear, no," said the Reverend. "Is the invasion coming here?"

"No, sir. We hope not. It does have a way of following us around, though. But we don't think so. No, sir, we came to ask you a question or two."

Latham's face went from sun-burned red to snow white. "Oh?" he asked nervously. "Whatever could you want to ask me? I haven't seen any Japanese since the war began."

Hawk thought about springing the question on Latham and getting the hell out of here. He still had the green bottle and wondered if Latham would be at all interested in having it. After all, the cleric had gone to Papanuca on some mysterious pilgrimage to the less than Christian witch, with dark purposes known only to himself. He must have had some kind of faith in the powers of indigenous religion. Rather than pulling out the code on the spot, and unfolding it, as Hawk had done in the past, he thought he might make more of a ceremony of it. On the other occasions, he had been under a bit more pressure. Due to the wager with Joe and due to the witch's strange prophecy, he wanted to know a little more about this odd gentleman, and what he knew. One thing that had troubled Hawk, in trying to understand the matter of the code, was how Hoech knew all of these people. How did this all come about? How was the chaos reined into a logical message?

"Maybe you got a place we could sit down and

discuss this, out of the sun?" Hawk said. This sounded ominous to Latham, but he showed no defiance.

"Oh, certainly. Let's go to my house. We can sit on the lanai."

"Yeah, okay. Lead the way. Joe, you might want to hear this, too," Hawk turned to Canlon, and gestured with his head. As they followed the pastor, Hawk said in a lower voice: "in case you ever get ahold of two hundred bucks?" As they left, Hawk waved at the other men to sit on the grass.

The host led his two guests to a table under the roof of the rear patio, and had them sit down. He called to a young manservant and asked that two lemonades be brought for the visitors.

"Dear God, what is this all about? You have me nervous as a cat," said Latham, sitting down with them. *In a room full of rocking chairs*, Hawk thought.

"Ain't nothing to be nervous about. Just this government thing they sent us on. Having to do with the war and all. It's like a code, you see?" Hawk said.

"It *is* a code," Joe Canlon corrected. Hawk turned sideways in his chair to look at Joe.

"Maybe your...self...would be more comfortable out on the grass?" he asked Joe.

"I'm fine," said Joe. "This is okay."

"Yessir. That's a fact. It *is* a code," Hawk continued. "To figure it out, we need your help. The code gives a few words that have something to do with a person, but only one other person knows who it is. You follow me?"

"Not entirely. I'm afraid not. I'm terrible at puzzles," said Latham. "Is this a word puzzle? I'm better with numbers. Are there pictures with it? I have trouble figuring things out."

"Oh, I know, me, too," said Hawk. "All that readin' and stuff." He shifted in his chair and searched in his pocket for the green bottle. "But it'll all make sense when I read the line of code to you. We hope." Hawk abandoned the search for the bottle, and reached instead for the paper with the code written on it. Latham watched all this aimless hand movement with increasing agitation. Hawk sensed a guilty conscience.

Hawk unfolded the paper and squinted. "It...uh... says 'only one could be student president.' Now...uh... does that make any sense, or make you think of anybody you've ever known in your life?" Hawk looked at Joe with a closed eye, as if to say, *"Like Melvin Singer?"*

"Why, yes, yes it does," said Latham. "I went to college with a man. We both ran for president of the senior class. The campaign was a little contentious for a minor office like that. He won, and that was a recurring line in his victory speech. It was supposed to be consoling to me, as I took it. But it wasn't. It was rather irritating. It was like he was needling me."

"I could see how that might be," said Hawk. His own clue had been the repetitive phrase used by the often irritating Vera Orr. "I reckon you remember this fella's name pretty well then?"

"Oh, yes. On top of all that, he's quite famous, and almost a neighbor. Melvin Singer. You've probably heard of him?"

"Melvin Singer?" Hawk asked, looking at Joe. "I'll swan. Mr. Canlon here was just telling me about him. Weren't you, Mr. Canlon? Mr. Canlon is kind of an amateur anthropologist himself. Yeah, we have heard of him."

"Oh, really?" Latham looked at Joe with large, helpless eyes. He wanted to look anywhere other than at the riveting gaze of the sergeant.

"Well, not really," said Joe. "That's just a little joke between me and the sergeant. He's a real joker. I'm not even sure what an anthropologist is."

"Oh," said Latham, still uneasy with the matter.

"I was thinking, not to change the subject," said Hawk. "Did you ever know a fella named Maxwell Hoech?"

"Uh...no. No, I didn't. But I know who he is, and I believe Singer knew him. He was a busybody sort, into everyone's business."

Hawk nodded. "Small world, ain't it? Oh." He suddenly pulled out the bottle. "Speakin' of which, we ran across another friend of yours, when we was asking around, to everybody about these questions. She said to ask you if you wanted your soul back. Ain't that something?" He put the green bottle on the table a little heavily. Latham half stood, and then quickly sat back down. Hawk noticed the reaction. The bottle had an unmistakable impact.

"You went to Papanuca?" Latham was barely able to gasp. "How...how did you get *this*?"

"It wasn't easy," said Hawk. "I had to kill a man for it."

"You had to kill? I could never...she would never have given it to me," Latham stammered.

"I was thinking you might like it back. As sort of a gift, for being so cooperative with the government, and all. Fact is, believe it or not, I ain't got much use for it. The witch thought I didn't have a soul, so she give it to me, but the joke was on her. I already got a damned good one."

Latham reached out with both hands and grabbed the bottle, as a man falling from a cliff might grab a rope. "Yes, yes, I will take it. Thank you. Thank you, this means a lot to me, actually. I know it must seem silly to you. It's sort of...sentimental reasons."

"That's awright, Reverend, you've filled in a lot of blank spots for us," said Hawk. He stood. "We probably ought to shove off. You've got stuff to do, and so do we. Time is money, as Mr. Canlon is always sayin'. I don't why, since he poops all his away—on gambling."

"You mean...that's all you wanted from me? That's all you came here for?" Hawk nodded, without speaking. His lips were tightly closed.

"That's about it, sir. It's a little more important than it looks."

"The Vuniwai didn't say anything about me? About this?" He held up the bottle.

"Oh, she said a lot of sh...stuff. We had to ignore a lot of that ignurnt talk, you know. This code thing can be a real time killer if you go listening to everybody's horse...manure."

"Yes. I understand. You are focused on your duty, of course, and not personal matters," said Latham, sighing with relief.

"You know"—Hawk nodded thoughtfully, rummaging for tobacco—"that's the honest to God's truth."

* * *

VERA WAS ESCORTED down the mud street of Papeete by Colonel Clark and Melvin Singer. The town had been shelled by the Germans in the First World War and had never fully recovered. Singer invited them to his favorite French café, where Singer understood they were to discuss some sort of war business. He had avoided the war, having seen all that he wanted of such matters in 1918. There was no step up to the wooden sidewalk, and Singer climbed the ramp constructed there. Clark followed, but Vera, younger and more adventurous, merely leaped up onto the porch. They climbed to the second story of the building as Singer regaled them with stories of the customs in Tahiti. Clark was glad that he had brought Vera along, as she listened attentively to these anecdotes, while he was free to tune them out. He spent most of his time staring at Vera. She looked her best when pretending to be interested in something.

Clark rejoined the conversation over dinner, however, bringing up the subject of the code, and laying the printed passage out before them on the candlelit table. The colonel's explanation was rather short, as he had grown weary of the subject of the code. It was left to Vera to fill in a few details. Although Singer was very bright and educated, he seemed to have difficulty understanding the workings of the whole matter. Perhaps, he wanted to know too much. While others had merely accepted the mysterious nature of the code, Singer wanted explanations. Of course, he would not get them. They finally arrived at the portion of the explanation that had made everyone, the bright and the not so bright, seem to understand what was required of them: the reading of the clue. What made this segment of the exercise a little more interesting was the fact that Singer may well not have been the subject of the clue at all. They only had the word of an addled witch doctor, insisting that Singer was the next in line. Clark had not received any confirmation of that designation from Hawk as of yet.

"And so, Mr. Singer, we will ask you this question, and you will identify the person that it reminds you of," said Clark, adjusting the paper in front of him.

"Very well," said Singer, flashing an exasperated but resigned smile at Vera.

"'Saved by the enemy's syringe,'" read Clark.

Singer nodded. "Yes, I know to whom that refers," he said right away. "I served in France in the First War with a man named Steven Jefferson. We had assaulted the German trenches when he was wounded. An awful affair, actually. I found a German syringe of morphine there, and waited with him for the medics. He was eternally grateful, but I'm not sure for what. I didn't do anything, really. Morphine doesn't keep you from dying."

"Interesting," said Clark. What interested him the most, and Vera, as well, was that the witch had been right. Vera also noticed that Hawk had been right, although this would have been beyond the powers of concession for Clark, had it even occurred to him. "Is this friend of yours still alive? We must contact him, of course."

"Yes," said Singer. "He is a meteorologist on an island south of New Zealand. Now, *there* is a solitary existence. I think the war did something to his mind. Way down there, on a barren rock in the middle of the ocean, nothing south of him but Antarctica. I get a letter from him now and then. As I said, he considered me a hero for some unknown reason. He even put me in for a medal, but nothing came of it. I heard a year or two ago that they were reviewing that, probably because I've become something of a celebrity. It would draw donations, you know, for our foundation."

"No doubt," said Clark. "Well deserved, too. We might put your radio to use with this information. It could expedite the process quite a bit."

"By all means, whatever has to be done," Singer agreed.

"Do we want to do that?" Vera asked. "I believe radio communication has been ruled out."

"Well," Clark coughed, "I meant with proper precautions and all. I wanted to contact Hawk and get him off his duff, you know. He should have been to Latham by now, and could check this one out. It's more relevant, than his traipsing about for nonsense. And you and I are so far away from this Jefferson to be of any use."

"Yes, well," Vera replied, "we can see what the situation is back in the Helvedes. I'm not sure the sergeant is any closer to Jefferson than we are, if the man is sitting on the South Pole."

Singer laughed. "Maybe not that far south. I don't want to give you the wrong impression. It just seems like it. I would say it's comparable in loneliness. I don't know how he is ever supplied down there. I'm sure he just does without for months. Several governments pay him for his weather reports, however, and he was always tight with a nickel."

The evening meal drew to a close, as Clark decided to check in with headquarters on Singer's radio. They returned with their host to his well-furnished tropical themed home on the beach. Torch light illuminated the outside. The colonel requested privacy as he contacted the base, while Vera entertained Singer in a nearby sitting room, set apart with bamboo walls. Clark came to the door several minutes later. He motioned Vera into the radio room.

"Excuse me, Mr. Singer, the war beckons," she said. Singer rose and remained standing until she left the room.

"Hawk contacted Latham. I suppose that's good," the colonel announced, upon her entering the room. "He must have found out that the information from Papanuca was correct. It's a good thing, too."

"Why, because of the time saved?" Vera asked.

"Yes, there's that. And something else. They've picked up a light cruiser, two destroyers and some Japanese troop ships headed for Salvation Island. They believe it's all part of the Helvedes campaign, but I suspect they're after Hawk. I feel certain now that they're trying to stop us from decoding the message. That's been the history of this thing. He and Latham could easily be killed by a force that size. You know how it is, catching them there by surprise and all. There could even be air support. We were very lucky on this one."

Vera blanched. "Uh...how are we *lucky*? That sounds awful."

"I mean to say, we don't need the information, or Latham for that matter. All is well. That was a close call."

"Bennie, I think we should be going," said Vera.

"No, no, the night is young, I think I'll have another little drinkie." The colonel laughed. Vera smiled, linked the colonel's arm with hers, and they returned to the sitting room where Melvin Singer waited.

"You have been enormously helpful, Mr. Singer. This information could advance the war effort. I'm afraid the colonel and I have to leave now," she said. "We've received some disturbing information regarding the current campaign in the Helvedes."

"Oh, no. I was just settling in for an evening of conversation. It's not often I have such a beautiful visitor." The torches flickered outside the window. Vera looked especially good by torch light.

"You are *too* kind," she said, "but it's sort of an emergency."

"Perhaps we could have another round," the colonel suggested.

"*Sort of an emergency*," Vera repeated.

* * *

HAWK REPLACED the headset on the radio. He had a strange frown on his face as he crouched next to the apparatus on the wet sand.

"So, is the guy on his way?" Joe Canlon asked, referring to the pilot of the Higgins boat. Several of the men stood behind the corporal on the beach, casually paying attention.

"No, the guy *ain't* on his way," said Hawk. "But the Jap fleet is. It's heading right for us. They said we just have to hold on, because the boat can't get through."

"What? The what? *Hold on to what*?" Joe exclaimed. "Is this gonna be the rest of my life? Everywhere I go, the all of damn Japan follows me."

"I don't know. But it looks like it did this time," Hawk answered. He looked at the crates of ammunition stacked on the beach where the Higgins boat crew had left them earlier. "I get the feeling not everybody was as surprised by this as we are," said Hawk. "Better go tell the preacher. He might want to say his prayers. And tell him to get the people as far away from the beach as he can. They'll probably shell it, way before they get here."

"I can't believe this, I just can't believe this. What about this top-secret information we have? Nobody cares about that?" Joe asked.

"I guess not. They didn't need it anyway. But we ain't got time to shoot the shit about it. Get the men to digging some holes, a hundred yards from the water-line. Break out them grenades and pass out every damn one of them. We're gonna be seeing a lot of ships out on the water pretty soon."

Joe paced in a circle, temporarily too overwhelmed to decide what to do first. Hawk repeated the orders to Baker and went to tell Latham himself. As he walked away, he heard Baker talking to the men and saw their concerned expressions. Hawk grew angry. As it turned out, they had all come here for no reason. This was a rotten place, and it was a rotten way to die.

As usual, things proceeded to get worse really fast. An aircraft appeared on the threatening gray horizon. It could only mean that the fleet would have air cover, and it would likely bombard the island. Aerial bombard-ment, naval gunfire support, and an all-out assault were minutes away. Twenty men on an open beach would be obliterated in seconds. Salvation Island had no interior. It was small, and vegetation was sparse, consisting of a few well spaced palm trees. The plane drew closer, and yet the enemy fleet had not appeared in the distance. It was a single plane, and judging by the high pitch of its engine, it was a mere spotter craft, sent to get a report on its prey.

Hawk searched the numerous crates resting in the

rising tide. He recalled seeing a machine gun in one of them. It would be nice to knock that little bastard out of the sky, even if they never got off another shot. But the plane swung in low and rapidly. Hawk shaded his eyes. The Catalina glided along, parallel to the beach before striking the water carefully and sliding by like an ice dancer. It turned around, cutting its engine and allowing the waves to push it closer to shore.

"Son of a bitch!" Hawk muttered. "That *stupid* woman." He turned to the men. "Get on the plane! Move it! On the plane! We ain't got time for horse shit!" A door swung open on the Catalina. Joe was the first aboard, reaching down to help the others climb in. Hawk ran into the church and found Latham there.

"Mr. Latham, you gotta come with us. The Japs are on the way. We just gotta flight outta here. Let's go," Hawk told him. Latham froze with shock.

"I...I can't leave here," he said. "My people are here."

"This is their island, not yours. You're leaving, if I have to tote you. Now, get moving." Hawk was not one to argue with, and Latham immediately sensed it. If he were able to put up a squawk, the sergeant might have left him. But one slap would end any argument or resistance.

"I'll have to get a few things," Latham said.

"You ain't gettin' shit. Last call. Are you going conscious or unconscious?"

"Yes. Very well," Latham followed him out to the water's edge. They waded out to the plane, the last two to clamber aboard.

Vera lounged patiently in the pilot's seat, limbs stretched out on the armrests. "I thought you were going down with the ship there for a minute, Captain," Vera said to Hawk as he closed the door.

"Yeah, so did I. Had trouble with this...fella. Good to see you, Vera."

"Do you love me now?"

"More than ever, baby," he growled. "Let's get the hell out of here."

The engines roared to life. Hawk swung to the back to look out over the ocean through the waist gunner's blister. The waves rolled in peacefully, rocking the plane. The horizon remained clear of ships. Perhaps it had all been a mistake. He had no intention of finding out. His horizons were about to expand.

* * *

Myrtle Thorpe returned home after a hard day, and part of a night, as a nurse at Bethesda Naval Hospital. Her ordeals with unsolvable medical problems did not end there, however. Myrtle enjoyed little peace or rest. Her mother, Beatrice, had been bed ridden and seriously ill for over a year now. Myrtle had been fortunate to find someone to care for Beatrice during her long hours of work in the cardiology unit. She was more than fortunate, in fact, because she found someone willing to watch over her mother for almost nothing. While taking advanced classes at nursing school, Myrtle had met young Setskuo Takemitsu, and the two immediately became friends.

Setsuko was not only an economical convenience for Myrtle, she was a talented nursing student, and had become a good friend and confidant. She confided in Myrtle about the death of her own dear mother back in

Japan, and the trying times toward the end. Although decades younger, Myrtle felt a bond with Setsuko. They talked openly about Myrtle's patients, and Myrtle was impressed with the medical knowledge, and genuine caring wisdom, that young Setsuko possessed. Myrtle was on the brink of asking the student for advice about a very serious professional dilemma she was having at work, but had not summoned the courage. Myrtle was the trusted assistant to Admiral Jones, head of cardiology, although Myrtle wasn't so sure he deserved that position. She had taken an oath of confidentiality administered by the United States government. Of course, she knew many of her colleagues who paid little attention to that, and gossiped to anyone who would listen. It did not seem quite right that an oath should protect Admiral Jones, when someone needed advice.

As the weeks wore on, Beatrice actually improved under the care of Setsuko. Myrtle had been advised by her mother's physicians that Beatrice would never get any better, and to prepare for the worst. And yet, every day, or night nowadays, when Myrtle returned home, Setsuko and Beatrice would be laughing and talking, and Beatrice looked more fit than ever. In fact, Beatrice was starting to look better than Myrtle. Myrtle was ready for a little bed rest herself.

"I don't know how you do it," Myrtle said to Setsuko. "You seem to have some magical power over her. She loves you." Myrtle leaned over confidentially. "And, so do I."

"She is responding to vitamins and Japanese herbs I have been giving her. I started out gradually, as I did not want to build up hope. But I think she will fully recover," said the girl. "I hope you are not angry with me. Some would not approve of this method."

"I should say not," said Myrtle. As a nurse, however, she wondered about this sudden revelation of a new treatment. Myrtle had been well trained in the infallible wisdom of doctors and the necessity for strict adherence to their every dictate. She had also witnessed the failure of this infallibility on too many occasions. She now took their pronouncements with a grain of salt. Patients often did better by *not* following medical advice, or doing the exact opposite. Myrtle never spoke such heresy to anyone else, it was merely a growing outlook she had developed.

"In medicine, my philosophy is to go with whatever works," said Myrtle. "It is more art than science."

"We agree on so many things," said Setsuko.

"Yes. And you are a great artist."

10

SHOWDOWN AT THE EARTH'S EDGE

HAWK STEPPED INTO THE OFFICE OF COLONEL CLARK. OF late, he had been dreading these meetings. The series of assignments Clark had been giving him had grown increasingly deadly. What began as an interesting departure from Hawk's dangerous routine had evolved into grappling with an even more dangerous and unpredictable routine, with unknown goals. Colonels were usually an inspiring presence to a fighting man on the front lines. Hawk had never had the pleasure of encountering Colonel Clark on a front line.

"It appears that the witch on Papanuca was right about that last name. I don't know how she did it," said Clark. "We didn't need that preacher, Latham, at all, as it turns out."

Hawk took some satisfaction from the colonel's admitting the witch was right, even if he would not admit that Hawk had been right. The opinion that Hawk's efforts had been unnecessary was nothing new, and only another unsurprising example of Clark's take on the matter. Clark's summation of the situation, as if it were now all his personal deduction, was an irritation that had become expected.

"I don't know how she did it either, sir. But I figured she was right. I figured she didn't just come up with a name like that out of thin air."

"Yes. Well, yes. Water under the bridge. Now, we have our next client. Got to move forward. I did save a little time by going to Tahiti, that was a stroke of genius. I can tell you, it was a long and trying journey," said the officer. Hawk had no good answer for that, so he said nothing. "I received the next entry from Singer. He was a quite intelligent fellow, and well respected in his field. A famous spokesperson, of sorts. It was probably better that I handled that one alone. It was a little more delicate, don't you know?"

"Yessir," said Hawk.

"The name he gave me is an old war buddy of his, a man about the same age, I suppose, named Steven Jefferson. It's strange how these people are scattered all over the Pacific. And I do mean, *all over*. This fellow is south of New Zealand, south of the Auckland Islands even. I don't know how these academic types get away with this foolishness in the middle of a war. No sense of duty whatsoever. You'll need a submarine to take your men there this time."

"A submarine?" Hawk noticed that it was taken for granted that he was going to this godforsaken place. "That's...uh...a little past the Helvedes, sir," the sergeant observed, with the intention of implying that it was not his sort of destination. To his way of thinking, it was a nice safe place for a colonel and Vera Orr to visit; maybe take a few photographs.

"I know what you mean. You better take your long

johns. Maybe you can see Antarctica, eh? Although, it says here the temperature is rather mild. Probably because it's summer. The islands are completely uninhabited and barren. The man has a weather station there. I think he's on the New Zealand payroll, I never got that part straight. Strange how a nut can find his calling, right?"

Yes, it is, Hawk thought.

"I probably shouldn't mention this." Clark leaned forward and lowered his voice. "But would you believe that the British have a base on Antarctica, to keep the strait at the tip of South America open? They say the Germans are there, too."

Hawk paid little attention to the news flash. He was more concerned about his own immediate future. "No, I missed that. All of these places were supposed to be uninhabited, sir. But we still got some pretty good reception committees everywhere we went."

"I've noticed that. I'm way ahead of you, of course. Now, to be precise, no one said that they were uninhabited, just unoccupied by the Japanese. Let me correct you there. This time, these southern islands are actually *uninhabited*, and likely *uninhabitable*. It's just a rock, the jumping off place for the end of the world. A place for penguins to breed, I would guess. One thing is for certain this time: you will *not* be bothered by Japanese down there, under any circumstances." The colonel shoved a large photograph across the table. "Here's Jefferson's meteorological station. They get some rough weather that far south, so he has this concrete bunker."

Hawk nodded. "Reminds me of that fort in Galveston. I guess they get typhoons. Does this fella have a radio, sir?"

"Indeed. But we are *not* putting the code on the air, if that's what you're asking."

"No, sir. I was just asking because a lot of things happen on these details. It's not such a good idea to be without radio contact. I mean, *a lot of things*, have happened."

"Know what you mean. But, you must realize, Sergeant, if these missions were easy we would be sending the Girl Scouts out to do them."

"Yessir." It seemed like the colonel used to refer to sending in the Boy Scouts. Hawk started to call that to his attention, but thought it better not to joke with the colonel. He didn't like him enough for that. He couldn't think of a way to work it into a joke anyway. "What I meant, sir, is that a radio can be used for a lot of things, besides broadcasting the code. Things like, say, rescue instructions. Those have kind of been going south on us here lately."

"Rescues aren't the mission, Sergeant. Let's not miss the point, and get sidetracked with minor details. That's how failure happens. We're seeing the light at the end of the tunnel, here," said the colonel. "We are about to solve this little riddle."

Hawk rubbed his nose. "I was looking at the code, sir. I had an idea that there might be more than one way to crack it. Maybe Hoech built in other ways to get to the answer," Hawk said. "It's kind of a feeling you get, the more you read it. And I've had a chance to read it a lot."

"Oh, probably," Clark huffed dismissively. "These code masters are always coming up with crap. But we've done it this way, and it's almost over. We've played it straight. So, no need to change horses in midstream, or try to get all fancy, so to speak."

"Yessir."

"The submarine leaves tomorrow."

* * *

A HEAVY HAND knocked on Vera Orr's thin door. It sounded as if a piece of wood had hit it. She opened it a few inches.

"You wanted to see me?" Sergeant Hawk stood outside, the fading lights of the base behind him, his features sharpened by the odd light, and his eyes shaded.

"Always. Come on in."

The curtains were tightly drawn and an oil lamp lit. On the windowsill, a scented candle burned. Vera Orr had left the camp early for her quarters on Greater Helvedes. Clark had assigned her a small, newly constructed, three-room wooden residence. It smelled like freshly cut lumber. She moved the drapery, looking timidly out the window, as Hawk crossed the room and sat down in her large, but only chair.

"The day is done and the darkness falls from the wings of night," she said as she turned from the curtain while closing it.

"Is that from the Bible?" Hawk asked, sitting at the table.

"Immediate recognition! A scholar!" she exclaimed. "Finally, someone to appreciate my erudition."

"Lady, I appreciate everything you got. I read shit. Speaking of which, look at this." He set the code on the table before him. He had made notes up and down the page itself, which was no doubt forbidden heresy in some government office.

"Wouldn't you like to unwind from your little scare?" she said, producing, and setting a new bottle of whiskey on the table. "I'll get a glass." He opened the bottle, his thumbnail cutting the seal as easily as a knife.

"Damn. How do you get all this stuff? I don't use glasses much." He tilted the bottle back.

"Uh...right. It looks like you don't use bottles much, either. People give me things. They like me. It's something that would be hard to explain to you."

"Starting kinda early with the low shots, ain't you?" He took another long drink. "Want a snort?"

"No, thanks. I'm the champagne type. That smells like an outstanding after shave lotion, though. I don't know why I'm so crazy about you. I keep expecting the great reveal: to find out that you're actually a hooved animal they shaved because they were a man short."

"Another good one. Hey, listen, did you ever notice that all of these things in the code have a certain number of words in them?" He tapped the code sheet.

"Lover, everything has a certain number of words in it," she said. "Education is an amazing thing, isn't it?"

"No, dammit, look. Each one has three, four, five or six words. That could mean something," he said. "Why would that be? Hoech was telling us something. He could have made the clues any length, but he didn't. They're all three to six words. Get it?"

"Iambic pentameter?" She smiled. "An imitation of the Jesus prayer? Actually, it just means he was keeping the clues short."

"No, look. It's like this *thing*. I forget what you call it, when things match up. See, if you count the words, in order, it's four for Clark, four for me, five for you, three, three, six, six, five, five, four, four. And it's eleven people.

That means something. He showed her where he had written the numbers down."

"My heart flutters as I watch the inscrutable Mr. Moto at work. Will I ever have such a learning experience again? You are saying it's a *pattern*, or a *sequence*? Is that the big ol' word that was stumping you?" She picked up the paper. "I don't think you're supposed to be writing your A, B, C's on this official government document, Baby Snookums."

"Yeah, it's a *pattern*. That ain't exactly the word, but that's the right idea. There's a shortcut in there, I tell you. Hoech put a way in here to figure it all out," he said. "On paper."

"You are *sooo* smart."

"And by that you mean you don't think so, right? I'm talking about the shortcut, I already got the message about the me being smart part." He looked around. "Hey, get another bottle of that shit."

"No, I don't think there's a shortcut. The codebreakers would have seen that, right off. That's the first thing they look for. Like that opening line at the beginning: 'Helvedes coordinates'? What does that mean? They've decided it doesn't mean anything. If you look up the coordinates, latitude and so forth, the numbers are just random and don't signify anything. It's a dead end they put into codes, sometimes. To slow you down. To throw off the gullible? Ever hear that word?" She sat on the table beside him. "I will admit that it's fascinating how Hoech knew all of these emotionally charged little catch phrases, obscured in intimacy, that meant so much to each of these people that they instantly recognized them; and then, was even able to combine them. How could he do that? Frankly, it seems more devious than ingenious."

Hawk shrugged. "There was a time I would have told you that it's over my head. I've had to get past that. Kind of like when you take the engine out of your car. You gotta get past giving up on putting it back together, or you ain't going nowhere."

"Why do you care so much about this? I've never seen you care about anything, unless you could eat it or drink it. Or kill it."

"Well, hell. People *are* getting killed over this stupid shit. And more will be, the way it's going. *Somebody* should put a little thought into it." He guzzled the last of the bottle. "It's all a kid's game, until people get killed, see? It's like poker. It's just a game, till you're bettin' the rent on it." Another bottle stood at attention nearby. "The way we're doing it, all of this is kind of for nothing, until you get to the last person."

"Baby, they have dozens of experts all over the world putting more than a little thought into this code. Rooms full. They'll figure out what it means. All you have to do is give them the names," she said. "Be satisfied that you had an important part in it all. Believe me, it's a part that no one else could do, or wants to do. Consider that maybe, just maybe, *you* can't do *their* part, either?"

"Yeah, but they ain't gettin' shot at. You think a lot faster when a bullet's chasing you. And you're surrounded, and trapped, and drowned, and burying people...and every other kind of no good shit."

"Now, don't worry, we're getting close to the answer. Where are we? About three names from the end? How many were there to start with, a dozen? Things are looking up. Relax. It's all velvet from here. They'll probably have the experts dealing with the ones at the end. These are the big ones that explain it all. You're almost through with it. Just put your little bullets in your gun and settle back. Which reminds me. Did I ever tell you that you're the velvet in my life?" She leaned over and looked into his eyes.

"No, I don't think you have."

"Well, you are. I risked my life for you, you know? And I don't recall any mention of where I rank in your life."

"You're pretty high up there, that's for sure. Don't ever do nothing like that again. That was ignorant. I can take care of myself." He waved an increasingly uncoordinated hand at her. "I wonder if they'll tell us how this code message thing ends. Or, one day, will it just be: so long, suckers. You mean to tell me you don't think the Hoech guy put a shortcut in it? A way to get around all this trouble? He writes this stuff for studious types sitting around desks...in code rooms...not people like me. I think the route we're taking, going after all these people, was meant to make the Japs chase around—not us."

"You know, on second thought, that's almost insightful. You may be onto something. Maybe he did. Maybe he put more than one other way to do it. And you're right, the Japs *are* chasing you around. But I'll tell you what I would be checking out, instead of arithmetic problems," she said.

He put an arm around her and pulled her off the table. "What? You?" It felt as if a hydraulic machine had picked her up.

"Definitely. No, I would be figuring out how the voodoo queen knew what she knew. Did she sit around the kitchen table adding up the numbers on dominoes, like you're doing? Or did somebody tell her something? We may have let that part of it go too easily. Here's this illiterate woman, in the middle of the ocean..."

"Yeah, that's a fact. I done told you that. I think she's got the magic from uptown hell. Like you." He kissed her for a long time.

"Oh, boy. Let me go. I have another present for you."

"Yeah? Is it an autographed picture of Clark?"

She walked across the room and opened a drawer. "No, I would never let that go." She took a small object out of the drawer and tossed it at him. He slapped it down with a one-handed grab. "I believe it's your brand: Old Dog Manure?"

He held up his hand to find a block of chewing tobacco there. "Damn sure is. This is good stuff. It ain't what the government gives us. Where in the hell did you get this?"

"I get around."

"You sure do. Too damn much."

"Let's don't try to tick anybody off now, for no reason. When things are going so smoothly."

"You're right. I forgot the low blows are a one-way street." He began tearing at the wrapper.

"Whoa, whoa, mister. And that means that crap," she added, waving a hand at the tobacco. "You can put that away for your trip to Antarctica. None of that fool-ishness in here." She walked back to him and sat on his lap. "You know, you won't have anybody looking out for you down there in the frozen south: a guardian angel, like me. I don't like that. You're so stupid. *Really*...stupid. You remind me of—a dog. A really stupid dog."

"Ah," he muttered groggily.

"It's true. You'll have no one to think for you. By the way, that poem was not from the Bible. I don't want you going around a Jap prison camp sounding even dumber than you are. They'll probably be all over this awful place that you're going."

"Well, that's the best part. There won't be *anybody* in this place, period. It's too far off the beaten path." He looked thoughtfully again at the code. "Just me and the polar bears," he said under his breath. HIs thoughtful look changed into a cloudy emptiness. "Tell me something..." His head dropped, he mumbled, "God," and he fell asleep in the chair.

* * *

THE SURFACE TEMPERATURE may not have been freezing, as the map of the southern climates indicated that it should be, but the water temperature was frigid enough and it was cold enough on the submarine. The patrol had not been issued long johns, as Clark had suggested, but they were requisitioned an extra set of their light jackets. The boat, departing from Brisbane, was able to sail on the surface the entire trip. There had been little enemy activity in the vast waters to the south. The last sighting of an enemy submarine, in fact, had been that of a German U-boat.

Joe Canlon, long advocating for an overdue trip to Australia, finally got his wish—if only for a few hours. The plane trip down from the Helvedes had been uneventful. The skies had been thinned of Japanese planes south of New Guinea. During the lazy sea excursion even farther southward, the Marines were allowed to climb up to the deck of the underwater boat to see the whales enjoying their lonesome playground, and to see isolated and thin patches of ice float by. They were assured that there would be no icebergs, although that night, they could possibly see the electric wizardry of the polar lights in the sky, the Aurora Australis. They were assured that this was a memorable experience, in case they didn't think they had a few others ahead of them.

Hawk clung to the wavering cable line serving as a railing on the deck and looked out upon the empty wasteland of water rising and falling beneath him. The cool, strong ocean wind blew his hair askew, and sliced into his squinting eyes. The endless, bluish-purple water looked deadly. He had seen miles of the Pacific, but nothing of this color or brooding texture.

"God!" was all that he could say, possibly with the emphasis that Magellan himself might have used. He hoped that these eerie, newcomer types of observations and feelings were to be the worst part of the mission. And yet, there was a bad feeling to it all, one that he was going deep into something terrible. He had also noticed a now familiar sight in the cargo hold: crates of ammunition, grenades, and a machine gun. He was guaranteed this was merely standard operating procedure; as he had been assured on Salvation Island, where he nearly met the Japanese fleet head on. He was not naïve enough to believe that the cargo was there to keep the more aggressive penguins away.

When it seemed as if they would never stop sailing south, the submarine finally sighted its destination: Pricekeep Island, the home of Steven Jefferson. The brown rock, perching atop the ice-blue ocean, made a poor first impression. It contained a few stunted trees and hardy shrubs, with a fair covering of tough grasses. But most of the ground was bare, grim, rock and gravel. The cold sky above the land pressed downward, gray and unfriendly. Though one would expect pristine views of endless clear air and blue ocean, the sky was not clear. It was a foggy mass of ugly floating cotton balls, rimmed in brown.

"This looks like hell," said Joe. "They aren't going to leave us here, are they?" He well remembered the sudden departures of the Higgins boat pilots.

"No." Hawk spat thoughtfully into the ocean. "They said they would hang around. They brought this weatherman his mail and some supplies. They got stuff to keep them busy for a couple hours. They ain't supposed to go runnin' off this time."

"Do we have to unload all that shit in the cargo room, just to be here a few minutes?"

"No, we're just going to get this over with. The Jefferson fella is expecting us, he just doesn't know why we're here." Hawk stretched. Perhaps the journey had been the worst part of this. What could go wrong? Who in creation would be careless enough to come here, other than Steven Jefferson, or James Hawk?

"We can keep our ass on the ship, too, then, right?" Joe asked. "While you're doing your shit with the guy?"

"No, shit no. That ain't in the deal. We gotta parade in there like MacArthur. This is government business."

"Government business." Joe lifted his rifle. "This is our only business. Where is this asshole? I don't see nothing but birds. Hey, and seals! Or something. What are them things? Is that a building up on that hill?"

"Yeah, he's got a weather station, to get in outta the

rain. Some kind of storm proof thing. They must get some pretty good blows here."

"Looks like it. Looks damn solid."

The captain of the submarine had the inflatable LCRs tossed into the water. Each held ten men. Hawk and Joe were the last to board them. Everyone was armed, with the ammunition they could carry. Marines had a habit of carrying a lot of ammunition, because they also had a habit of using it. Hawk was going to be prepared, but not to the degree that it became burdensome. They quickly paddled ashore, the freezing water broadcasting its inhospitable temperature through the thin bottoms of the boats. As predicted, however, the temperature ashore felt no worse than the high forties or low fifties degree mark. Nevertheless, it was a good deal cooler than the blood of the Marines had been accustomed to.

They climbed out onto the sharp, clean and untrod gravel of a narrow beach, avoiding any wading or wet feet. Hawk led the way up the slope toward the castle-like weather station. A wind velocity gauge spun on the top of it.

"Watch him shoot our ass," said Joe.

Hawk said nothing. He supposed it was possible that the lone man here kept a pistol, to kill himself with. Hawk did not want to jinx the expedition by saying good or ill of any of it. He only wanted to move it along, and leave this place behind, on memory lane. As he came to the base of the structure, he noted that most of the concrete was buried beneath the ground. It had a thick roof set atop huge pilings, and a narrow view space about a foot to two feet high, all the way around, just above ground. Hawk bent over to peer inside the brooding monolith. It looked rather dark within, although he could see light on the far side. He supposed the blockhouse was hexagonal, or of a similar geometrical shape. He could not see all the way around it.

"I guess the guy ain't home," said Joe.

"I don't see him. Or anything," Hawk answered.

"Maybe he's out chasing the chicks," said Joe.

"Maybe," Hawk answered, going to one knee to get a better look inside. "Or the seals."

A seal barked in the background.

"Anybody home!" Hawk called.

A chorus of seals barked. Several of the men laughed.

"Ahoy!" a voice called from a distance.

More seals responded. It sounded as if the man was on the far side of the edifice. Hawk motioned for the men to follow him as he circled the building. Several stepped up on the flat top of the massive stone fortress, stomping on it, as if testing it, for no particular reason. They were young, and perhaps they thought it a good place for a jitterbug contest.

Before he got to the other side, Hawk saw a middle-aged man with a salt and pepper beard wearing a heavy coat approaching him. "I think we found our guy," Joe said in a low voice. "The weatherman."

"Hey there," Hawk called and waved. "Mr. Jefferson?"

"That is my name. Who do I have the pleasure of meeting here?" The man called breathlessly, obviously surprised, and excited.

"Sergeant James Hawk, US Marine Corps. Pleased to meet you, sir," he greeted the man, as he climbed around the jumble of rocks. They finally reached one another and shook hands.

"I had no idea that an entire army was coming to see me," said Jefferson. "I don't have much food. Or water, or anything, you know?"

"Oh, yeah. We know," said Hawk. "We don't need nothing. We brought you some supplies, and I think they said they even got your mail and stuff. Some scientific equipment, or something. How you been?"

"Wonderful. Just wonderful. I love it here—my home, you know. It's rather lonely, though. I've forgotten how to talk, much less converse, I'm afraid. I never was one to talk to myself, so I'm really out of practice. It's been...let's see...three months since a ship stopped by."

"Damn. You got a lot of time to kill, I reckon," said the sergeant.

"Oh, I stay busy," Jefferson answered, waving at the sky. "There's always the weather, you know."

"Ain't that the truth?" Hawk agreed. There was a pause. "If you got a place in outta the wind, we gotta a couple questions for you, sir." The wind was rather high, and they were fairly screaming at one another.

"Oh, sure. That's one thing I do have. A two hundred mile an hour wind couldn't get in there." Jefferson walked toward a rear opening to his weather station. It had a labyrinth concrete entrance, concealing the interior, without any sort of door that could be closed. All of the men filed inside to get out of the gale. While it was not freezing cold, the hard wind blasting across the bare stone of the earth left the atmosphere on the verge of uncomfortable.

"I'm sorry I don't have chairs for everyone. Or

anyone, actually," said Jefferson. "There's only myself here, of course."

"That's fine," Hawk said, and turned to Joe. "Watch the front and back," he told the corporal beneath his breath.

"What for?"

"You goddam..."

"Okay, okay," said Joe. He sent Baker and Blackwell back outside to watch the beach and the wastelands. Hawk walked to the edge of the large open room and looked out of the wide, open portals, across the island, and to the ocean beyond. The thick, reinforced ceiling lay just inches above his head.

"It must get nippy in this icebox at night," said Hawk, noticing that he could still feel the wind whipping across the ground outside, and swirling, wet and biting, inside.

"Oh, there are quarters below," said Jefferson. "It's quite comfortable down there." He pointed to a concrete stairway leading down into the earth. "I've even built a fire up here on the concrete for sport," he added. "You do a lot of things when you have the time."

"I imagine so." Hawk got to the point. "The reason we're here has to do with a military code we've picked up out of Japan. We're trying to figure out what it means. It's these groups of words that identify certain people, but only certain other people know who they are. Your name was on the list, and we think you can identify the next person for us."

"I see," said Jefferson. "That seems strange to me."

Hawk nodded. Good reaction. "Yessir, and to a lot of other people. It's been getting stranger all the time. The last person, the one that gave us your name, was Mr.

Melvin Singer. He said y'all had been in the war together. And all."

"My goodness! Melvin Singer! My old friend. My dear, dear old friend. And I suppose then I am to name yet another friend of ours?"

"Yessir. But it don't have to be no friend. It's just somebody that you, yourself, know."

"Melvin Singer. Imagine that. I wouldn't mind seeing him again. How is he? He's like a brother. Is he still in Samoa?"

"I believe it was Tahiti, sir."

"Ah, yes. Tahiti. My mistake. Like a brother. He's been there for years, you know. I have to get up there sometime. To the frozen northlands of Polynesia."

"Yeah. Folks need to get together," said Hawk, who had never gotten together with anyone for any reason. "Maybe for Christmas or something, y'all could do something. So...here...what I'll do is read this line to you off the paper and then you tell me who the line of words is talking about." Hawk reached within his jacket and pulled out the paper.

"Yes. Yes, indeed. Ready." Jefferson had an expectant half smile on his face. This was the most excitement he had experienced in years. He seemed to understand and like the game, which made him somewhat unique in this endless process. Hawk glanced twice at the child-like expression. Yep, *the fella's lost his marbles, stuck out here. If, he ever had any.*

"It...uh...says here, 'robber messenger of the sea.'" Hawk folded the paper up and returned it to his pocket. Jefferson continued staring at him with the same expression.

"That's *it*?" Jefferson asked.

Hawk nodded.

"That doesn't sound like any of *my* friends."

Hawk cleared his throat. "No, sir. It don't have to be a friend. It could be anybody you know, or even heard of, I guess." Hawk took off his helmet. He seriously doubted Jefferson had any friends.

"That doesn't sound like anyone I would know."

Hawk shuffled and took the paper out again. "I probably done read it too fast." He read it again. Jefferson slowly shook his head back and forth.

"No, doesn't ring a bell."

Hawk stood dumbfounded. Everyone else had answered their clues with immediate recognition. Their eyes had lit up, some even laughed warmly. Not this guy. Hawk did not know how to react to this response.

"Doesn't ring a bell?"

"Doesn't ring a bell."

Hawk read it again. Joe Canlon came and looked over his shoulder.

"That's what it says, all right," said Joe. Hawk looked at him. "I thought maybe you skipped one or something," said Joe. "The man said it doesn't ring a bell."

"I heard what the man said," Hawk replied.

"Give him a minute. Sometimes you have to think about this stuff, I guess," said the sergeant.

"You think about that one, sir," Hawk suggested.

What would he do if he did not receive an answer? End of the line? There were no instructions on that score.

As they discussed the clue, Baker came back inside and signaled Canlon. Joe walked over and spoke briefly with Baker. Joe returned to Hawk's side.

"Something came up. You want to come outside a minute?" Joe said.

"Now? We're kind of in the middle of something important here."

"Yeah," said Joe.

"Yeah, okay. You just relax and think on that, Mr. Jefferson. I'll be right back," said Hawk. "A penguin is chasing somebody or something." Hawk followed Joe and Baker outside, and around to the front of the bunker. There on the beach he saw stacks of crates. His now familiar ammunition, grenades and machine gun had been unloaded. The submarine no longer lay at anchor offshore.

"Uh...what in the hell?" Hawk walked down the slope toward the abandoned supplies.

"This was nailed on one of the boxes," said Baker, handing him a sheet of paper.

Hawk read: "Enemy ships approaching from east. Could not locate you. Seeking deeper water. Will return at earliest convenience." He handed it to Joe. Joe read it and slapped his thigh with the crumpled page.

"They did it again! They followed us *again*. To the end of the world. From the east? Where were they? South America?" Joe paced around the supplies. "They dumped the guy's shit here, too, along with ours."

"Did they have to run off?" Baker asked. "They took the time to unload all this shit and they couldn't just come get us?"

"Could not locate you," Hawk repeated the words on the note. "I told you bastards to be watchin'. Sounds to me like they just wanted to get the hell out of here." The sergeant looked over the crates. "They may have wanted to get a shot at the Japs before they get here," Hawk said, trying to give the submarine commander every benefit of the doubt. "Maybe he can stop them, or lead them away from us."

"I think I would rather take my chances on the sub than being stuck here," said Joe.

"Yeah, except for one thing. We *are* stuck here," said Hawk. "We ain't got no answer yet from the cross-eyed weather man. If he had just answered the goddam question, we would be gone by now."

"You know damn good and well he knows what you're talking about," said Joe. "I can tell he knows. He just wants company or something. He's gonna get it, too, real soon. Let's beat it out of him. *Doesn't ring a bell?* He needs his stupid bell rung."

"I don't know what his deal is." Hawk paced back and forth. "Get the men out here and get this shit inside. I wish I knew what the boat was doing. He didn't actually say they left us for good. I gotta figure they'll be back soon."

"Yeah, they just unloaded all these boxes for the exercise," said Baker. "So, they can come back and load them again."

"I don't know. They wanted to deliver the guy's stuff, and maybe they just threw ours in with it because it was sitting on top," said Hawk. "Who knows what the shitbag was thinking. He wanted out of here. I wonder if that's the same bunch of Japs that followed us to Salvation. What was that, a cruiser and two destroyers? That's a *lot* of shit. And there ain't no Battle of the Helvedes here. Those bastards came here just for us."

"A nightmare. This is a nightmare," said Joe.

"Pretty much," Baker agreed. "It says, 'could not locate you'? On a two-foot-long rock? With one goddam building on it? What was he looking for, a sign with an address?"

They had just enough time to get their supplies under cover. Though several lookouts watched the horizon, no one had seen any approaching ships.

A 4.7 inch shell from a naval gun weighs fifty pounds. The men on Pricekeep Island never saw it coming, as it was fired from a destroyer eight miles away. They didn't hear it being fired either, as the sound had not yet arrived. Fortunately, although the blast was terrifying, the accuracy of the unseen assault left a lot to be desired. The explosion struck the far side of the island, causing the ground to shake and killing a number of seals. The gun fired fifteen rounds a minute, crossing the island diagonally, covering it in smoke and rock dust, and leaving it vibrating like a tuning fork. None of the rounds struck the weather station, leaving its massive roof untested. With a fleeting look out the front portal, Hawk saw the horizon flashing madly as the bombardment increased to full capacity. The men descended below, while the earth, and the structure itself, rose and fell under the impact of dozens of shells. Even below ground, the men were shaken like dice in a cup. The top floor was filled with choking smoke and dust. A door on the single landing of the stairway was closed to keep the fuming miasma outside. After an hour, the shelling stopped. Pulling protective cigar butts out of his ears, Hawk rushed up the stairs to see if the enemy had advanced on the island.

When he reached the top floor, a last convulsive salvo erupted from afar. The sky outside went black. Hawk flattened on the floor, realizing that he had prematurely climbed to the outer level. A silver sheet of shrapnel, lit by red flame, came in a straight cutting scythe through the openings on all sides, just above his body. The world outside succumbed to illumination by a searing, lightning-colored whiteness. The bunker rose and fell under the shock of the blast. A moment later, he raised his head to see the sharp, triangular pieces of smoking steel embedded in the concrete walls in a hundred places. Chunks of sizzling metal fell out of the walls and from the ceiling, where they had failed to stick, some landing only inches from his face.

"Shit." He rose again, and went to the wall in a crouch, to look outside.

The swirling smoke covered the beach and all points between the ocean and the bunker, reducing visibility to only a few feet. Hawk announced to the men below that he was going outside, to the beach, to see if anything could be seen on the ocean. He hoped that the wind and open spaces above the pounding waves had caused the smoke to dissipate out there. Stepping out into the alien world of devastation, the first thing he saw was a deep gash carved along the heavy roof, where a shell had skidded across it.

Running forward, through the ringing mist, he avoided craters gouged by the naval shells, scattered in a moonscape across the island. Shrubs and splintered trees still flamed from the igniting explosions. A black lid of lingering gunpowder pressed low, hiding the sky, and it was painful to breathe in the sulfurous atmosphere. He reached the beach, and visibility immediately improved. The shelling had not affected the ocean. The view from here was no more comforting, however. He could see a dozen or more diesel-powered landing barges rushing toward the island, with white wakes like tails behind them. About fifty feet long, they could hold one or two platoons each. Widely spaced in an arc before him, there was no indication that the barges were limited to the area of his sight on the gray horizon. The Japanese could well be landing on every inch of the beach, all around the island. The Americans were, without a doubt, surrounded. Other than observing the gut-wrenching horror of it, he could do little else but return rapidly to the blockhouse.

When he returned, the men had again climbed up into the ground floor room. They peered out the openings on all sides at the devastation caused by the shelling, leaning on the thick concrete pilings that supported the slab of a roof above them. Some knocked away the sharp pieces of metal jutting from the walls. The shrapnel remained scalding to the touch. The blasts had peppered the walls with small rocks and even wooden sticks jutted out, driven into the concrete like arrows by the enormous force.

"They're landing," Hawk announced. "They got us surrounded. Let's get spaced out here, all around the perimeter of the wall. About ten feet apart. Without that shelling, we can give them a good fight," he said.

"What about the door?" Joe Canon asked. "We ain't got no goddam door on that rear opening. You turn a corner and you're inside."

"Yeah, see if you can get some rocks outside to block it. Don't go too far and get lost. We can use the crates, or the shit in here, if we have to," Hawk replied. He walked to the labyrinth entrance to oversee the stacking of the barricade. "Osage, bust open that machine gun."

"At least they can't shell us any more if they're landing," said Joe, carrying in a massive stone and dropping it on the floor.

"Goddam Japs can do anything," Hawk answered. "You think they give a shit?"

Hawk heard a series of thumps. The men looked at one another. Everyone knew what the loud knocking meant. Seconds later, mortar rounds exploded along the front of the bunker, tossing in more dirt and smoke. The men ducked along the walls, and under any slashing metal. The Japanese weapons units had already assembled on the beach. Another round of explosions hit closer, right up against the open portal in the rear, and onto the roof itself. The explosions were not as powerful as those from the naval guns but were sufficiently deadly. Hawk felt certain, however, that mortars would not crack the thick roof. He had not been as confident about the 4.7-inch shells from the destroyer. It grew difficult to breathe in the increasing clouds of curling smoke and dust.

"Better get down in your bunk below," Hawk told Jefferson. "It's gonna be gettin' kind of bad up here. We might be down there with you pretty soon." Jefferson needed no encouragement. He ran in a crouch for the stairway and the safety below.

"When those mortars stop, they'll come running on up in here," Hawk called out. He helped Baker and Osage set up the thirty-caliber machine gun, pointing it from the front of the bunker. The tables were turned for Hawk and most of the Marines there. It had usually been the Americans who were attacking defensive Japanese pillboxes after a landing. The lack of mobility, and facing superior numbers, gave the Marines a new appreciation for what the Japanese had to contend with during the island campaigns.

Between the mortar explosions, Hawk looked out to see if the enemy approached. The Japanese would have to advance up a gently rising slope to get to the bunker. The weather station had been as well constructed as a military installation as it had been for a refuge from arctic storms.

"Aw'ight," he called out, pulling back the bolt on the Thompson. "There they are. The mortars will stop. Let's cut the son of bitches down. Plenty of targets, you can't miss. Fire at will."

Joe rose to a knee and looked over the wall. He saw dozens of helmeted soldiers darting from crater to stone outcropping, as they climbed up toward him. Some flattened out on the cold ground for a few seconds, before proceeding up. His gullet constricted with raw fear. He was not looking at approaching humans, he was looking at a tide of death rising toward him. He picked a target, an advancing man bolder than the rest, who had never sought cover of any sort. Joe squeezed the trigger of his MI and the man dropped like a bag of garbage, draped across a high, pointed stone. That was the beginning of the small arms fire. The Japanese immediately responded, returning a concentrated volley directed at the position of Joe Canlon. He ducked behind the wall as the raging bullets bounced off the front of the blockhouse, or entered it just above his head. Ricochets sang across the room, ping-ponging from one wall to the next. The advance halted about halfway up the hill on the way toward the Marine position, as the opposing forces traded shots on all sides of the reinforced concrete building.

"Hurry up with the gun," Hawk shouted to Osage. "Blackwell, feed the belt."

"They're coming up the rear. Fast," Murdoch said, firing from the side opposite the beach. Hawk ran to have a look. It looked as if there were twice as many soldiers attacking the rear as were massed in the front. The crate of grenades, each in their cardboard packing, lay open next to Murdoch. It was almost impossible to throw them because of the low ceiling. The wall of the bunker was sunken to almost ground level. A well aimed and powerfully thrown side arm pitch could thread the needle between the top of the wall and the slab overhead, thereby reaching the outside. This was asking a lot of a timed bomb, however, that could kill them all if it accidentally snagged the wall or the ceiling and fell inside. The Americans' best defense for the moment was their automatic weapons, as several carried M3 grease guns. The limited range for these was ideal, as they were soon to be face to face with the attackers.

The automatic fire reached a feverish level as the Japanese closed in on the fortress. The Americans fell into a panic in the effort to keep the enemy away. The chattering roar and its echo in the closed concrete container went beyond deafening. The bodies of the enemy lay strewn up and down the hillside, and yet they continued forward. Hawk pulled a grenade out of the crate and shook the packing loose. He crouched beneath the protection of the wall, pulled the pin, and leaped into the opening, whipping the grenade through it as hard as he could, with his arm almost entirely within the opening to prevent any mishap. Standing back even a few inches from the window risked banging the grenade against the overhead. The pineapple swirled far down the hill, exploding in the ranks of the charging enemy.

Hawk fell to a knee, guiding the spewing Thompson back and forth across the oncoming horde. He saw only the tops of helmets, but it was enough for devastating accuracy. The bodies fell close around the blockhouse's open sides. Among the roar of weapons, an even louder roar was discernible in the area of the doorless rear entrance. Hawk crawled under the lightning trajectories of the fire slashing across the upper area of the building to check the doorway. Marchand and Joe were firing hysterically at a dozen of the enemy trying to breach the doorway barricade—more intent upon the output of their shots rather than the accuracy. Hawk tossed a grenade just outside the opening, sweeping all of those outside away with the single blast.

As the sound of the grenade died away, the firing almost came to a complete stop everywhere. The charge had ended as suddenly as it began. When Hawk looked outside, he saw no one retreating. He could only surmise that the defenders had dispatched all of the attackers. Joe stood beside him, looking out from beneath the low, concrete slab ceiling. The smoke from the naval fire had cleared, and they could see the ocean. The silhouettes of two darkly menacing ships floated a mile or two out on the cold blue and distant water.

"Did we stop them?" Joe asked breathlessly.

As he spoke, a bloody hand and arm flashed from the roof above them and a round ceramic grenade crashed into his helmet. Hawk reflexively swung at the arm, latching onto it, and pulling the Japanese soldier down and through the window as if he weighed nothing. Joe tossed the grenade back outside, where it failed to detonate. Hawk stomped the Japanese soldier twice in the chest with his boot, as if the man were a misbehaving reptile. As the man groaned and tried to roll away, the Thompson flew from Hawk's shoulder and he fired a three-round burst into the retreating soldier's head, splattering more sticky gore to be tracked underfoot on the hard surface.

"Son of a bitches might be on the roof," Hawk said. "I'll go look." He climbed over the barricade in the doorway and left the building, to return shortly. "No, that was the only one. There's about a hundred and something of them dead out there, though."

"I'm afraid there's more live ones somewhere," said Joe.

As they spoke, the two ships floated peacefully in the background, between, and far behind them. A flash erupted from the middle of one, and black smoke rose above it. A secondary explosion flickered near the bow. Neither Joe nor the sergeant had seen it occur. Seconds later, the rumbling thunder of the blast reached them, and they turned simultaneously toward the ocean to see what had happened.

"Shit!" Joe exclaimed. "That Jap ship blew up!"

Hawk slung the Thompson, fascinated by the sight. "That must be our submarine. They got him with a torpedo," he said.

"Reminds me of Guadalcanal. That's the last time I seen a ship get hit like that," said Joe. "Did you hear that shit? I hope it goes down fast and they hit that ice water."

"Yeah. That looks pretty damn good," said Hawk. "Goddam son of bitches."

"Uh oh," said Joe, nudging Hawk. "Look." He gestured toward the beach. More of the enemy troops were massing and climbing upward. Arms and legs were moving feverishly around, like the limbs in a disturbed nest of insects.

"Where the hell did *they* come from?" Hawk unslung the submachine gun. "I gotta get some ammo. Did you see any landing craft? Where did they come from?"

"Shit, I wasn't looking, but there they are." Joe shook his head. "A lot of them."

"Get to the wall," Hawk ordered the others. "They're back. We stopped them before, we'll do it again. Don't throw a grenade unless you're standing right there against the wall in the opening. Be damn sure what you're doing. We don't want them things bouncing back in here. One mistake blows us all to hell."

"And don't let them get too close this time," said Joe. "They got grenades, too." A mortar round hit the roof, shaking the structure, and shooting white dust through the portals. Two more exploded outside, sending shrapnel flying across the room. The men flattened on the filth strewn floor and crawled to the walls. The enemy outside broke out with piercing screams as they launched their attack. The animalistic howls froze the nerves of the defenders. The words of the Japanese were incomprehensible, if they were words.

Osage opened up with the machine gun, swinging it back and forth at the advancing climbers. Blackwell broke open another crate of ammunition for the gun and draped himself with belts of it. The gun shook and jumped as the young gunner pressed the trigger constantly, in violation of all training and common sense. The steady fire signaled to the enemy where the thirty caliber weapon was located, and drew their fire and grenade throws. Osage never slowed, however, as line after line of the Japanese fell under the relentless stream of lead. Smoke rose from the perforated barrel and it glowed a fiery metallic color.

After the onslaught began, Hawk slowed his fire, picking his targets more carefully. He moved around the perimeter of the walls, to assess the assault as it progressed along all fronts. Marchand called for help in the entranceway, and Hawk ended up there, battling the greatest pressure from without.

"Getting closer over here," Joe shouted from the front of the blockhouse. He grabbed a grenade and slung it out toward the grimacing enemy charging upward, only a few feet from him, with their long, fixed bayonets. The most threatening group disappeared in the blast, and Joe rose to fire into those still advancing behind them. They seemed impossible to stop.

The Japanese jumped and stumbled over one another trying to get through the barricaded entrance-way. One would occasionally vault over the rest and be cut to pieces by the Marines guarding the doorway. Hawk changed magazines and fired it into the ceaseless outpouring of humanity. They dropped back for only seconds, and he had to change it again. He knew that the submachine gun could jam any minute now, it had been reliable for far too long. Marchand fired his semi-automatic M1 with greater care, picking his targets as they burst to the forefront of the pressing mob. Hawk had lost track of what was going on behind him as he became preoccupied with the overwhelming force at the doorway and labyrinth lobby. The Japanese climbed through the window on one side, driving the Americans toward the middle of the room.

Hawk glanced behind himself to observe the dire situation that had developed. The distraction was long enough for the enemy to surge savagely through the entrance and over the barricade. Unable to fire, he swung the Thompson ferociously at them, beating them back over the pile of rocks blocking the entrance.

"We gotta pull back, and go down in the hold," he told Marchand. The two backed away firing, and the enemy flooded in, stepping on and ignoring the dead men falling before the defensive fusillade.

"Into the hold!" Hawk shouted at the others in the main room as the enemy breached another side. His men were grouped in the middle of the room, around the stairway, afraid to climb down because of the time it would take to abandon the attention they were giving the Japanese. Osage dragged the machine gun to the stairway and let it slide roughly down. Hawk lobbed a grenade over the heads of the attackers into the entranceway lobby. The blast knocked a half dozen Japanese forward, who in turn knocked down Hawk and Marchand. The force blasted just as many of the enemy toward the rear and back outside.

Hawk rose groggily to one knee, twisting and firing to every side as his men filed down the stairway. The Japanese were relying on their bayonets to avoid shooting one another in the crowded interior. Three Americans lay dead under the slashing stampede of enraged enemy troops. Once again Hawk had to search for ammunition, as the last man retreated down the stairs. When he had earlier loaded his pockets, he had not made provision for this number of shots. He swung the weapon like a club at the array of bayonets while they surrounded him for a final lunge. Backing toward the steps, he tried to turn the Thompson around, in order to fire it again. A group jumped at him, attempting to tackle him, as every other method had failed to drop him. As the weight of the men hit him, Hawk stumbled back on the top step. He fell backward down the stairway, his shoulders hitting each hard stone step, and he began to slide downward. The Japanese continued to charge down after him, inches away, and he fired up into their enraged and twisted faces as he slid down to the landing below, holding up his head to let his shoulders absorb the jolt of each step, and waving the muzzle from one madman to the next. He slid past the bodies of at least two dead Americans on the way down.

Canlon and Osage seized him under the arms as he lay flat on the landing, pulled him through the heavy door there, and slammed it shut. It had a bar, possibly to keep the door fastened against high winds, and they shoved the bar across its braces to lock the entrance. Almost immediately, shots and the banging of heavy objects could be heard colliding with the wood. In a terrified frenzy, the two left the big door on the landing, shoving Hawk ahead of them, and proceeded down toward the additional safety behind the smaller door to the room of Jefferson below.

11

THE LIARS WITHIN THE CODE

THE TELEPHONE RANG. RUTH NAGLE LOWERED HER BLIND and lifted the receiver. Lenora looked up at her. The dog had never quite figured out the telephone, why people talked to it, and why they ran to it as if were so important. She always barked dutifully when it rang, however, as it obviously meant something significant to Ruth.

"Hello. Oh, hello, Myrtle. No, I've been so busy, you know. Go away, Lenora, not now. This dog. All she does is eat," said Ruth, taking a bite out of a cinnamon roll. "And how is Beatrice?"

"She has been doing so well, Ruth. That's part of the reason I called. You know I haven't had time off in weeks, and I can't call you at night. I know you go to bed with the chickens," said Myrtle.

"I do not go to bed with chickens," Ruth protested. "Just because I don't work a night shift at a hospital. I stay up until they put that infernal music on the radio. Who wants to hear that? Does anybody listen to that... whatever it is...Beethoven or something? And even before that, they put on those scary programs. I don't like all that, with the spooky voices and all."

"I don't listen to the radio," said Myrtle quickly. "No time for that silliness. Listen, I've been wanting to talk to you. It's kind of important. Something has been bothering me."

"About Beatrice?" Ruth couldn't think of anything else that would be important to Myrtle.

"In a way," Myrtle answered. "You know that girl that watches Beatrice? Yes, her. Beatrice adores her, and I'm quite fond of her, too. Anyway, she's been giving Beatrice these vitamins or something and it has done her a world of good. You can tell the difference on the days when she gets them and the days when she is on her old medicine. I'm thinking of getting rid of the old medicine all together." Myrtle waited for a reaction.

"Oh, I don't know, Myrtle. I wouldn't do that. I've thought about doing that myself, but the doctor says you don't just stop taking those things, you know. There are side effects with stopping something that you've been taking for a long time," Ruth said. *Honestly, the woman is a nurse!* Ruth thought. That was the advantage of old age: with age comes wisdom. Myrtle, in her sixties, was still young and stupid.

"Ah," said Myrtle. "Doctors! What do they know? I could tell you stories of how many people I've seen doctors kill. People don't want to hear about that, though. But that's not the problem, I don't want to argue with you about that. We could go on forever. I know what I'm talking about."

"Okay, okay. Fine," said Ruth. "What do you want to argue about? Go away, Lenora. Now, you're not hungry. You just think you are."

"You better quit feeding that damn dog before she pops," said Myrtle. "The problem is Admiral Jones. Now, I'm not supposed to talk to anybody about him, or the job, you know that. So don't you say *anything* to anybody. I would lose my job, or go to jail. But the man is incompetent, and there they go giving him the most important patient in the world."

"Wait. Wait," said Ruth. "Don't go telling me anything that will have the police knocking on my door. I've told you about that. I don't want to be mixed up in anything like that. I don't go out, and I don't want anybody coming in here. I haven't cleaned up in years."

"Ruth, I have to talk to someone or I'll explode. Like that dog of yours."

Ruth paused. *This must really be good.* "Well, all right, don't explode."

"I think Admiral Jones is letting our patient die. Have you seen him lately? He looks terrible. His blood pressure is through the roof."

"You know I don't get out, Myrtle."

"I meant in the papers."

"I quit the newspaper. Do you know it's twenty-five cents to have the two dailies and Sunday delivered? I said, no way, mister. I wasn't born yesterday," said Ruth. "For a piece of paper?" Of course, she thought, a young person working in a hospital could throw away their money on that kind of foolishness. All that was in the damned paper anyway was the war. Who cared about that?

"Okay, never mind the newspaper. The thing is, I was talking to Setsuko about it..." Myrtle began.

"What? You just said you couldn't talk about it. Now, you say you've been talking to that foreigner about it."

"She's not a foreigner. She was born here just like you and me. And she's the sweetest girl in the world. And so, I was talking to her and she said she could get me a shot of these vitamins and herbs she has been giving Beatrice. She thinks maybe it would help...*the Admiral's patient*. You know who I'm talking about."

"*What*? Are you crazy? You would do that without telling the Admiral? What if he...died...or something? You'd go to prison, or get hung, probably." Ruth finished her roll. Lenora looked to the side in disgust. Sometimes, Ruth could not believe how stupid Myrtle was. She put her hand over the mouthpiece and whispered to Lenora. "She goes to a church with a bunch of simpletons, that are just like her!" Lenora was not interested. She was in no mood to be confidential, after Ruth had hogged all of the cinnamon roll.

"You didn't listen to a word I said, did you?" Myrtle sounded angry. She was not getting a sympathetic hearing. She knew Ruth was talking to the dog.

"I heard every word. And I'm telling you to stay away from something like that."

"Here comes my girl," Myrtle said suddenly. "She has the cutest little cream-colored Studebaker. Well, I have to go, Ruth. I have a job, you know. And a sick mother. Talk to you later." The phone clicked.

"Well!" said Ruth. "That was rude. I guess I should have told her to go on ahead and give people shots of God knows what. Right, Lenora?" Lenora barked. "I know what Bert would say about that," Ruth mused. Then she shook her head. "No, Bert was a jackass. He would have said to go ahead and do it. No, come to think of it, he would have said, 'just stay out of it, Ruth.' He was an asshole."

* * *

A SHOT PENETRATED the door on the landing, striking Joe Canlon in the leg as he tried to retreat. The wood slowed the bullet down, but it still felt as if he had been clubbed with an iron pipe. He was able to limp down the stairs to the room below, the last refuge of the defenders. The men descended the steps, into the bowels of the fortress, in an effort to regroup and meet the endless onslaught from above. They gathered Jefferson's meager supply of furniture to use for cover when the last door at the bottom of the stairwell would be breached. A heavy desk and couch afforded the most stopping power for the bullets that were to come. The enemy continued to bash at the other door on the landing above.

"Blackwell, rig a grenade up on that first landing," Hawk ordered. "Fix it so they kick it over when they bust the door down up there." The sergeant picked up a heavy book from the floor. "Here, pull the pin and set this on the spoon." Blackwell took the book, opened the door of the room and ran up to the landing. He pulled the grenade's pin, but while he prepared to set it gently on the floor as a booby trap, the great pressure of the attackers from without forced the landing door off its hinges, and it went up and then down, falling on top of him. Crushed beneath the weight of the door and the mass of men behind it, Blackwell was barely able to thrust a clawing hand containing the grenade on the top side of the thick, broken portal, before he was completely flattened under the weight and onto the floor of the landing. The blast lifted the Japanese from atop the door, and other than the men mangled and killed, knocked them from the landing itself. Shielded from the blast, but not the concussion, the Marine beneath groaned and tried to lift the weight of the door and several bodies from his back. Groggily, Blackwell caused the heavy wood to rise and fall only a few inches. Finally, however, he fell unconscious beneath it. The weight was too much for him in his weakened condition. Mindless of the slaughter of their comrades, the attackers surged over the fallen door, and the unseen Blackwell, as they rumbled down the stairs to the last ditch refuge of the defenders.

As the enemy massed at the bottom of the stairs against the last door, it opened and another grenade flew out. In a panicked effort to retreat, the Japanese ran into each other, stumbled and screamed, only to be torn to pieces by the blast. Nevertheless, more attackers piled down the stairs, ignoring and stepping on the dead, hurling themselves at the door.

Hawk lined the men and their automatic weapons to face the door. They propped the machine gun on the overturned desk. While the enemy had far superior numbers, the battle was far from over. Many would die at point-blank range before they could subdue the well ensconced defensive force. The door buckled as more and more furious pressure struck it from the exterior. The enemy screamed like starved predators with an all-consuming bloodlust. The grenades would be of little use now, here in the interior, as the twenty to thirty feet long room left the Marines within the range of their own bombs.

The door collapsed. The machine gun erupted. A tangle of bodies fell in the opening. Automatic fire blazed through every square inch of the open door, pushing the attackers back. The small room disappeared in hot, swirling gun smoke. The Japanese ran directly into the fire and tried to crawl under it. Finally, enough of them succeeded, and a hand came up from the floor to seize the scalding barrel of the machine gun, and pulled it from the grasp of Osage, off the desk, and onto the floor. The weapon had been silenced forever. Marchand pulled the meteorologist, Jefferson, to the wall farthest from the door, and shoved him behind himself to protect him. A bullet struck his chest and he fell across Jefferson, who himself took a bullet between the neck and shoulder. Osage, now without a weapon, received a bayonet thrust in the arm, and retreated backward, desperately seeking something to fight with. Hawk climbed onto the desk and began mechanically clubbing the men pouring through the door. The desk rode across the floor, here and there, as dozens of men fell or threw themselves against it. The stock of Hawk's Thompson shattered and separated from the frame, but he continued to swing the sharp metal frame at them in a last raging effort, cutting and chopping them as much as clubbing them. Desperate, zombie-from-the-grave-hands stabbed upward, ripping at his flesh and tearing his jacket to pieces.

Baker struggled up onto the desk beside Hawk, to join in bashing the heads and faces still pouring through the doorway. He carried a broken Japanese rifle stock. Almost immediately, as he twisted himself around to swing downward, a shot from the door struck the back of his shoulder with a wooden drumbeat. He spun around and flew into the crowd of men charging at the back of Hawk, knocking them down, and enabling the sergeant to continue his relentless chopping into the attackers in front of him. He aimed at the angry eyes and heads on the forward swing, and at anything he could hit on the backward swing. Twice, the sharp twisted metal in his hand became entangled in the thrusting rifles and he jerked it free. He ignored the burning, and the pounding sensations, first behind his head and then in his back.

Murdoch took a point-blank rifle blast, catapulted backward, holding his side, and knocked Hawk from the top of the desk. The back of the sergeant's head whipped roughly against the floor. Joe Canlon fired his last clip. All of the Marines were dead or injured, but the attack had ceased at the same time, and the smoke-filled bunker fell quiet.

Hawk rose to all fours and shook his head. He had nothing in his black, bloody hands to fight with. He searched in panic for anything that would inflict damage. It was only then that he noticed, he also had no one to fight. He saw Joe propped against the back wall, still holding his empty rifle with one hand and pointing it toward the vacant doorway.

"Are you hit?" Hawk gasped.

"Yeah. I got one in the leg, but my goddam arm is the worst. I think it's broke. I hit one of 'em so hard I broke my arm. Can't move it too good." Hawk crawled over to him and lifted the arm. Joe sucked air through his teeth.

"Nah, it's okay. Maybe you busted your hand. Listen, I gotta go up top and see what's going on. More of 'em are probably coming. I hear some kind of firing up there." His muffled hearing could not clearly identify what was happening. He could hear men groaning throughout the room, but didn't know how many of them were his, or how many were alive. He climbed the stairs, crawling over dozens of dead Japanese, and several Americans. He could not understand who would still be fighting outside the bunker.

When he got to the viewports above, and looked out, he saw the submarine, close in toward the shore with its 5-inch deck gun blazing, rumbling twenty shells a minute into fleeing Japanese troops. The huge explosions dropped clumps of the enemy at each blow. He leaned on the concrete for a minute to observe the carnage. The entry of the deck gun into the contest had ended the assault. The Japanese who had not entered the building were stricken on the open slope, while still trying to climb up to the bunker. Far out on the horizon, an enemy ship burned red, with a black plume of fumes above it. Hawk walked around the perimeter of the viewport. Seeing no one outside threatening to shoot him in the back or enter the fortress, he descended the stairs again, to assess the damage below.

The first man he encountered was Blackwell, trying to get the landing door off his back. His helmet, jammed between the door and the floor, had prevented the heavy barrier from fatally crushing him, and his skull, into the concrete under the tremendous weight that had been on top of him. Hawk kicked several bodies off and lifted the door with a superhuman effort to drag Blackwell free. The young man's leg was broken, but he had few complaints. Hawk left him sitting against the wall.

Down in the room below, the dead were lying three deep in places. Marchand was dead, and Jefferson lay beneath him, badly wounded. Murdoch had been shot and was stretched out on the floor. He did not look good. Baker had been hit, but failed to lose his deranged grin. Osage and Joe were wounded more than once, although not critically. The rest of Hawk's patrol were dead, killed in a matter of minutes.

The devastating combat had caused Hawk to momentarily lose all interest in his information-gathering mission. Dimly, his purpose for being here came back to him. As he saw Jefferson gasping for breath, he thought perhaps he could salvage something out of all of this. He knelt by the side of the weather scientist, and unbuttoned his coat.

"They nicked you, huh, sport?" Hawk asked him.

"I'm afraid so," said Jefferson. "I don't think I'll pull through, to be perfectly honest."

"Why? You're looking good. A little shoulder wound there," said Hawk, trying to encourage him. "We'll get some sulfa on it, and...good as new."

"No, I...can't see. My vision. I think I'm fading rather quickly, Sergeant. I have something to tell you...I'm afraid, before it's too late."

"What's that, podnuh?" Hawk asked, propping up the wounded man's head, and seeing a horrible neck wound for the first time. "Just rest easy. We got a boat out there full of corpsmen and medicine. They'll be here any minute."

"That question you asked me. I knew the answer. I knew what you were talking about," Jefferson said. He coughed.

"You did? You could have fooled me. What was the answer?"

"Garrotero. He's a Filipino pirate. He brings supplies to me sometimes."

Hawk grew quiet. He well knew of Garrotero, and how he was a smuggler, and a go between for black marketers trading with both sides of the war. He was also a thief and a murderer, among numerous other things. His pejorative titles and categorizations were limitless. That Hoech would name him, or that Jefferson would know him, were both somewhat unusual. It was perhaps the only name on the code's list of names, so far, that was of worse public repute than that of James Hawk himself.

"I've heard of him," said Hawk. "You dealt with this fella?"

"You may as well know. It doesn't matter anymore. I wasn't going to tell you. Yes, I did business with him. He took weather reports to the Japanese. I made a little extra money and got supplies, contraband, from him."

"Damn. You sold weather reports to the Japs? I'm surprised they'd buy stuff like that. They wanted to know when to get their parasols out, I guess? Don't worry, there's folks that's done worse." Hawk didn't actually know of anyone more disloyal, but he was certain that there were some.

"Maybe not," Jefferson choked. "You see, I made little notations on the reports sometimes, about radio messages I had heard. Shipping and things like that. It may have been treason, I don't know. When you're out here by yourself, you kind of lose your moral compass. People are people. You lose track of sides. They were all...social calls. And I needed the money."

Hawk nodded. What the hell did this guy need money for? Bird seed to feed the seagulls?

"I can't tell you where he is," said Jefferson weakly. "The rogue could be anywhere. He travels all over the Pacific."

"Oh, I reckon they can find him," said Hawk.

"They'll just put a piece of cheese in the trap, and he'll bite it. It's kind of hard to imagine asking a bastard like that about any more names, though. Or gettin' a straight answer about anything. He's kind of...unreliable."

"Yes, yes," Jefferson whispered. "I thought of that. He's an evil fellow. I was always relieved when he left. I was afraid of him. I don't see anyone negotiating with him." He winced. "I feel like I'm evaporating...my thoughts are disconnected. I'm...hardly here. Do you believe in an afterlife, Sergeant?" Jefferson's head dropped, he wretched twice, and then he was dead.

"Yeah," Hawk said solemnly, and lowered him to the floor. "In hell, anyway."

Joe Canlon stood over them, leaning on his rifle for a crutch. By then the medical personnel from the submarine had reached the bunker and were checking the wounded. "So, the poor old guy finally talked? Did he say who his person was? Like he was supposed to?" Joe wasn't just curious. He was second in command. It would be very easy for anyone to be killed that day. He might have to report to someone what had happened here on Pricekeep Island. Joe noticed a gash on the back of Hawk's head, extending down his neck. Neither of them knew at the time that there was a bullet under his scalp.

"Garrotero."

"Garrotero? That son of a bitch? That guy ain't talking to nobody. And ain't nobody gonna be talking to him," Joe said.

"No," said Hawk. "Unless it's us. At the end of a rifle."

* * *

COLONEL CLARK CONTACTED the American liaison with the Filipino resistance in Luzon. He had despaired of solving the code when he learned of the latest name. Garrotero had no permanent address. Authorities, armies, and navies had pursued him for years, without success, before and during the war. The colonel was doubly elated, therefore, to find that Garratero was alive with his wings clipped, and securely imprisoned by the resistance in recently fallen Manila. Clark boarded a plane for the Philippines without hesitating. Although it was an active war zone, he was expecting little danger, and big rewards.

The penal establishment in the Philippines was old and quite impressive in its historicity. Clark was granted entrance to the ancient and crumbling dungeon, and presented to the commandant there. In the newly placed bureaucrat's dark little office, Clark was told that perhaps it would be better for a jailer to speak with Garrotero. The pirate was too dangerous to take out of his cell, and the cell was located in a deep and unsavory part of the rambling structures. The prison consisted of a veritable casbah of add-ons, encompassing different levels in different states of decay. Japanese flags and posters still hung here and there.

Clark didn't like the conditions being placed on his authority. He liked the looks of the prison even less, however, and considered the possibility that the commandant might actually have Clark's welfare in mind. Commandant Abalos offered to take the top-secret message to the pirate personally, assuring Clark that no one else would have access to it. He did not see that this mattered a great deal, as once it was conveyed to Garrotero, there was no limit to the earthly scum who would have access to it. Clark agreed and chose to wait patiently in the commandant's dingy office while the latter conducted the interrogation. The colonel explained the code, and what was required, giving the puzzled Abalos only the single phrase that he would need to convey to Garrotero, rather than the entire code.

Abalos filed down one filth strewn stairway to the next, and through the maze of walls and cells to where the most dangerous prisoners languished. He found Garrotero sitting on the floor of his dim and airless cell, feasting on chicken and rice, with a bottle of wine at his side, all of which had without doubt been smuggled in to him, for a price.

"Come here, dog," said the commandant, gesturing for the prisoner to come to the bars. "I have a question for you. If you know what's good for you, you will answer truly." They spoke in Tagalog.

Garrotero smiled. "The only way I know how. God as my witness."

"If you refuse, or if you lie, I will get the right answer out of you. Do you understand?"

"Your hospitality is legendary," said Garrotero, still smiling.

"The Americans want to know this, and it is very important to them, so do not give me any of your foolishness. I am going to read you a line of words, and you are going to tell me what it means to you. You will tell me the person it describes. You will tell me all that you know about this person. Understand?"

Garrotero thrust out his lips and pulled his eyebrows together. "You want me to lie already? How can I understand this confusing talk? Do *you* understand any of this?"

"Shut up, you bastard, and listen. I warn you, do not test me. You will answer this one way or another."

"You are scaring me, Commandant. You know how sensitive I am," said the pirate.

"I know what a dog you are. The words are 'me like a bird.'" He read them in English. "What does that mean to you?" The commandant frowned at the odd words on the paper. He repeated them slowly, and in a low, questioning voice, mostly to himself.

Garrotero threw back his head and laughed.

"What is so funny? Do you know what that means?"

"Of course, I know what that means. Now, you tell me. Who wants to know? It could make a difference, as to whether you find out the answer or not."

The angry commandant started to issue threats, but decided against it. He wanted the matter settled. He wanted the Americans to go away, and he wanted to get out of this stinking pit with the filthy pirate. "An American colonel wants to know." He surprisingly submitted to Garrotero's inquiry.

"Then, bring me the American colonel. I will tell him. This information could ruin reputations, you know. I can't tell just anyone these things. Anyone—like *you*. I have a reputation to uphold, too." Garrotero smiled. "What if certain people learned the commandant and I were sharing confidences? My life would be worthless. Sir...my *reputation*. Before God and man."

"Your reputation as a dog. The colonel will never come here to this dirty hole. He is afraid of this place. You must tell *me* your answer," said the commandant.

"Very well, *here* is my answer. Bring me outside the gates of your delightful prison. Bring this honorable colonel to speak with me there. Two of my friends will meet me out there on the road in a motor car. I will tell the colonel what he wishes to know, absolutely everything he wishes to know, and then I will ride off with my friends, never to see you or your accommodations again. Although, we can still exchange good wishes occasionally, if you like. You are in a position to help me quite a lot. I believe we have your address. It is good for old friends to stay in contact." He leaned over and added in a low voice, "And we have your home address."

"You must be insane. I am not going to do any of that. I will beat you to death first," said Abalos.

"I don't blame you," said Garrotero. "I would do the same, if I were in your position. I am just no good. Even my mother says so. But, I promise you this. Neither you nor your colonel will get this information, and the colonel will cause you a great deal of trouble, perhaps for years, if you do not do this my way. I know how these matters work. You do not. You do not understand the arrogance of these people. I am trying to help you, as much as myself. You must use some common sense."

Abalos thought about that. "I will ask the colonel. If he thinks this bit of nonsense is worth letting you go free, I will do it. If he does not, you will be dead tomorrow morning. First, you will have a very long night. You think about that while I am gone. You have my promise on it."

"You know how sensitive I am," said Garrotero. "I wish you would not say such scary things to me. I may have to tell my confessor. He says he can still get me into heaven—or the outskirts."

Abalos left to discuss the matter with Clark. Clark, unused to criminals, and having dealt only with subservient yes men for most of his life, was livid. He and Abalos discussed advanced interrogation and torture at length. Finally, Clark tired of the subject.

"What is he charged with?" Clark asked.

"Piracy, treason, and murder," said Abalos. "Among other things. There is nothing he hasn't done. He will die here."

"All right, we will meet his conditions. This code is too important for any more delays. We are nearing our deadline. You realize that, otherwise, the matter of this man's fate means nothing to the United States. We will help you, of course, to resolve it. Once he tells us the name, and drives off, I can have a bazooka team take care of the car, and him in it. The city is a shambles. No one will know the difference. He's more likely than not to be executed anyway. We merely expedite it. It gets rid of his henchmen, as well."

Abalos nodded. "I like this. Very much."

Garrotero had an entire night to think over what was being asked of him. His mind quickly ran to how to make a profit off it. This code business was evidently worth a lot to someone. He saw a golden moment.

The arrangements were made, and the next day Garrotero met with Colonel Clark in the middle of the shell pocked road in back of the prison. The pirate's long hair was greased back and he wore the same flowery and billowing shirt he had been wearing when arrested days before. On the road behind them was parked an American Jeep, its motor running, and two of the pirate's former colleagues sat in it. Abalos had two sleepy guards standing with placidly slung rifles between the prisoner and the Jeep.

"You'll never make it to the bay if you lie to me," said

the colonel. "We can check the authenticity of the name you give us immediately."

"Me? Lie?" Garrotero laughed. "You have me mistaken for someone else. I would lie if I had any reason to lie, but why should I? I have no interest in any of this, or war secrets. I don't care who wins or loses."

"I won't quibble with you. Let's get to the point. What is the name?" the colonel asked.

"'Me, like a bird' is something I used to call one of your American pilots. He was a businessman, much like myself, only with his airplane, he could do so much more than I could do, and much faster. Many times he helped me do my work. I used to say to him, every time we concluded our business: 'ah, you are me, but like a bird. If only I could fly. How much more I could do.'"

"The name?" Clark pressed.

"The name is John Starr. A lieutenant, I believe. You may have difficulty finding him. I heard the Army Air Corps was trying to detain him for some unpleasantness. He probably would not let that happen. You see, he was me, but like a bird. He could disappear like the angels. But make no mistake, he was not an angel. Not like me." Garrotero placed his hand on his chest with feigned innocence.

"John Starr? Where did you last see this pilot?" Clark asked.

"Samar," Garrotero answered quickly. "But he would have no reason to still be there."

"Very well. We will find him. You are free to go. I would advise you to be more careful in your endeavors from here on out. I've heard that they had plans for your future that were rather short term," said the colonel.

The pirate let this pass, bowed, and approached the

Jeep as the guards parted to let him walk by. He received elaborate hugs and grunted greetings from his waiting comrades.

"Thank you for your advice," the pirate called to Clark. Then with a confident nod of his head, he took several steps back toward the colonel, and raised a finger. "You could do one more favor for me, sir. The city is too much different now. I wonder if you would mind guiding me to the bay. I have a boat waiting there. My mother is so old, she will worry, if I should get lost in this disgusting rubble."

"That is out of the question," said Clark. "If I were you, I would not waste any more time. Someone may change their mind about what to do with you, now that we have what we want." Clark smiled to himself, as that plan was already in the works, with the assistance of a skilled bazooka team.

"Strange. I was thinking that very thing. This *very* thing you say occurred to me. We are so much alike, you and I. You are me, with a belly," said Garrotero. He pulled a 1911 .45 automatic from his waistband and pointed it at the colonel. "Get in the car," the pirate ordered.

Clark's knees almost gave way under the shock. "Wha...wha...?"

"No more words. Get in the car," said the pirate, seizing Clark's loose uniform around the neck and shoulder area, and pulling him forward. Abalos and his armed guards stood by helplessly. They never changed their posture as the drama unfolded. Garrotero and Clark climbed into the Jeep, and it sped off, leaving the commandant standing in gray dust and exhaust fumes. Abalos shrugged. He dusted off his white uniform. He rather hoped that the bazooka team lying in wait would recognize their colonel in the open vehicle. If not, there could be a scandal.

Abalos turned to the guard next to him. "John Starr. US Army Air Corps. Write that down. Someone will be wanting that," he said. "God knows why. But I'll probably be getting another American visitor. A different one, of course. I don't like trouble."

12

THE WAY IT SOMETIMES ENDS

JAMES HAWK SAT AGAINST THE TAUT CANVAS WALL OF THE mobile hospital tent on Greater Helvedes. The canvas had a little give to it and it was kind of comfortable, but it was hot, and it had that hot canvas smell that was everywhere, and even stuck to your clothes. His evacuation had been decided against, since he could be treated here. He had a headache since leaving Pricekeep Island. A slug nestled in his scalp, a little above his neck, and another one lay in the muscles of his upper back. The one in his back itched occasionally, and he rubbed his back on the tent brace, as a horse might do. He spat the tasty tobacco that Vera had given him between his knees. His view of the camp was less than entertaining, and he wanted out of it. He didn't know anybody here, and he didn't know what was going on in his unit, or what had happened with regard to the code. His hands often reached for a Thompson submachine gun, that wasn't there. And he had way too much time to think.

"There you are. You aren't supposed to be outside. Are you crazy? I was looking all over for you. They said you're never in the bed." Vera Orr looked down at him. She held a clipboard and was not wearing her customary flight jump suit. She instead wore a tight dress, looking like a well-to-do civilian, and standing out in the bustling military crowd.

"Hey, Vera, you look nice. All painted up like a French battleship," he greeted her.

"My, what a compliment! If only Attila the Hun were alive, you could give him some pointers on how to flatter the ladies. Look, I have your medical chart. It was hanging on your cot."

"What are you doing with that? That's private information. There could be embarrassing stuff in there."

"Yes, you are so easily embarrassed. Did you know that you've been shot nine times?"

"Damn! On Pricekeep? They told me it was just twice. Lyin' bastards. Hell, I didn't even know I got shot at all, till I got on the sub. I was just hurtin' all over."

"Not on Pricekeep. I meant all together in your life. Your life, being the last two years. Guadalcanal isn't on here. Or Cape Gloucester."

"Oh, yeah. Well, it may be more than that. Maybe they meant on nine different days. And it's the ones I got treated for. I try not to say nothing about that kind of stuff. Keep all that under your hat. You can't tell the son of a bitches nothing, or they'll take you out of your company, and send you off to some damn hospital in Australia—for months. I gotta get out of this place. And pretty damn quick."

"That's just ridiculous. It only took one shot to kill Dillinger. You know, a cat only has nine lives."

"Yeah. That's why they don't let them bastards in the Marine Corps."

"Did it ever occur to you to avoid guns that are shooting at you? You're just...just a mess," she said, frustration in her voice. "Look at you." She appeared sad. Vera was never sad.

"Nah, I'm awright. What do you mean? I'll be outta here in a day or so. This ain't nothin'. Hell, I could walk off right now if I wanted to. Kirk would take me back. I'm just kind of puttin' up with their shit, you know, till I got a plan," he spat. "You gotta have a plan with these shitheads. They're as bad as Japs. It's hard to think penned up here, you don't know what's going on and they give you shit about damn near everything." Hawk smiled. "Hey, what's wrong, kid? You look down. Somebody steal your joy buzzer?"

She shook her head, and tried to shake off the mood his appearance had put her in. "They got the last name out of that pirate," she informed him. "Correction, the second to last name. They don't have the 'big one' yet. But we're on the way. It's a matter of days."

"No kidding? I never thought that pirate asshole would talk, or that anybody would ever listen to him, as far as that goes."

"No. What was even more amazing, is that they think he told the truth. There *was* one amusing little incident involving him," she said.

"What was that?"

"He kidnapped Colonel Clark at the prison and held him for six hours on a boat in Manila Bay. The Coast Guard had to rescue him. The pirate threw him in the water." Hawk and Vera looked at one another for a long moment. They both burst out laughing at the same time.

"Aw, *shit*!" Tears rolled down Hawk's face as the

laughter continued. "That's about the funniest thing I ever heard in my life."

"I thought you might appreciate that. It was actually even funnier. I messed it up, in the telling. I should have first mentioned that they traded a crate of baloney for him."

"Aw, *shit!*" Hawk laughed, rolling back a little, until the pain shot up his neck and ended the merriment.

"You wanted to know how this ends, and I may be able to tell you pretty soon. The last name—sorry—the second to last name, is a Lieutenant John Starr. He's also in a prison, only this time in California. Clark wants me to go home and talk to him. I know someone in Washington. I can find out what happens to the code breaking after that. The only thing is..."

"What?"

"I don't know if I can come *back*. Here. I've kind of used up my bag of tricks, I'm afraid. People are asking questions about me."

"Why? You ain't done nothing? You're in the WASPs or something. Ain'tcha?"

"Yes, well. That I am. I'm the *only* WASP in the South Pacific. Or not in the States. They don't go overseas. I...seem to stick out."

"No kidding."

"Listen, here's something else. Latham went to Papanuca to see the witch woman," she said.

"He, what? That crazy bastard. What did he do that for?"

"Because he's a crazy bastard. There's a lot going on in that little pointy head. He had to go thank her for giving him his soul back. Like they go to the Pope, to kiss his ring. Get it?"

"No. *What*? *I'm* the one that gave him his goddam soul back. She wouldn't have given him shit. Even if he kissed her ass."

"Yes, well. Be that as it may, he did it. And the witch wants me to go there and be her daughter and heir to her fabulous estate," Vera smiled. "Princess of Papanuca." She handed him a letter signed by Latham. "Unfortunately, it's not the worst offer I've ever had."

"Not much chance of that." Hawk looked at the lengthy letter for a second, without reading any of the scribbling on it. He supposed the witch had dictated it to Latham. He handed it back.

"No, but here's the part you might like. She says she will tell Latham the last name, 'the big one', and what the message means, if I'll go there." Vera nodded in affirmation. "That's right. I think she knows everything. I think she may even know what the last person knows. I don't know if she got it from Hoech, or the Japanese, or what, but she knows. This is it: it's that other shortcut I had considered."

"Oh, now it's '*you* considered.' I *knew* it. She's got the hoo doo magic, is what it is. Direct line to the devil."

"Yes, okay. No backwoods corn pone, please. Not today. There's something else. Do you still have the code?"

"Yeah." He pulled a folded paper out of his open, white hospital jacket pocket. "I don't go nowhere without it. Like my St. Christopher's medal, and my serial number, tattooed over here. That's in them records."

"You were right about the numbers at the top of the page, too. They actually *do* mean something."

"What? I knew it. Remember how you called me stupid and all that shit? You and Clark?."

"Yes. Nothing changed there. That's solid: you *are* stupid. Mr. 'shot nine times'? Look at this. This is from Washington, so you can't tell anybody about it, or we would all be sent to a firing squad. That 'Helvedes coordinate' line at the top was encrypted in artillery coordinates, not latitude and longitude. That's why there were so many numbers."

"No, shit? Damn. I should have thought of that. I was close," said Hawk.

"Close to what? You weren't close to anything. Do you want to hear this or not? The coordinates were in the Japanese way of doing them, not the American. No one would have *ever* figured that out. Especially you."

"I might have. I know how the wrong end of artillery looks. We shoot it in a square pattern target, and the Japs shoot us in a half circle."

"*Nobody* could have figured it out."

"You just got through telling me that somebody did."

"Accidentally. They stumbled on it, they didn't sit down and figure it out, like Mr. Moto. Somebody accidentally knew all that. Isn't that something? Okay, look at this." She handed him a slip of paper with the numbers 33-1-34-39-40 written on it.

"Hunh. It ain't in no set pattern. I got a headache. There's a ball bearing stuck on my brain. What the hell does it mean?"

"Look at the code, and count the words that fall in that order," she said.

Hawk squinted at the lines of clues in the code. "Hell, I can't keep track of all that. Got a pencil?"

"Yes." She found one in her purse. He counted out

each of the words on the lengthy code, the thirty-third word first, the first word second, and so forth. He circled each of the five words. "This better be good," he muttered halfway through.

"Awright. It says, 'Students kill President with syringe.'" He frowned at it, and then at Vera.

"That's Hoech's message out of Japan. You lived to see it. Through no fault of your own."

"But...uh...what do they do about it? I mean, what *is* it? Are they talking about Roosevelt? There's no details."

"Yes, the President, no, no details. So, it's not a *huge* shortcut. They still need that last person to tell them everything about how it's to be done. They couldn't have figured any of it out without you, and without having *all* of the names. This is more like a headline or a title, than an actual shortcut. They can be on a general alert to guard the President, especially regarding medical treatment. But it tells us what we were trying to stop, the object of the whole mission."

"That's a lot of information. You know more about this thing than anybody. Which, ain't no surprise to me," he said, closing one eye and looking up at her.

"I'm going to know a lot more. I'm off to sunny California. I'll have a lot more to tell you after that. If I can get back, and if you're still alive."

"I'll be alive. You know...they went to a lot of trouble to stop me from getting that information. You better be damn careful. If the Japs can send an army and navy to the South Pole, they can send a guy to bump you off anywhere between here and California." He shook his head. "You ain't never seen so many Japs in your life, as they put on that island. This ain't nothing to mess with, Vera. This is the big leagues. Look what happened to

Clark. He thought he was going to be a hero and got the shit scared out of him. I'm surprised that damn Garrotero didn't kill his ugly ass. Clark's lucky it wasn't Japs. They don't play walk the plank. If I was you, I would let *him* do this. They got guys that do this kind of thing. Ain't the general in charge of this? Call that damn general. Why the hell has Clark got you mixed up in any of it anyway? You need to get loose from that guy."

"I have a theory on that. He hates you."

"Sounds about right. Everybody does. So, what?"

"He doesn't want me around you. That's why I may not be able to get back. The old green-eyed monster. It's a terrible feeling, jealousy. Have you ever been jealous?"

"Jealous? I don't know." He appeared to be thinking. Vera looked skyward.

"No. I guess you haven't." She kneeled down and kissed his cheek. "Why do you chew that dirty, filthy, nasty stuff? The most important moment in our lives, and I can't even kiss you. You're a mess. Just a mess! If you weren't so pathetic, I would hate you, too. Sitting there, shot to pieces. You don't even know how many times. Drooling black sap, like a moron." She stood back, surveying him with a bit of a sneer.

"Well, yeah," he said. "Be careful. That's all I got to say."

"That's *all* you have to say?" She put a hand on her hip. "I tell you I may never see you again, and that's all you have to say?"

"You don't listen to nothin' anyway."

* * *

VOLMER WAITED in the foyer for Setsuko. They had spoken only on the phone for the last week to avoid attracting any attention. The German had the ricin injection ready for delivery in a valise. Setsuko was becoming nervous about the number of meth-amphetamine injections given to Beatrice. She was afraid Myrtle's mother would die any minute now, and ruin the entire operation. Myrtle had to remain convinced of the efficacy of the shots, in order to stay motivated enough to administer a drug to the President. Volmer decided that now was the time to act. Every-thing was in place. Timing was crucial.

Ruth Nagle saw the car pull up next door and rushed to the window to see who it was. She was surprised to see the young Asian woman. The girl had not been around for over a week, and Ruth thought perhaps the students next door had some sort of parting of the ways. Wilhelm Volmer came out on the porch to meet Setsuko, handing her a small medical house call bag. Ruth thought that was strange. It was usually the girl bringing him gifts. What happened next was even stranger. Setsuko turned around and returned to her car. The two did not talk for hours as they usually did, even though they had not seen one another in a long time. Ruth looked for a pen. She had better write this down. She had not seen Calvino lately, either.

She opened her blue notebook to the middle. She had taken quite a few notes now. What was the sneaky Volmer doing with a medical bag? It dawned on Ruth that they might all three be medical students. She peered out the window again, for a final look at Setsuko. She was getting into her cream-colored Studebaker.

Cream-colored Studebaker? "Oh...my...god!" Ruth

stood and lifted the blind, to watch the girl pull away. To her horror, when she looked over at the porch, Wilhelm Volmer was still standing there and had turned, and was looking Ruth right in the eye. She quickly closed the blinds.

"Bert, Lenora—that's the *girl*! That's the one Myrtle was talking about." Ruth sat back down. She didn't even know what to write. Myrtle was not a part of her journal. Yet. Myrtle had no relevance, until now. What were the chances of Myrtle Thorpe having a connection to those three hooligans? Quickly, Ruth filled in the missing details, about Beatrice, and about Myrtle's job requiring her to visit the White House. She became more and more fearful as she wrote. Usually writing calmed her, but not today. Her hand shook as she recorded the story of Setsuko convincing Myrtle to give the President a shot of "vitamins."

"I'm keeping my mouth shut about this, Lenora," she said. "I am not the kind to carry tales. This is Myrtle's business. What would I say? Who would I tell? I just don't get involved in this kind of thing. I am too busy to be bothered with all of that. I have things to do. I didn't get to be eighty-one years old by poking my nose where it doesn't belong. That's just not me. It's all probably harmless anyway. Maybe it *is* vitamins." Ruth leaned over and whispered to Lenora. "She's not Chinese. She's *Japanese*!" Lenora cocked her head with obvious suspicion. "Why does Myrtle have to be so stupid? There is something wrong with her. That's how those people from West Virginia are. They are so stupid, handling snakes, and catching the Holy Ghost and all of that business. And her, a nurse in a big government hospital. Attached to an admiral, no less. To the *President!*"

Ruth looked at her notebook. Maybe she should get rid of it. She looked back at the old fireplace, which had not been used in years. She was afraid the chimney would catch fire. Bert had not cleaned it in decades. Bert, again, ruining her life.

"That shiftless asshole," she whispered.

* * *

VERA ORR WAS SMARTLY ATTIRED with a feathered hat, gloves, pleated black cocktail dress, and high heels when escorted by a guard into the non-contact visiting room at a Southern California prison. Her wardrobe could have been done by Orry-Kelly. She sat down to face a hardware cloth screen behind a little counter in front of her. Shortly after, John Starr was escorted to the seat behind the screen. An overhead fan threw jittery shadows across the gray walls, and them. The prisoner smiled broadly. *He looks like Tyrone Power*, she thought.

"Wow, I wasn't expecting a movie star," said the pilot.

"Why, thank you!" said Vera. "You aren't so bad yourself, big boy," she said. "But all you pilots are dashing."

"Ah, the ladies! How these bars bring out their candor," he said.

"Yes. It's a sad state of affairs, isn't it? Mr. Starr, I am Vera Orr, WASP, here on behalf of the United States Marine Corps. I believe you have been briefed on the reason?"

"I have. I'm told that I am going to win the war. I had

to wait until I was in prison to aid the war effort." He laughed.

"You seem to be in high spirits, nonetheless," she said.

"It doesn't help to cry over spilled milk, does it?"

"No, indeed. Very insightful. I'll get to the point. We have intercepted a message from Japan. It is in the form of a code that consists of a series of names. We were given your name by an associate of yours, in the Philippines. A Mr. Garrotero—no first name—I believe?"

"Never heard of him," said Starr.

"Yes, I see. Be that as it may, it's neither here nor there to me. I am going to read a phrase to you, and I would ask you what person comes to your mind."

"Is this like one of those word association psychological things? I took one of those three days ago. They said I was nuts."

"Far be it from me to dispute the experts. But no, it is not a psychological test. It is a factual determination." She knew the code by heart, but opened out the paper on the counter anyway, to show him that this was not just something off the top of her feathered head.

"You know, you don't look like any Marine I ever saw," he said.

"You would like to see my credentials?"

"Would I? Break 'em out, baby." They both laughed.

"Very amusing," she said. "To clarify, I am not a Marine. I am with the Women's Auxiliary Service Pilots. Shall we proceed?"

"Sure. Take your best shot. I'm all yours. Those gals are doing an excellent job, by the way. I know all about them."

"Mm. Why, thank you. I appreciate that. Your

portion of the code reads, 'summer lake apple pie.' Who does that remind you of?"

"You smell good. Like a rose. A real rose. You know, I could show a classy dame like you a good time," he said.

"Really? Would that by any chance involve a beer joint, a dartboard, and a bowl of peanuts?" she asked. "Shall I repeat it? 'Summer lake apple pie.'"

"Wow. Does that take me back? I mean, wow, lady. You really know how to make a guy think of the old times. Before all this happened."

"Yes, just another of my many talents. And the name is...?"

"Yeah, well." He slid a business card through the little opening at the bottom of the hardware cloth. "That's my attorney. He's dying to get me out of here, for some reason. He seems to think this apple pie name might do the trick. He wanted you to call him. Maybe you two can work out a deal. He'll have the name, so you don't have to come back to me. Unless, you want to." He winked. "Of course, if things go right, I won't be here, will I? Don't worry, baby, we can still meet somewhere else. Where are you staying?"

"I don't think that's going to work," she said.

"Oh, I don't know. The word is, this is a *big* deal. And it's a big deal that's happening in three days. All just waiting on big old me to flip the switch. I'm like...indispensable! Don't act so fancy!"

She nodded and looked at the card. "Unfortunately, you're right. You could have done us and the country a great service. Judging by your history, that's not much of a priority with you. If this falls through, you're going to have a little more egg thrown in your face than you

already have. And you likely will never get out of here."
She stood and began to walk away.

"Hey, hey, don't leave mad!" He stopped her. "I don't want that. You're too good looking. Tell you what. You go see the lawyer, and do what you can for me, and I'll tell you the name right here and now. I trust you. You got nice...eyes."

She sat down. "I will speak to the man," she said. "I'm in town for a few days, anyway. I hear the zoo is spectacular."

"Yeah. Check out the monkeys. Don't stand too close, though. Listen, next time you leave, walk a little slower, okay?" They stared at one another for a moment. She did not look as amused as before. "All right," he said. "The name is this old lady. Me and a buddy used to see her down at the lake in New York. Green...something...Lake. Not far from the city. We'd go in the summer. She would make these apple pies for all us kids. She lived in Maryland during the rest of the year. She's probably in the phone book, under the husband's name. Bert, it was. Her name was Ruth Nagle. She'd be a really old bag by now. Might be dead. Now, you can't blame me for that."

"I might. N-A-G-L-E?"

"Yeah, probably. I mean, how many ways can you spell it? Is spelling part of this deal, or what? Do I get half credit? It could be E-L, you know."

"No, spelling is not crucial." She stood. "Thanks." She set the business card on the counter and walked away—quickly.

"Hey!" He shouted. The dozing guard stood and approached the prisoner. "Don't be that way! I helped you, didn't I? We had a deal!" he pleaded. She came back.

"Just wanted a little respect, big guy," she said, and picked up the business card. "Since I'm not allowed to slap the shit out of you. Actually, I am, but I can't get my arm up that little opening."

* * *

MYRTLE THORPE GOT into the back seat of the Lincoln Continental. Admiral Jones sat on the opposite side of the seat, as far away from her as he could get. They never spoke on these drives to the White House. He noticed that she carried a new medical bag, but he said nothing, even though he kind of liked it. He didn't like Myrtle, and he knew that she didn't like him.

Myrtle had made up her mind that today was the day she would give the President the shot given to her by Setsuko. Roosevelt was looking, and acting, worse and worse, declining much the same as Beatrice had done. And Beatrice had almost died. The Admiral didn't visit every week, so time was of the essence. The President might leave the country, and then what? He could die overseas, and it would be on her conscience. She only wished that the Admiral were a more approachable doctor, so she could discuss the matter with him.

* * *

THERE WAS a knock on Ruth's door. Her heart stopped. Rarely did anyone knock on her door, and if they did, she rarely answered it. It was probably the Fuller Brush man or something just as aggravating. Lenora barked loudly, but the old dog's stamina was low. She had to pause occasionally and whine before continuing with her outrage.

"Shut up, Lenora!" Ruth ordered. "Don't let them know we're here."

But the knock was persistent, and Lenora did not stop. Ruth decided to look past the curtain at the porch. She saw two men in suits. At least, it wasn't the police. She didn't want anyone coming in her house. They were likely selling vacuum cleaners, or insurance. She would have to get rid of them, or Lenora might have a heart attack. Why didn't men get decent salaried jobs and stop knocking on people's doors?

As she went to unlock the door, she saw the giveaway fan on her end table, with the picture of Jesus on it, knocking on a door, and the name of a local funeral home under the picture. It said: "knock and the door will be opened."

"Oh, my," she said. "That's a sign." She opened the door only a few inches, so that Lenora could not pounce, which would be an inglorious spectacle. The two men took off their hats, both looking first at the enormous and distorted face of the gasping dog.

"Ruth H. Nagle?" one of them asked.

It didn't sound like a Fuller Brush man. He wouldn't know her name. "Yes. What is it? I'm busy."

"Ruth Hoech Nagle?" the other man said.

"I said, yes. Are you those damned deaf people? I don't give away money from my home, and I don't want your sign language card. I do all my giving at the church."

"No, ma'am, I'm Agent Murphy, and this is Agent

Costello. We're with the FBI, and I wonder if we could have a word with you?"

"Oh...my...god. Whatever for? I don't let people in my house. This isn't some charity thing? I don't give from home."

"No, ma'am, it isn't. You can come sit with us on the porch, if you like. We just have a few questions for you."

"Oh, dear. You've frightened the bejabbers out of me. What is this about?"

"We're hoping that you can tell us that," Murphy said. Lenora continued barking intently. Ruth picked up the cardboard fan from the funeral home, and slipped out onto the porch, while holding a foot in Lenora's face. She sat down heavily in her porch chair. She pushed Bert's chair farther away from her.

"We have intercepted a message out of Japan, Mrs. Nagle. It originated with your nephew, we believe. Maxwell? We have been trying to decode it for several weeks. You seem to be the key to the whole thing. Have you heard from Maxwell? I should begin by asking if you have observed any activity out of the ordinary lately? Anything that could be remotely connected to a national threat of some sort?"

"I...I'm not one to meddle, or carry tales," said Ruth. "I mind my own business. I would never have said anything, but since you asked. Just a minute. Let me get my notebook. I have this friend, who is a nurse at Bethesda, you see?" She shuffled quickly toward the door. Lenora saw the door open slightly, and Ruth's foot was in her face again.

Ruth nervously picked up the notebook and it fell open to the first page. Toward the bottom, her eyes fell upon the line she had written when she first began this scholarly work: "Sent Max letter. Mentioned those hooligans in the rooming house next door where his friend Mr. Carswell used to live."

"Oh, Lord!" she exclaimed. "Saints preserve us."

* * *

MYRTLE ALWAYS FELT a ripple of excitement, no matter how many times she had entered the White House grounds. Admiral Jones sat like a stone statue in the car as the guard spoke with the driver. Jones probably felt nothing, she thought. She was thinking of sweet Setsuko, and the injection she was planning on giving the President, when the rear door of the car swung open and a uniformed officer stood before her. She was obviously startled. The Admiral looked over with little interest.

"Myrtle Thorpe?" the officer asked.

"Yes, that's me," said Myrtle amiably. She clutched her medical bag.

"Get out of the car, please." He didn't say it very nicely.

* * *

WHEN HAWK REJOINED HIS COMPANY, Joe Canlon had already returned. Joe had a slight limp, but was otherwise ready for duty. Joe quickly arranged for them to share a tent in order to catch up on the news.

"Did you hear about Turnage?" Joe asked.

"No. I looked for him. He died?" Hawk asked. *What the hell else happens to people in this place?*

"No, he's doing good. They put him somewhere in

headquarters, I think. Typing or something. He said he's coming back, though. He's just not up to all the runnin' and jumpin' yet," said Joe.

"I'll be damned. I have to go see him. I was worried about that kid. He had a shithead for a doctor. How about Murdoch, how is he doing?"

"He's doing good, but they haven't let him go yet. Too soon. Did they operate on you?"

"Sort of. I guess they call it that. They got the bullets out anyway. They didn't knock me out or nothing," said Hawk.

"How'd they do that?"

"Shit. Just said, lay on your stomach, and started chopping on me. It was that same shithead surgeon Turnage had."

"He probably figured he wouldn't waste any ether on a pile of crap like you. Too many sick people around."

"Yeah. I might just tie a knot in that guy's stethoscope. Speaking of Murdoch. You remember him saying all that shit about how they oughta just kill the leaders of countries, instead of everybody else killing each other? That's exactly what the Japs were trying to do. That was what the code was all about."

"No, shit? Did they get Hitler? That guy's slick. Hey, look who's here. You gotta visitor. Is she decked out or what? *What a babe!*" Joe lowered his voice. "Too bad she's nuts."

* * *

THE HIGHEST POINT in the Helvedes is on Klippetopf Island. There is a cliff on its northern coast that has a spectacular view of about seven of the islands in the chain, most of which had been untouched by the campaign. You can see smaller islands, too, but they consist of only little more than a rock jutting from the water, with an occasional tree or two hanging from the sides. The ocean is a beautiful turquoise color, and the islands are emerald green. In those days, few people visited the Helvedes, and almost no one went to Klippetopf. Only the youngest, the most fit, and the most adventurous would climb the cliff for its rewarding view. Atop the cliff, the ground was no longer as rocky, as it was covered with thick layers of dark green grass. The grass was so green, and so uniformly green, that it did not look like part of nature. At the base of the cliff lapped a little inlet, protected from the ocean by a hook-shaped peninsula. On the gentle waters there, a Catalina flying boat bobbed peacefully, as it waited for the return of its occupants on the cliff high above. The silhouette of a man and a woman could be seen standing against the blue sky behind them. Her right knee bent backward as she stretched up to kiss him. Another daylight moon, soon to be a nighttime moon, stood vigilantly on guard, protecting them from the violent world in which they lived.

"I thought you told me you weren't ever coming back," Hawk said.

"And never see my man again? You know I'm crazy about you, don't you?"

"I knew you were crazy."

"Besides, you wanted to know how the code turned out, remember? Who else could tell you? Or, I should say, who else *would* tell you? I had to go to a lot of trouble to find all this out."

"Nobody would tell me crap. They're done with me," he said.

"Exactly. They shoot you nine times and turn you out to pasture. In fact, they don't even do that. They send you back into combat. What's the deal on that? You get two points for every month overseas, five points for battle stars, points for wounds, points for decorations— shouldn't you have enough points to have gone home about twelve years ago? Isn't it only like ninety points total?"

"I think you have to ask. I ain't askin' 'em for nothin'. Even if you got the points, it ain't for sure."

"Well, *ask*. What's wrong with you?"

"Let's don't get into all that. Do you always have to stir up shit? What about the code? There wasn't nothing in the newspapers about it that I saw."

"As a matter of fact, I just happen to have an article from the paper to show you. You're right. The assassination plot hasn't come out yet. I guess they don't want anyone to know about that. They especially don't want the Japanese and Germans to know that they broke it up. Let's see, four conspirators and three arrests. They arrested two non-citizen medical students and an American nurse in the plot to kill the President. I don't know who or what that other one was, or if they ever got her."

"Hunh. So, they already figured out who they were? And how they were going to do it?"

"Oh, yes. The last person on the list told them everything. She knew all about it. Names, dates, how it would happen, everything. She was a relative of Hoech. And guess who was the crafty person who gave the FBI her name? A true lady sleuth of distinction, world traveler, and of remarkable intelligence. Coincidentally, devastatingly beautiful. *Nooo*, not Mata Hari. Try again. Think *more* beautiful, this time. Someday, *I'll* be in the history books."

"What the hell? Sounds like they should have arrested that Hoech woman, too—the last name—if she knew all that guff. Why didn't she tell somebody, instead of letting us get our ass shot off digging it up? Was she in on it or something?"

"She was a hundred years old or something. And kind of a lunatic. They had to actually go to her house and question her. Just think, *you* saved FDR's life. He's sixty-three now, and you bought him another twenty years, probably. He'll run for a fifth, sixth, or seventh term, till he's eighty something. It'll be 1960 before there's another president. Can you imagine what would have happened if he had died in the middle of the war? We would all be speaking Japanese this time next year."

"Not me. I can't even speak English, so I damn sure ain't speakin' no Japanese. And listen. Don't be going around saying shit like that to your stupid friends. I didn't do nothing on this code. The men that died doing this, they're the ones that did all that. I just did what I was supposed to do. I don't want no funny business."

"Well, don't worry, sweetheart. I'm sure the people that sent you out there like a dodo bird feel the same way. Your humility could never exceed their ingratitude. Plenty others will take the credit. You can consider it forgotten. Let me show you a little *something else*, that *is* in this newspaper. This is good. Don't let your mind wander, now, and go off grazing with the goats." She reached into a carrying bag, opened up the newspaper, and pointed to the bottom of the front page. "This code thing never dies. I'm starting to think it came from God or something. I'll bet they eventually trace it back to Winston Churchill someday. Wait and see. Isn't he mysterious?"

"Who? The guy in England?" Hawk read the headline above a short article: 'Kidnapped Codebreaker Rescued from Pacific Island.'

"What! Hoech? He got away?" He scanned through it. "Maxwell Hoech...dramatic rescue from isolated island of Papanuca..."

"I love how your lips move when you read. It's so... stupid. Need me to point at the words as you sound them out? Or lick the pages, so you can turn them?"

"Is this a real paper? It says Honolulu? They have newspapers?"

"Yes, dear, of course. It's almost like a city there. Hula girls need banks and grocery stores, too, you know. And newspapers. How do you think they get the ads for those grass skirts?"

"I can't believe this. That damn fool had to be there when we were dealing with the witch," Hawk said.

"Darn. All that work with the lip reading and you still missed the point. Looks like you get an F for word comprehension. That surprises me. You did so well in finger painting. It says here, you will *now* note upon second reading, with my help, that he was almost killed in an American air raid on the island. Now, *that* was *us!*"

"Yeah, you're right. I didn't read the whole thing. What was he doing there?"

"Since you asked, here's what I think. He wouldn't talk. The Japs were reverse constructing the code. They didn't know what kind of beans he had been spilling. That's why they were tailing you. They were dragging him around with them, until you kind of messed them up. He got stuck there when they all got killed. Did they ever tell you at the beginning of this little venture that the ultimate message might be the rescue of Hoech? As opposed to, killing a president. Or, that Hoech had to be rescued first, to tell us the final message?"

"Hell. I don't know. Maybe. Sounds familiar. Somebody said something about that."

"I think that's exactly what Hoech did. He was trying to be rescued. Only he wasn't waiting until the end. He worked it into the middle of the deciphering, somehow, and got himself to Papanuca. The man is the kind of a genius that doesn't just operate on paper. He's very practical and knows how people think. He puts ideas into practice."

"Yeah, he's a genius awright. At least he impressed you. Did you know this Hoech or something?"

"I think I may have met him at a party once. He was just another bug-eyed, bow-tied, bore. I can't remember. Maybe a Somerset Maugham type, with a sneaky little diary. Never ask a lady about that kind of thing, she may have been tipsy. It's bad form for a gentleman of your caliber."

"Hunh. But, the paper, it doesn't say any of that stuff about Hoech trying to get rescued, though."

"History is written between the lines. They didn't put our names in it, either, did they? Do you think, perhaps because they didn't know how to spell them? Never fear, however, when Colonel Clark reads this, I feel certain that at least *one name* will be added to round out the piece. There will be a much larger article in the Marine Corps Chevron, with an even larger photo."

"Yeah. You got that part right. He'll put Sergeant

York outta business on the war bond tours. He'll be playing John Wayne in the movie version." Hawk dropped the paper to his side. "I told you the damn witch was getting her information from the Japs or something. And all you could say was that was stupid."

"No, no, no, I said that *you* were stupid. The two aren't the same. You mixed all that up. A minor correction, *s'il vous plaît*? I do believe that you said the witch was getting her information from the devil, *not* the Japanese. Which, is somewhat different, as it implies a certain degree of...medieval...how shall we put it politely...*naivete*? They can take the boy out of Mississippi—but—as I believe the expression goes?"

"I was joking when I said that," he said.

"Right. You old jokester. You and the devil." She waved a finger at him. "You're ready for a comedy act. People often tell me that you should be Edgar Bergen's dummy. But you're no Charlie McCarthy, of course. He's too sophisticated. You have more of the Mortimer Snerd elan."

Vera had forgotten that humor, or rather, a sense of humor, was not one of Hawk's strong points. It only triggered darker emotions. Her memory was about to be refreshed. He frowned.

"What's that on your hand?" After being with her for over two hours, he now noticed a large diamond ring.

"That's my finger, doll. This part here, see, *this* is my hand? Got time for a little anatomy? Let's find a room."

"Where did you get that?

"From Bennie. It was his mother's wedding ring. He said it cost five thousand dollars. That had to be in the 1800s. Think of what it's worth now?"

"Hunh."

"That sounded vaguely accusatory." She flaunted the ring in the waning light.

"He just *gave* you a five-thousand-dollar wedding ring from the 1800s, that belonged to his mother?"

"I told you people give me things. Because people like me. We're old friends. And I'm stunningly attractive, as you yourself are constantly reminding me." She smiled. "Although, not lately. Isn't it about time?" She pressed against him.

"Hunh."

"What is that obnoxious noise you keep making? Does that mean something?"

"No, it don't mean a thing."

"Am I detecting a sudden proprietary interest? Don't like the ring? That's it, isn't it?" She stepped back, holding up her hand. "Don't like the ring? Here, it's yours." She slid it easily off her finger and held it out to him.

"It ain't my size."

"Take it."

"It ain't my style."

"Take it!"

"I don't want the goddam ring. What the hell am I gonna do with a ring? I ain't never had no ring. Get that son of a bitch out of my face."

"Sell it. Buy a case of Old Dog Manure tobacky. By cracky. They can size rings, you know? And change settings to suit your style. Make it into a cowbell. What are you so mad about?"

"I ain't mad about nothing. You would know if I was mad. I just asked you a question. And I don't remember much of an answer."

"You *are* mad. I told you. He wanted me to have it.

That's what gratitude looks like, in case you were wondering. I have a half dozen rings, a lot better than this one." She looked hurt. "You never did understand me. I do things for people, so they'll like me, and then they treat me like...I'm nothing."

"I understand you. You were showing off."

"Maybe. Just like if I wore any of the other rings. Why do you think you wear a ring? What's wrong with that?"

"Yeah? If you got a half dozen other rings that are so great, why are you wearing *that* one?"

"I just thought...it looked good. I just got it. It's old-fashioned. Kind of Victorian." Her voice weakened. "You have to wear things like this when you're young."

"Mm hmm. Ain't that bastard married?"

"I seem to recall reading something about that."

"I wonder how the wife would like this conversation. He just gave her ring to *you* because he likes you? She's probably shaking the dresser drawer upside down like a cross-eyed bitch right now, lookin' for it."

"I said it was his *mother's*. I don't know anything about the wife. But I know she wouldn't fly ten thousand miles a half dozen times through a war to come see him. Or join the WASPs. Or save his life. Or pretend he's not the stupidest human being God ever created. Do you *want* it or not? *Stupid*."

"Hell, no. I told you fifty times, I don't want the bastard. Keep it in your treasure chest with your other crap. It ain't nothing to me what you do." She turned away from him.

"Then I'll throw it off the cliff," she said with tears in her voice. "It's nothing to me, either." Emotions were beginning to run high. "After all I've done for you, after

I came all this way, at all this risk. After all I had to do to get here. This is how you act? Clark could have loused the whole thing up, you know?" She sobbed, and her body shook. "Sometimes people have to act civilized to other people, if you can *imagine* that. If you can imagine anything that decent people do. Besides...*killing* each other."

He looked up at the endless sky. His upper lip tightened inward against his teeth. Then he took her shoulders and turned her around. He put his arms around her. "Okay. Give me the stupid assed, son of a bitchin' ring."

IF YOU LIKE THIS, YOU MAY ALSO ENJOY BLAZER: GHOSTS OF WAR

A COP THRILLER BY G.C. HARMON

GO BACK IN TIME WITH BLAZER AS THIS HEART-STOPPING ACTION TAKES A CLEVER LOOK AT HISTORY.

Before Steve Blazer was given command of SFPD's Special Forces—before he was a crack Homicide Inspector—he was an elite up and comer on the Vice Squad.

During an Asian drug smuggler bust, two Vice cops are murdered. The killer leaves a signature—one that means something to Blazer's mentor, Captain John Stanson—leading him to believe the smuggler gang is tied to a wealthy Vietnamese businessman who rules San Francisco's Little Saigon district with an iron fist. As Blazer dives deeper into the investigation, he clashes with the Federal Agency providing his protection, and when the Vietnamese businessman is murdered, the feds put Blazer on the top of their suspect list.

While the Vice squad pursues a drug ring from the Golden Triangle and a cop killer, Stanson goes on a perilous journey of his own, reliving parts of his violent pas where he was taken as a prisoner of the Vietnam War. Blazer takes notice and sets out to prevent Stanson from crossing a line he can't come back from.

But will Blazer get to him in time? Will the mysterious killer connected to Stanson's perilous past be brought to justice once and for all?

AVAILABLE NOW

ABOUT THE AUTHOR

Patrick Clay was born a fifth generation Texan, in Galena Park, Texas. He received a scholarship to the University of St. Thomas and graduated cum laude from there. He then graduated magna cum laude from South Texas College of Law, where he was fourth in his class and a member of the law journal. During the time he waited for the bar results, he began writing fiction.

Patrick became a captain in the Civil Air Patrol and was Houston chess player in 1990, more for his tournament directing ability than playing skills. After fourteen years, he gave up the private law practice, and worked as an attorney for the federal government for the next thirty years.

Patrick met his beautiful wife at Astroworld in Houston, the first year that the amusement park opened. When he began writing in 1977, he had no children, and by the time he stopped writing in 1983, he had three daughters; he now has nine grandchildren.